KU-152-581

ONLY US

By the same author:

English for Communication, John Murray, 1970

Over to You, John Murray, 1980

Targets 1,2,3,4. Spartacus Books, 1991

Collins Study Guides, Harper Collins, 1999, 2000, 2001, 2002, 2003, 2004, 2005, 2006.

ONLY US

A. A. Coleby

AS

1 5 5 4 2 9   E

Book Guild Publishing
Sussex, England

First published in Great Britain in 2010 by
The Book Guild Ltd
Pavilion View
19 New Road
Brighton, BN1 1UF

Copyright © A. A. Coleby 2010

The right of A. A. Coleby to be identified as the author of this
work has been asserted by him in accordance with the Copyright,
Designs and Patents Act 1988.

All rights reserved. No part of this publication may be
reproduced, transmitted, or stored in a retrieval system, in any
form or by any means, without permission in writing from the
publisher or the author, nor be otherwise circulated in any form
of binding or cover other than that in which it is published and
without a similar condition being imposed on the subsequent
purchaser.

All characters in this publication are fictitious and any
resemblance to real people, alive or dead, is purely coincidental.

Typesetting in Baskerville by
Nat-Type, Cheshire

Printed in Great Britain by
CPI Antony Rowe

A catalogue record for this book is available from
The British Library.

ISBN 978 1 84624 446 9

1

It's that barn, thought Hazel. Oh, God! It's that barn. It's every time I've been in there.

She tried to breathe, slowly and deeply, but the back of her throat stung. She held a handkerchief to her mouth, but breathing through the nose caught her throat just as sharply. Like a thousand tiny needles stabbing her. Like an unseen hand gripping her throat, closing it down.

Hazel had unloaded the Saturday shopping, and parked the car in the barn. Now she ran back across the lane to her house. Once inside, she grabbed a glass and reached for the relief of the cold water tap.

The water was cool, and the stinging lessened, but she found it hard to swallow because her throat had swollen. She stood for two or three minutes at the sink, and kept drinking cold water, but her swollen throat did not ease. It even got a little worse, and then her whole mouth and tongue and face felt hot, as if they, too, were swelling.

She found a chair and sat down, still clutching the glass of water. She deliberately tried to keep calm and took deep, measured breaths: it was all she could think of doing. But her breathing was getting harder, and her nose and nasal passages felt hot. They were clogged and bunged up.

Fear of choking caused the start of panic.

Then Hazel caught sight of herself in a mirror, which hung on the end wall of the kitchen. Even her eyelids and lips were puffed up. Her face was patchy red. She looked

1

grotesque. She was really alarmed. Panic was beginning to rise.

She knew her husband, Sam, was in the lounge, watching sport on television.

She got up from the chair and carefully, slowly walked to the doorway. Sam sat casually, gazing at the screen. When he turned to look at Hazel, his expression and manner changed in an instant.

'What on earth is the matter with you?' Tension sharpened and hardened his face.

'Dunno. Been in the barn,' she gasped.

'Can you breathe OK?'

Hazel shook her head. She was trying to stop the panic rising too far.

Sam thought hard. He tried to stay calm.

'Shall we try steam, like my mum did for bad chests?'

Again, Hazel shook her head. She was trying to breathe deeply and regularly. She knew instinctively that that was the priority and the swelling could wait until later. But how much would the swelling increase? Would it close her throat completely?

'What about that vaporiser we used for Andrew's bronchitis? It's antiseptic.'

'No time.'

Air rasped in and out of her mouth, while Sam looked on helplessly. He was rigid with concentration, almost paralysed with fear.

'This is really serious.' Hazel managed to push the words out between breaths.

Sam hesitated between ringing for an ambulance and taking Hazel to hospital himself. He thought the Saturday afternoon traffic would be heavy, and that an ambulance would have a hard time forcing its way through.

'Andrew!' He called to their son, upstairs. 'I'm taking Mum to Casualty. You look after the house.'

By the time Sam had run to the barn and brought his car round to the door, Andrew, alerted by the urgency of Sam's tone, had raced downstairs and was helping his mother to the door.

Sam swore at the traffic as he drove as fast as he could to Thorby. His heart thudded in his chest. Hazel concentrated on steady breathing and felt as if she was passing out. The energy was being sucked out of her. She thought she was dying. She looked down at her lap dimly, through swollen lids. Great waves of darkness threatened to swallow her.

When Sam eventually arrived at the Thorby General Hospital Accident and Emergency unit, he drove straight into the nearest parking bay next to an ambulance and shouted for help. He saw for an instant the disapproving look on the face of a paramedic who, as soon as he saw Hazel, changed his expression immediately and rushed to help get her inside the building.

Everything seemed to be swept aside as she was whisked straight into an examination bay. Within seconds, a doctor was injecting her with antihistamine, and then another injection followed after a blood-pressure check.

The doctor was calm, steady and reassuring.

'She got here in time,' he said. 'She'll be all right now.'

Tight cords of tension loosened. Sam felt his whole body wilt, and he slumped into a nearby chair.

It was later, when he was giving registration details, that the triage nurse asked him why he had not called an ambulance.

'I just thought the quickest way to get here was for me to drive,' he explained tonelessly.

'No. The paramedics would have known what to do, and they would have kept her safe until she got here,' she said. 'Please, next time you have an emergency of any kind, dial 999. An anaphylactic attack can be fatal.'

'OK,' replied Sam. 'Anything you say. Anything that's best for my wife.'

His voice shook and his throat hurt: it was nearly closed with emotion. There was no doubting his sincerity. His whole mind and body were flooded with relief and gratitude to the hospital. All he wanted was to be with Hazel. The spectre of losing her would haunt him for some time.

2

The hospital insisted that Hazel consult her own doctor. The symptoms had subsided and she had been allowed to go home late on Saturday evening.

Sam and Hazel Dent lived in a new house on the edge of the village of Thoreswood, five miles to the south of Thorby. They both worked in Thorby, Hazel as customer services manager at Pine Property Services, and Sam as a project manager for Thorby Computer Services, known everywhere as TCS.

Hazel made an appointment to see Dr McCurrach at the Thoreswood surgery on Tuesday, and told her the story of Saturday afternoon.

'It must have been a severe allergic reaction to something you had eaten or something in the environment,' said the doctor. 'You say it started with a stinging sensation in the back of your throat?'

'Yes.'

'And you've had that before?'

'Yes, but it has not developed and got so much worse, as it did this time.'

'It may be that you had more of the allergen this time, or you're getting more sensitive to it. There could be a build-up of it, though that only applies to a food allergen. Where were you when the stinging sensation started, at home or at work?'

'I had finished work, but I had been shopping in town, and had then driven home. I had parked the car in the barn at the back of the houses, and what this has made me realise is that I have parked the car in the barn each time I have felt the stinging.'

'Aha. I see. What's in the barn?'

'Nothing much. The floor is earth. There are all the neighbours' cars. We all park them in the barn, two spaces for each house.'

'What are the walls made of? Brick?'

'Stone.'

'The roof?'

'Pantiles.'

'And what is the other side of the barn?'

'Well, Mr Brewster's farm. The bit we live on was originally his land. The houses are new.'

'So, are there outbuildings?'

'The nearest things are some chicken huts. Battery houses, they are called. Hundreds of hens in two long huts, all crowded together.'

'That could well be it. Feathers and organisms and dust are borne on the wind, and you could be allergic to just a trace of any of them. Had you been in the barn longer than usual on Saturday afternoon?'

'Yes. I had lost some coins on the floor, and I was poking about looking for them for a few minutes.'

'Right.' Dr McCurrach obviously had no more time for speculation. 'I could refer you to the allergy consultant at Thorby General. They'll test you for all sorts of foodstuffs that are common allergens nowadays. But if the source of the trouble is those chicken huts, it will be a matter for the Environmental Health department at the Council in Thorby.

'Now, what you had better do is this. I'll refer you to the consultant, but things will happen only slowly, and we don't want to risk another one of those attacks. You can't mess about with anaphylaxis.'

The doctor raised her voice a little, widened her eyes

slightly and leaned towards Hazel. 'It can be fatal. You should get in touch with the Environmental Health at Thorby Council. Explain the problem and tell them what you have told me. They have to respond to you, and I think they'll come and have a look and try to assess the situation. You may have to do some tests for them, and you can tell them that they can ask me for a letter if that will help. Meanwhile, I'll prescribe you some Piriton tablets. They are a mild anti-histamine. Take two with water if you feel another attack coming on. In fact, you can buy them over the counter if you run out.'

The smile and the thanks that Hazel expressed were heartfelt. The doctor had confirmed what she had suspected.

'Well, shall I speak to Mr Brewster myself first?' she asked, thinking that it would be best to handle the matter tactfully, and in a neighbourly way. The doctor, however, was firm and emphatic.

'No. Let Environmental Health handle it. They handle problems every day.'

'Thank you again,' said Hazel, and left the surgery.

Marie Pocklington, the Environmental Health officer assigned to Hazel's enquiry, had promised to call at ten-thirty the following Tuesday morning, but she was now late. H a z e l wanted to make a good impression, and sat at her dressing table, putting the finishing touches to her appearance. She had on the same open-necked white blouse that she would have worn to work on any other morning of the week. The collar spread slightly across the shoulders, and at the back it was just touched by Hazel's dark brown hair as it fell straight from the back of her head. Hazel did not like the close-cut hair fashion favoured by most girls these days. She took great care to keep a soft, just-washed look all the time. She felt that this complimented her thick but loosely styled hair: straight at the back, but swept across her forehead to show a good expanse of skin above the brow in both directions. Then it curved round each temple so that, as it fell, it showed the soft thickness to its best advantage. The rounded impression this hairstyle gave expanded the slight thinness of her cheeks as they fell from high cheekbones past a thin mouth to a strong and well-rounded chin.

To balance the strong colour and texture of her hair, she used a porcelain foundation to tone down her cheeks, and for the same reason always wore a very pale pastel-pink lipstick. She always kept her eyebrows thin and unobtrusive, hoping that her blue eyes and the evenness of her teeth when she smiled would be the facial characteristics most remembered by her customers and friends. They might distract attention, she hoped, from her nose, which was too sharp and thin.

A loose-fitting beige jumper and mid-grey slacks completed her selection of clothes for today. After eighteen years of marriage, her figure was still thin, lithe and well proportioned.

The house was warm. She wanted to put her visitor at ease. She went downstairs to wait.

Sam and Hazel were happy with the house. After fifteen years in a semi-detached house on a crowded estate in Thorby, it was just what they had longed for.

It was built in a conservation area, and so the outside walls were of grey stone, and the roof was pantiled.

It was one of four similar houses built on an area that had been sliced from the land of Charles Brewster, who farmed a thousand acres on the north side of Thoreswood, and had sold the land with planning permission to a local builder two years ago. A tarmac drive, Brewster Lane, led from the main Rowle Road, and after some thirty yards, it became block-paved and was flanked by the four houses, two on each side.

Some distance away, beyond two poultry sheds, was Charles's own house, large and traditional, standing on a small rise at the end of a tree-lined drive. Between the new houses and the poultry sheds was a barn, which had been included in the plot of land and had been left as a farmyard feature by the builder. It was situated on the property of the first of the houses, but all four houses had access by a narrow drive, for the barn had been divided into four sections, one for each household, as a sheltered parking space. There were no garaging facilities at any of the four houses. Cars could not be left on Brewster Lane because it was too narrow for two cars to pass each other.

Hazel studied the framed photograph on the mantelpiece as she waited. It was one of the few they had of all three of them together: Hazel in the middle between her two men, for Andrew, though only fourteen, was now as tall as she was.

Hazel reflected briefly on how similar Sam and Andrew were. Like her, they both had thick, dark brown hair, and both had it brushed forward with no parting, so that it fell over a low forehead. In addition, a few strands of hair had blown across Sam's forehead, which emphasised a natural, casual look, for he, as usual, had a broad, happy smile. Both father and son almost closed their eyes into narrow slits as they smiled, and, though just forty, Sam had already developed the crow's feet round the eye corners, which Hazel had thought were the attraction of his father's face when he was alive. It was one of the features of men's faces that Hazel always noticed: the skin round the eyes, was it full and creased, or thinly stretched over the bone? Strong lines ran from Sam's nose to each corner of his mouth, though these were disguised now by the smile. He and Andrew smiled in the same way – mouth slightly open and teeth showing.

Hazel loved having this photograph there for the happiness it showed. The nearly closed eyes and slightly open mouths showed, she thought, the forthright and open characters that both Sam and Andrew had. They could both show a stormy, intimidating expression when concentrating on work, or in an aggressive or unhappy mood, but at other times there was a mental and physical looseness that always made for a healthy, relaxed atmosphere in the home.

The doorbell chimed. Hazel had been so absorbed that she had not noticed a car come along Brewster Lane, and park with the nearside wheels on the grassy area that stretched from the road to the house and then round the side of it.

The interview was as pleasant as Hazel had hoped. Marie made copious notes while Hazel told the story of Saturday and what the doctor had said. She recalled all the occasions when her throat had stung after she had parked her car in the barn.

'I will certainly want a letter from the doctor,' Marie said, 'and could I have the names and house numbers of all the neighbours, please? I will have to call on them. I hope you appreciate that this is usual in cases of atmospheric or environmental pollution. The trouble is,' she explained, 'that if Dr McCurrach is correct in her suspicion of the cause of your attack, none of the neighbours will have been affected and this might well complicate matters and cause us a problem – unless, of course, they consider just the smell from the chickens to be unpleasant, and that would probably help us.' She put her hand to her chin and looked thoughtful.

They walked to the barn so that Marie could inspect the situation, and she continued to make notes and observations. There was a fairly strong wind, and so there was some smell, although it was blowing directly into the back of the barn. There was an area between the top of the wall and the roof, which was designed so that the wind could blow straight through, and so the smell was quickly dispersed. Marie checked to verify that the smell never came into or around the house, and that Hazel did not suffer any adverse effects, except when she came to the barn. She noted that all this was so.

Within a fairly short time, Hazel's throat began to sting, so that Marie went on her own round the end of the barn to estimate the distance between it and the chicken huts, while Hazel went back to the house to make some coffee.

Before she returned, Marie spoke with Ray Towers, who had been in the barn, servicing one of his two motorcycles. He was a very pleasant and friendly man in his late middle age, who had not worked since he suffered a severe heart attack three years previously. His bikes were his pride and joy, the love of his life, and he always seemed to be in the barn taking them to pieces and reassembling them. Hazel was not at all surprised to see him there and realised that, though he appeared to be busy, he was listening to their conversation. Later, he told Marie that his wife, Judith, a hairdresser, was not at home. He said that he always noticed a smell, but agreed with Marie's suggestion that, as he was so often in the barn, it seemed that he did not find it offensive.

When Marie returned to the house, Hazel gave her details of the neighbours, together with a guess about whether they were at home.

The Towers, she said, lived in the corner house nearest the farmhouse. Ray Towers did not work, but his wife worked long hours as a hairdresser, at a shop in Thorby, and also with clients in their homes at the weekends and in the evenings. They had two grown-up sons who were married and did not live there.

In the other house on the barn side, nearest the road, lived Mike Davies, who was a travelling salesman for a brewery, and his wife, Sue. Marie said she knew Sue Davies, who worked as a receptionist and clerk in the housing department at the Council offices. Hazel had seen Mike setting off for work that morning, and Sue worked regularly from nine to five every day. Both their two children would be at school in Thorby.

In the other house on Hazel's side of Brewster Lane, furthest away from the barn, lived Jack and Jean Hunt, a childless couple in their early thirties. Jean was a teacher at a secondary school in Thorby, and would certainly be out at this time of day. Jack was a bit more unpredictable. He worked in the computer industry, like Sam, but for a multinational company, Global Computers. He travelled abroad frequently, updating branches of the company in other countries about innovative software applications, and sorting out various problems that they always seemed to have. Hazel explained that if he was in between trips abroad, Marie might well find him at home, but she advised her to be careful. He might be still in bed, for he sometimes arrived home in the middle of the night.

'Shall I go and have a word with Charles Brewster about it – as a neighbour, of course?' asked Hazel. 'I would be quite friendly and tactful about it.'

'Absolutely not.' Marie raised her voice to emphasise the point, and Hazel thought she seemed more animated than she had done for the whole visit. 'You must let me handle this, Mrs Dent. I'll speak to Mr Brewster at the appropriate time, which is not yet. The best thing you can do is to keep a list of every occasion you go to the barn, with times and dates, together with a note about any effects you might suffer. And could you get that letter for me from the doctor, please?'

'Oh, certainly,' Hazel promised. 'That will be no trouble at all.'

Hazel liked the firm, warm handshake as Marie left. She had also liked the way Marie looked steadily into her eyes when she spoke to her.

3

'She said what?'

Sam's eyes burned into Hazel's face. His jaw dropped. Hazel sat silently. She knew that Sam had heard exactly what she had said. Now the passion was rising. She looked impassive and despondent.

'I can't believe it,' he said, his voice thick with swelling anger. 'She said she would take no action?'

Hazel nodded. A month had passed since Marie Pocklington had made her visit. Hazel had seen her call on the neighbours and one of her colleagues had called twice to take readings of the air quality in and around the barn. Hazel had kept a diary of her own visits to the barn, with a record of her throat symptoms. Now Marie had phoned to say that she could not take Hazel's enquiry any further on environmental health grounds. A letter to confirm this would follow.

Hazel had waited until the best time to tell Sam, the moment he was winding down to relax for the evening. They had eaten a meal – Sam's favourite, beef stroganoff. Andrew had gone upstairs to immerse himself in his school work and his computer. Now, Hazel knew, Sam would help her clear away the meal – or do it all himself, if she had work to do. Occasionally, she had to work on customers' accounts at home, and had various passwords to access Pine Properties' database over the Internet. But what effect this piece of news would have on Sam, Hazel now waited to see. She knew all the signs of his shock and anger: reddening of cheeks and neck, widening eyes, a piercing gaze as his eyes seemed to bore straight through hers. She felt she had to break the silence.

'Yes. After full consideration of our complaint about Charles Brewster's chicken huts, she felt she could take no action.'

'Reasons?' Sam's mouth tightened, his eyes screwed up. He was now looking down at the table.

'She has been to see Brewster. He said he had kept chickens in those sheds for over forty years and no one else had ever complained. He was not moving them. He said it had not been proved that they made anyone ill, and if they did, it was up to that person to do something about it. He had been very angry and told her to get out of the house. He said that if she took him to court, she wouldn't stand a chance. And he told her not to forget that he was a councillor and could bring influence to bear on her department.'

'Oh? Up to that one, is he?'

Hazel knew that that would make Sam even angrier, but she felt she had to tell him everything, just as Marie Pocklington had told her. He would only blame her if she came out with something later that she had not told him.

'Yes, but Marie said that she never listened to that kind of threat, and it wouldn't get him anywhere. She said that the important point was that he would fight against anything she did, in court if necessary, and he could afford the best lawyers.'

'And what about the doctor's letter, and this diary you have kept?'

'She said that Dr McCurrach's letter referred to the evidence of the anaphylactic attack and of my diary, but said only that a newly acquired allergy *could* have been caused by dust and micro-organisms borne on the wind from the chicken huts.'

'Huh!' Sam snorted. 'So much for her support.'

'She has to cover herself, and be careful what she says,' said Hazel, with a sigh. She raised her eyebrows, and let her hands fall limply into her lap. She seemed tired with the hopelessness of it all.

'But I assume the neighbours spoke up for us, and said about the smell,' persisted Sam.

Hazel sighed again, slowly. She knew this next bit would make him seethe. How long would he stay on the boil?

'She said none of the neighbours had had their health affected by it, and only one of them said the smell was unpleasant. I didn't expect her to say which one. What she did say was that, because we don't have a lot of evidence and support, Brewster has a very strong case. It's not worth taking any action. We would lose. It's just my individual reaction that is unfortunate.'

Sam's thump on the table seemed to drive him to his feet, and he stalked around the dining area.

'Pah!' He snorted again. 'After all that garbage about supporting us. We could count on them. They would support us. What's that all worth? It's different when they have to be counted.' His eyes darted about restlessly. They had in them the gleam that Hazel always saw when he was gripped by feeling.

Hazel thought that she had better get something done. It might calm Sam. She gathered up dishes, cloths, cutlery, everything she could find, and whisked it all to the kitchen end of the room.

She kept busy and did not meet Sam's eyes. She knew he had been raised to a pitch. She had been confident in her timing, but would have to be very careful in handling Sam's mood now. There was always that bit of uncertainty, wondering how far his anger would take him. He seemed to fill with a dangerous energy at times like this.

Soon, Sam sat down again, looked at the newspaper and seemed deep in thought. Hazel ran out of chores to do.

15

'Well, what are we gonna do?'

Hazel shrugged. 'We'll have to carry on as before, and I'll have to be careful. I'll have to stay away from the barn.'

'You won't be able to go near it.'

'No. I'll have to park my car alongside the house, as I have been doing since the attack, and mess up that precious grassy area that stretches down to the road.'

'Yeah,' said Sam. 'There were all sorts of agreements in the deeds about looking after that bit of land, but they can go to hell.'

'Oh, yes. I'm not going near the barn,' Hazel repeated.

'There's one thing we've found out. We can't rely on the neighbours.'

'No. That's that,' said Hazel, flatly, resignation in her voice. She hoped Sam would let it rest.

'I'll have to tackle them about it,' continued Sam. 'They're not getting away with that.'

Hazel's hopes collapsed. It was just like Sam. He had to pursue everything to the bitter end. He couldn't just leave it.

'Oh, don't bother,' she said. 'We've got to live with them, and we may need them sometime.'

'You could say that about anything,' snapped Sam. 'I'll see them sometime.'

Hazel decided that, having told Sam the news, she would now let it rest. Sam also seemed to have said all he wanted to say for the moment, and went to the end of the dining-room area, where he had a desk pushed against the wall, with a small range of bookshelves above it. He sat down and powered up the computer.

'What are you doing?'

'Just sorting out little piles of grubby bits of paper,' was the gruff reply. 'Thought I'd better get on with the village newsletter tonight, so I can get that out on time this month. Besides, it might take my mind off that damned Council.'

Hazel knew it was best for him to be doing something, to be thinking of something else. One of the ways Sam had tried to settle into village life, when the family first arrived in Thoreswood, was to volunteer to compose, print and distribute a monthly village newsletter. In spite of his moods, he was a public-spirited man and enjoyed being able to use his IT skills to serve the community in this way.

It did indeed put him in touch with many different aspects of village life. For the November edition, Sam gathered together the contributions from various villagers which would be the substance of the newsletter. If he did not have enough to fill four A4 pages, he would pad it out with word-searches, crosswords and jokes that he kept in reserve. But, as he shuffled and arranged different papers, he thought he was doing quite well this month. The committee secretary had written an update on progress on the village hall. A steering group from the Parish Council was organising funding for and planning of a skate-park for the youngsters. The Neighbourhood Watch secretary had written a report of various petty crimes and acts of vandalism that had occurred during the last three months, and there was an article by the community police officer giving advice about safeguarding property.

There was also a framed advertisement for Thoreswood History Society's Christmas social. One of the aspects of village life that the newsletter kept Sam in touch with was this History Society. At the end of November, it was the first of the local clubs and societies to hold its Christmas social. It was held in what were known by the villagers as the church rooms, although they did not belong to the church any more. They had been bought by a wealthy parish councillor about forty years ago and, although he still legally owned them, he simply made them available for village activities, free of charge. There was now a new committee trying to build a new village hall because the church rooms were quite small, unsuitable for energetic games like badminton, and the heating was weak and inefficient.

Still, for the moment, that was the only place village clubs had to meet. The History Society this year had had the new idea of having the social on a Saturday evening and holding an open day during the morning and afternoon, partly to recruit new members and partly as a service to the village. Now, in good time, it was advertising the event.

Sam thought he had almost enough material. A small crossword and that will be it, he thought. He needed a quick glance at a past newsletter to make sure he had got the fonts and column widths right, and then he could save it all ready for printing another time.

Sam shut down the computer and went into the lounge. Hazel sat in front of the television watching an old film. She felt more tired than she expected. She was glad she had told Sam everything that Marie had told her on the phone, and he seemed to have got over it – partly, at least.

Sam sat beside her on the sofa. She was surprised when his hand closed over hers. She was first surprised, and then relieved. Relief flooded through her. All her muscles and joints, even her nerves, loosened and relaxed. Hazel was so glad Sam was not going to keep up his aggression. He wouldn't let it rest, but at least the personal tension seemed to have dissolved.

Sam twisted round to face her, and his eyes looked straight into hers. She gave a smile of gentle happiness.

'Close your eyes,' he said, softly. Then his lips brushed against each eyelid in turn. Hazel loved it when he kissed her eyes like that. She remembered telling him before they were married that no other boyfriend had ever done that. It was the most tender and loving thing he ever did. She thought of how he was a man of such contrasts. He could be so soft and sensitive at times, and at other times so menacing and frightening. His kiss on the eyes was like falling thistledown.

Hazel opened her eyes and he was still gazing at her face. She reached forward to touch his forehead with her fingertips. Then, she traced, with her forefinger, around the hairline to his ears, down along the jawline and then round his lips. That was also a tender thing to do. For a minute, her mouth closed over his.

'You know,' she said, as she pulled away from him, but still in a soothing mood, 'there's nobody who is completely on your side. When it comes down to it, there's only us – together.'

'Yes,' said Sam. 'We're on our own with a problem that won't go away.' It seemed that there was nowhere to turn. The hospital could not identify what Hazel was allergic to; the doctor confined herself to facts and a carefully worded medical opinion; the Council said they had no case; and all their neighbours except one were afraid of Brewster. Brewster often boasted that he had a lot of influence in Thorby and Thoreswood. People were always aware of him, never wanted to offend him.

It's pretty much the law of the jungle set in modern times, thought Sam.

The experience lay like an ulcer on his heart.

'Still,' he said, with a sideways look at Hazel, 'I can think of something to do about it.'

Hazel said nothing.

Oh no, she thought. What can he have in mind now?

4

After his outburst and towering rage against the neighbours, Charles Brewster and the Environmental Health officer, Hazel thought that Sam would be in a silent, sullen mood for a while. She would get little more than grunts out of him while he brooded and looked sour, almost as if he was taking out the unhappiness on himself.

But it was not like that. He seemed to accept the new situation quite quickly. He did not brood. He knew what he wanted to do about it. He had had in the back of his mind an idea to build a garage at the side of the house. It would be between the house and the road, end on to Brewster Lane.

Now he decided to make the idea become a plan.

'I don't see how the neighbours can object,' he said to Hazel. 'Maybe they want to side with Brewster so that he doesn't have to move his chicken huts, but surely they can't object to us safeguarding your health by keeping your car well away from the barn. You can't leave it in the road because it's too narrow, so we'll have to build a garage.'

Hazel went along with this. She thought they had to move on to this next stage. They would have to leave until the appropriate time the question of whether the neighbours would support them.

In the evenings, Sam set to work. In his student days, he had worked on many building sites where new houses and separate garages were being constructed, and he was sure he knew enough about plans to be able to draw his own. A friend of a friend at work had built his own bungalow, and had promised to look over the plans before Sam submitted them to the Council planning committee. After all, a garage was a fairly simple thing to build.

He drew the plan of the foundations showing the depth of the trenches, the middle filled with hardcore and topped with a raft of concrete. Then he showed the side elevation from the damp course to the barge boards and soffits. End elevations showed a plain back wall and, at the front, an up-and-over door with a concrete lintel above. Finally, a pitched roof with pantiles completed what should have been a compact, secure garage, which was pleasing to the eye and in accordance with the conservation area regulations.

He drew the plans four times altogether, each time trying to make them more precise and more informative. He had bought a special new drawing board, set squares, pencils and mapping pens. All the time he imagined how it would look, and how he would be satisfied because he had conceived it and planned it from the beginning.

Then, all was ready. His friend checked it and made two suggestions which necessitated a fifth drawing. Then he submitted it for planning permission.

Sam, Hazel and Andrew were quite pleased when they saw the application displayed in a frame in the Public Notices section of the *Thorby Recorder* a few weeks later. The notice pointed out that the proposed garage was within the Thoreswood Conservation Area and that members of the public could see the full application at the Planning and Transportation Services offices at Thorby town hall. Anyone wishing to make representations could write, within twenty-one days, to the Head of Planning and Transportation Services at the town hall.

'Looks good, doesn't it?' said Andrew, looking at the notice.

'Quite professional,' agreed Hazel.

'Well, let's hope it takes us a further step along the way to solving this business,' said Sam, and then the phone rang.

'Hello. Mr Dent?' The voice at the other end of the line sounded soft and a little timid.

'Yes.'

'Oh. Hello again. My name is Mary Dyer. I have been looking at the Thoreswood newsletter. My neighbour picked it up at the Post Office yesterday and gave it to me. I notice that this is the number to ring if you want to send in a contribution,' she said.

'Yes. That's right.' Sam hoped he sounded encouraging.

'Well, I don't exactly want to be a contributor,' continued Mary, hurriedly, 'but I wanted to ask about this open day of the History Society. Would you be the person to ask?'

'What do you want to know?'

'It's just that I have a small antique object that has been in my family for many years, and I wondered if there would be someone there who could value it for me.'

'Well that's not quite the purpose of the open day,' said Sam, 'but Geoff Lowis, the chairman, is sure to be there. I know him personally, and I should think he will help you out if he can.'

'Oh, thank you.' The lady seemed really pleased and grateful. Her voice shook slightly, and Sam formed the impression that she was probably elderly.

'There's one other problem, though,' she continued. 'I'm afraid I don't know where the church rooms are – near the church, perhaps?' The rising intonation quite charmed Sam, and he felt sure this was an old lady on the line.

'You might think so,' he said, 'but in fact they are a little distance away. But there's no problem. You just tell me where you live, and I'll come and pick you up and take you there.'

'Oh, that's very kind of you, Mr Dent. Actually, I live a little way outside the village, about two miles along the Rowle Road towards the abbey. Could you manage that?'

'No trouble at all,' said Sam, full of good feeling. 'I'm sorry. I didn't catch your name?'

'Mrs Dyer. Mary Dyer,' she said. 'Look, about two miles along Rowle Road, you will see a pair of semi-detached cottages. Mine is the furthest one away from Thoreswood. It's called "Lilac Cottage".'

'That's fine,' said Sam. 'I think I remember seeing them. The open day is this coming Saturday, so I could fetch you at three o'clock. OK?'

'See you then, and thank you very much,' she said, with feeling.

So before Sam went to the open day on Saturday afternoon, he went to fetch Mary. Hazel was at work and Andrew did not want to go, and so just the two of them walked into the church rooms, to be welcomed by a member of the History Society and to be given two information sheets and two enrolment forms. Inside, there was a large number of photographs and written accounts of various sites of local interest, all professionally mounted on vertical display panels. Old parish registers of christenings, marriages and funerals were laid out as flat displays. One feature that Sam found fascinating was a display of accounts that were 250 years old. They were from a large estate, about five miles to the east of Thoreswood, which had been owned for centuries by the wealthy Rowlinson family. They lived in a mansion known as Rowle Hall, and situated on part of their land were the ruined foundations of Rowle Abbey.

In one part of the accounts were listed the annual salaries of estate workers:

	£	s.	d.
Mrs Brecken, Housekeeper	20	0	0
Sally Swann, Laundry maid	9	0	0
Diane Hewins, Housemaid	7	0	0
Mr Harvey, Groom of Chambers	35	0	0
Ronald Drakes, Footman	15	0	0
Jack Pritchard, Coachman	20	0	0

Kitchen expenditure of the same period included:

	s.	d.
7lb salmon	3	3
36 eggs at 3 a penny	1	0
5lb butter at 6d per lb	2	6
19lb of yeast at 2d per lb	3	2

Mary was also scrutinising the accounts. She wore no glasses, and was having to use a magnifying glass to read the figures. She had a sharply pointed nose and high cheek-bones. Geoff Lewis, the History Society chairman, was standing at the end of the display table. He said nothing as he looked at Sam and Mary, but his smile did the talking: he was asking if he could help with anything.

Suddenly, Mary shuffled sideways towards Geoff, fumbling in the pocket of the old brown coat she was wearing. Sam looked up from the estate accounts and watched with a casual interest as she pulled an object from her pocket and, with a hesitant, awkward movement, thrust it on to the display table in front of Geoff.

'Mr Lowis, would that be worth much?' she blurted out quickly, and Sam realised by the speed with which she spoke, and the unnaturally high pitch of her voice, that there was some tension and feeling behind the question. She put her hand to her face and rubbed her thumb lightly along her lips.

The effect on Geoff Lowis was traumatic. His smile vanished. His jaw dropped slightly, and there was a small but noticeable intake of breath. As Sam watched, he was struck by the fact that Geoff's face, arms, hands and indeed his whole body, seemed quite still. For a second or two, he was absolutely motionless. Sam looked back at the object. It was golden. It had a little loop, or ring, at the top, and its shape seemed to be that of a small ink bottle, or possibly a liqueur bottle. But there was no doubt, even at two or three yards' distance, that it was made of gold.

Geoff came out of his momentary trance. 'Good Lord!' he said emphatically, but softly. 'It looks like it...' But as he reached out to pick it up, Mary sprang into action. She snatched up the object and thrust it back into her pocket. 'You can't have it,' she snapped. She pushed past Geoff and scurried towards the door.

'Well, I only wanted to look at it,' he protested, and looked at Sam in bewilderment. Sam smiled, shrugged, and shook his head slightly. Geoff spread his hands in a gesture of helplessness. 'I thought she wanted me to look at it. It did look as if it had some value, but why should she just run off like that?'

'She seemed to take fright,' said Sam, eyebrows raised. Then he noticed that in her haste, she had left behind a small, navy blue handbag.

'She'll need that,' he said. 'I'd better get it to her. Do you know her, then, Geoff? She seemed to know you.'

Geoff shook his head. 'She will have seen my name on the sheet, and anyway, lots of people in Thoreswood know me without my knowing them. I've seen her about, and in the Post Office, and I think she lives on her own somewhere outside the village, but no more than that.'

'Well, I'm just getting to know her,' said Sam. 'Her name's

Mary Dyer, and she lives in Lilac Cottage, a couple of miles along the Rowle Road. I'll have to take her this handbag.'

He slipped out of a side door and quickly found his car. He moved off in the direction of Rowle Abbey, but, after only about fifty yards, he saw Mary walking at the side of the road towards him. She was obviously coming back to recover her bag.

Sam stopped and wound down the window. 'It's OK, Mary. I was just bringing you your bag,' he said. He saw her mouth contract, and the muscles of her mouth tighten slightly. 'Look, why don't you jump in and I'll run you home? It's a tidy step along this road.' Mary hesitated and glanced along the road. It was not yet four o'clock, but the dusk was gathering, and she knew she would have to walk most of the distance in the dark.

'OK,' she said, and clambered in, awkwardly, stiffly. 'I seem to be putting you to a lot of trouble this afternoon. I'm sorry about running out of there just now.'

'It's all right,' said Sam. He thought it best not to question her or talk about it. He engaged the clutch, and moved smoothly through the gears. He glanced at Mary. He thought it must have been a very old brown coat that she gathered round her thin, straight shoulders with a frail, bony hand. A wide-brimmed hat was pulled low on to her forehead, but Sam could still see the high, hard cheekbones and the pointed nose. She returned his glance, and the cracks round her old and knowing eyes darkened in a faint smile.

'How long have you lived out at Lilac Cottage?' Sam asked.

'All my married life,' she replied. 'I moved in there when I married Bill when I was twenty-five. He was killed in an accident when I was fifty. He was a few years older than me, though. We had only rented it, but they let me stay on after he died because they said they didn't need it for workers on the farm any more.' Then she dropped her eyes and watched her fingers as they wrestled sluggishly on her lap. A silence settled between them. Within two minutes, they approached the two semi-detached cottages, which fronted the main road.

Sam braked smoothly to a halt, and then reached across Mrs Dyer to release the door catch. He thought she would be eager to climb out and get into the warmth of her cottage, but she sat in silence for a few seconds, looking down into her lap. Sam looked intently at the side of her face.

'Are you all right?' he asked anxiously. 'Is anything the matter?'

When Mary spoke, Sam noticed how her voice had changed. Gone was the high-pitched tension with which she had spoken to Geoff Lowis. Gone, too, was the blunt flatness with which she spoke to Sam when he arrived with her bag. Sam sensed that she had relaxed during the three or four minutes' drive, and now the voice he heard was softer, more submissive.

'It's just – could you help me? Could you deal with something for me?'

'Yes, if I can. What is it?' Still they sat in the car.

'You see, there's only Mrs Pritchard next door, and she is no better with these things than I am.'

'Yes, but what is it?' persisted Sam. 'Have you got a problem of some sort?'

'It's the heating,' she said. 'You come into the cottage and I'll explain about it.'

As she was getting out, she turned back towards Sam.

'Look. If you take your car a few yards forward after I've got out, the road widens a bit, and you can put it off the road. It's where they sometimes leave piles of grit in the winter.'

Sam did this, as Mary Dyer unlocked her cottage and turned lights on. She went back and let him in at the front door.

'There's a water heater over the sink that gives me trouble,' she said. 'It gives hot water to the radiators as well, but the worst thing is the gas fire in my sitting room. It has a pilot, but I find it ever so hard to get it going. Sometimes I have to get Mr Steadman, the farmer, to see to it. He owns these cottages, you see, but he is always so grumpy because he has to come half a mile down the dirt track, and when he's done it, he says it's perfectly simple and even a child could do it.'

'OK, OK. Let's have a look.' Sam tried to reassure her, and told her that he had plenty of time, because he would have stayed at the exhibition if he had not chased after her.

With the help of instruction manuals, which Mary found for him in a kitchen drawer, Sam soon worked out how to position the two levers that moved across the wide slit at the bottom of the water heater before pressing the ignition button. He explained carefully and patiently to Mary that it was necessary to have the gas full on when the ignition button was pressed. She said she knew that, but claimed that it never worked when she did it, and then there was the smell of gas, and then she always got frightened.

In the same way, he explained that with the fire, the volume dial had to be held down in position for about twenty seconds after ignition so that there was enough gas to fill the flue and then it would stay alight.

She nodded as he was speaking, but put her head slowly on one side, closed her eyes briefly and then rubbed her knuckles slowly across her forehead. Sam could tell that she wasn't really following, but was so grateful to him for starting the fire.

Suddenly, as he looked down at this fragile, quiet, patient little lady, he was full of compassion for her. She has had her fill of everyday battles, he thought. She will have raised her children, brought them up on a farm worker's wages, fed and clothed them as well as she could, struggled to save the money to send them on school trips, put up with their children's tantrums and teenage wilfulness. And now, with her husband long dead and her children gone away, she will show more bravery every day in tackling her little problems with modern gadgets than I have had to show in all my life.

'Thank you so much. Now I'll be warm tonight.' The warmth of her gratitude stopped the flow of his reflections. The face he was looking at was relaxed now, and the relief was beaming out of those crinkled, smiling eyes.

'That's OK, Mrs Dyer,' said Sam, trying to mirror the smile. 'Look. I can see you're on your own out here and it must be difficult for you sometimes. Have this card, and you can give me a ring any time you want if you've got a problem or can't make things go right. This place is only a couple of miles away from my house.'

'Thank you. Thank you.' Again, he was touched by the simple gratitude.

She took the card readily, even eagerly, and showed him out.

As he was leaving, finding his car, turning in the road and heading back towards Thoreswood, Sam enjoyed a warm glow of satisfaction. He was halfway home before he remembered the golden object that Mary Dyer had snatched back from Geoff Lowis and had stuffed quickly into her coat pocket. He pictured again the look of amazement that seemed to deaden Geoff's ability to respond. He wondered what could have made a thing so small produce such astonishment.

5

A few days before Christmas, Geoff Lowis brought Sam the History Society report of the open day for the New Year edition of the village newsletter. It was early evening, and in view of the season, Sam asked him in and offered him a glass of wine.

Hazel joined them, and the three of them sat sipping wine and discussing how the society was flourishing. The conversation moved round to the open day and the incident involving Mary Dyer.

'Well, did you find that old lady to return her handbag?' asked Geoff. Sam had given Hazel a rather light-hearted account of the incident, and so she was not surprised.

'Oh, yes,' replied Sam, 'and I noticed how surprised you were by that gold object she showed you.'

'Well, what a carry-on,' laughed Geoff. 'She offered it to me one minute, and then, before I could pick it up, she snatched it back and pretty well ran out of the room. I've never seen a woman so old move so fast.'

'Yes. It was quite odd,' agreed Sam, 'but why were you so struck by it when you first saw it? You seemed to seize up.'

'For a start, it was made of very fine gold. It couldn't have been pure, because pure gold will not mould with precision, but it might have been almost pure,' said Geoff. The laughter had gone now, and he was in earnest. 'I didn't have a chance to examine it, but you have a sense of what's gold and what's not gold even at a distance, and what I am sure of is that it was gold.'

'But what was it?' asked Sam.

Geoff paused before he replied. He took a deep breath through closed teeth. 'It's difficult to say,' he said at last. 'If she's got a piece of gold that size, she should simply take it to a jeweller to have it valued, but the fact that she asked me and then behaved in such a secretive manner suggests that it's an antique that she's found or had in the family for a long time. Maybe she's hard up and wants to get some cash.'

'But supposing it's not an antique, what would it be?' Sam was puzzled.

Geoff spread his hands again, as he had done at the exhibition. 'I can't think of anything it could be used for except as a paperweight on a desk. But people use pretty things and novelties for paperweights, not anything valuable, because they just leave them around on a desk when they're not there.'

'It would be about the right size, though,' mused Sam.

'Yes, and very heavy, but you just wouldn't have anything of that value lying around in an office. It was quite a big lump of gold, you know.'

'H'mm.' Sam was thoughtful. The conversation died. There was silence for a short time, but not an uncomfortable one. Sam fiddled with the cuff of his shirt. Hazel glanced at the clock.

'But if it was an antique, what would it have been?' Sam returned to the subject of Mrs Dyer.

'I didn't get a close enough look,' said Geoff, without any enthusiasm. 'I couldn't tell for certain whether it was a container of any kind, but my guess is that it wasn't. That loop at the top looked more like something to hold it by, than something to pull up a lid.'

'Yes.' Sam still seemed lost in thought. 'It's obvious that we won't be any the wiser unless she lets us have another look at it – a closer look – a real examination.'

'And if Mrs Dyer really wants to have it valued, she'll have to take it to a jeweller or an antique dealer or to the museum in Thorby.' Geoff did not seem much excited by the matter, and the way he listed Mrs Dyer's options sounded as if he wanted to close the subject. Then he seemed to have second thoughts.

'Mind you,' Geoff continued, 'if it is really old, not only is it an antique, but it would count as treasure, and then she would have to report it by law.'

'What counts as "really old"?' asked Hazel.

'Over three hundred years,' said Geoff, 'and, as it's made of gold, it could easily be that old.'

'Yes. As you say,' went on Sam, 'if she is serious about having it valued, she really will have to let someone examine it. The way she carried on at the open day makes you think she's afraid to let anyone else get their hands on it.'

'It all rather makes me think that she is probably hard up for money and is thinking of trading it in.'

Each person looked at the table in silence. Each was, in their own way, thinking about a lonely old lady in an isolated cottage, and wondering how poor she was. They looked at drinks, emptied glasses, and soon Geoff Lowis was on his way with a cheery 'Goodnight, and a happy Christmas if I don't see you again.'

Quickly, Hazel prepared a meal. They had eaten, and were just relaxing with a glass of wine, when the phone rang.

The caller was obviously in some distress: 'Oh, I'm sorry, Mr Dent. This is Mary. I'm really sorry. I realise you must be busy, but I'm freezing. Could you come and fix my heating, please? I've phoned the farmer, but there's no reply.'

Sam paused for a second or two while he took a deep breath, but then gave the only answer possible.

'Of course, Mrs Dyer. I'll be there in a few minutes.' Anyone listening would have needed to know him as well as Hazel did, to notice the hesitation: the fact that he said 'Mrs Dyer' instead of 'Mary' showed the faintest hint of irritation.

When Sam explained, Hazel reflected the feeling. 'Of course. You can't just leave her.'

Sam soon covered the two miles along the Rowle Road. He took Hazel's car from the side of the house. She always left it there now since her allergic attack. Sam still put his in the barn to occupy his allotted space.

As he drove past the cottages into the rough space on the nearside of the road, he noticed that there were no lights in Mary's neighbour's window.

The doorway lit up as he approached. Mary waited on the step. 'So sorry to drag you out at this time of night,' she said, and dropped her head slightly so that she looked up more appealingly. 'I sat for an hour wondering if I dare phone you, but I had tried Mr Steadman several times.'

Again, Sam began to fill with a compassion that swamped all other feelings. He smiled as he entered and turned right into Mrs Dyer's small kitchen. It had been not so much modernised as made more functional and convenient over the years. A series of plain, wooden storage units had been mounted at shoulder height on the back wall, the wall adjoining the living room. Turquoise tiles, dated by colour and shape, covered all the walls from the ceiling down to waist height, but then there was a thin band of wood, below which it was thickly painted brick to the stout skirting board and floor. The only window, wooden-framed and single-glazed, with six small panels, was at the front, next to the door. A wooden draining board had been replaced by one of stainless steel. What had originally been only a standpipe at the back of the sink had been replaced by a 'hot' and 'cold' mixer tap beneath the water heater, which was mounted on to the outside wall so that the flue had a direct exit. This heater also provided hot water to radiators in each of the two downstairs rooms, and it was this that Mary had found difficult to start.

A plain gas cooker stood beside the sink and draining

board, and a fridge/freezer stood against the far wall. A small radiator occupied the middle of the back wall where a kitchen range had once been, and behind this was the large, wide grate and chimney breast of the fire, which warmed the adjacent living room. The old coal-fired heating system was therefore central to the arrangement of the cottage, and had been adapted when gas was introduced.

Sam went to the heater, moved both levers across to the closed position, and pulled one back for a wide-open flue as he pressed the ignition. A loud popping noise announced that the gas had lit.

He moved into the dining-room, knelt down in front of the fire, turned on the gas supply as he pressed the ignition, and then held the supply button down for fully half a minute while he looked up at Mary Dyer and smiled his sympathy. She looked back bashfully, slowly and gently shaking her head.

'Would you like a cup of tea?' Mary asked timidly, while Sam was still in the kneeling position. It occurred to Sam that he might have been the only person she had spoken to that day and he thought that he had better spend a few minutes with her.

'Yes, please, Mary.'

Five minutes later, Sam was cradling a mug of Mary's strong tea and sitting in one of her two easy chairs, looking at the fire he had just lit. It was a living flame fire and the effect was one of light and joy.

The recess into which the fire was set was very wide and a copper canopy hung over it at a height of rather less than three feet. The original brick wall had been left bare as the fire surround, to give a feeling of old-world stability, and of a solid structure. As Sam looked at it, it certainly gave a feeling of comfort.

At shoulder height above the fire, a thick mantel was in place, about six feet in length. Mary had a few Christmas cards standing on it, and a few red decorations hanging down the side supports. A carriage clock stood in the middle of it, flanked by family photographs – two girls in their late teens, Sam guessed. What was obviously Mary's regular, well-worn chair was to the left of the fireplace as Sam looked at it, because from that position, she could see out of the window, and had a clear view of anyone approaching the house.

'And who are the two girls?' asked Sam.

Mary's face lit up. 'My grandchildren.' The pride was clear. 'That's Maria on the left and she's my son's girl. Howard – that's my son – has done well for himself. He went to night school for years to study mining, and got to be a really well-qualified mining engineer. The trouble was that he then decided there were not any mining jobs in this country, so he's gone out to Australia. He and his wife, Joyce, they like it out there. They had Maria after they'd gone there, and I've only seen her once. They came back for a holiday five years ago, and they're hoping to come again next year. Maria's a bright girl and she has a good job in a bank.'

'And the other girl?' Sam prompted, after a lull.

'Oh, that's Sarah. She's my daughter's girl. Bridget is my daughter, and Sarah is very clever. She's really good at languages. She got 'A's in all her GCSE exams and this coming year she does her 'A' levels.'

A sudden energy seemed to course through Mary when she spoke about Sarah. Her eyes shone; she moved around in her chair, restlessly adjusting her position; her hands were constantly on the move, her fingers picking and clutching at the sleeves of her cardigan.

Sam sipped his tea. 'And what will she do eventually?' He was consciously trying to keep his voice gentle and his tone friendly. His interest in Mary's family was genuine.

'Ah, well. We don't know yet,' Mary said, and she seemed to subside a little. Then her eyes flashed up to look directly into Sam's face. 'I want her to go to university,' she said, with an intensity that really startled Sam. 'She's got the ability. She's good at languages and she would be able to read all those legal documents. She could be a lawyer or work in business. I've had enough of girls being trampled on in my family.' Then she took her eyes from Sam's face and peered into her cup.

'Bridget married a lad who was in the army – Brian,' went on Mary, in a rather flatter tone, the excitement gone from her eyes. 'They seemed all right while he was in the army, but he's not been able to get much of a job since he came out. At the moment, he drives a lorry for Gibson's, in Thorby. They live in Thorby and Bridget works part-time in a shop on the outskirts, but I don't see much of them. Brian never wants to come round here. It would be no good asking him to fix my heating. They have a younger lad, Kevin, but he doesn't seem to get on too well at school.' She looked down sadly, her voice trailed off and she seemed to retreat into her own thoughts.

'How old is he?' asked Sam. He thought he'd better keep the conversation going until he had finished his tea.

'Thirteen.' She smiled directly at Sam, seeming to come out of her dream, and her eyes began to shine again. 'Getting more expensive,' and the smile lit up again. Then she added, as if lingering on a picture that had stayed in her mind: 'Oh, Sarah, though – she could make so much of herself.'

'I'm sure she will.' Sam was trying to be encouraging, without engaging too strongly. 'And will you see them all on Christmas Day?'

'No. They always stay at home on Christmas mornings, and go to Brian's parents in the afternoon for tea. He comes from a big family, and I think they have quite a knees-up in the evening.'

Sam began to feel a little concerned. 'So what about your neighbour?' he asked. 'Will you see her on Christmas Day?'

'No, no. She's gone away to stay with her family for Christmas and New Year. They live down south, somewhere near London, and they came to fetch her yesterday.' Mary was quite animated and lively again. 'She gave me a lovely card this year, and a big tin of biscuits. That's it on the end of the mantelpiece. Don't you think that's a lovely card?'

'Yes, it is,' said Sam, with scarcely a glance. 'Look, does that mean you are on your own on Christmas Day?'

'Yes,' said Mary, with a shrug. 'But it's all right. I'm quite used to it. Bridget's family will be round on Boxing Day.'

'Yes. Would you excuse me while I use my phone?' asked Sam, as he got out of his chair and walked into the kitchen to ring Hazel.

6

Christmas was one of the best times of the year as far as Sam was concerned, perhaps the very best time, depending on how good the summer holiday had been. If the family had had a really good holiday, memories of warm days, alfresco food, spectacular sights and flaming sunsets fed his imagination for weeks as he sat in the dusty surroundings of the open-plan office, battling with the hard and unforgiving machine in front of him.

Christmas, though, was not dependent on the weather and Sam was able to plan it each year with happiness in mind. He always saved a few days of his annual holiday allowance so that he could use them up just before Christmas. The company closed down from Christmas Eve until January 2nd anyway, and so it was an easy calculation to leave three or four days to be spent before the close-down.

Hazel knew how much the season meant to Sam, and thought the explanation lay in his own lonely childhood. He had been an only child, and his mother had died suddenly when he was just ten years old. His father had done his best for him, but from the age of ten, Sam had had to manage many of the domestic chores and activities on his own. When he was older and looked back on his teenage years, he realised that he had missed, without being aware of it at the time, a sense of being looked after, the comforting presence of a mother's indulgent touch. Visits to his school friends at their homes always produced a slight envy of the gently pressing warmth of a crowded family life. Now, Sam was conscious of wanting to make his home more comfortable than at any other season of the year, and of thinking of his own small family more tenderly than he did at any other time.

The décor of the lounge of the Dents' house was a very light, but soft yellow. Hazel had called it ivory when choosing the wallpaper, though the label was 'Natural Hessian'. Certainly, the effect was to generate a bright, cheerful atmosphere and mood. The addition of splashes of red and areas of dark green at Christmas time was therefore strong in its provision of warmth and relaxation.

There were holly bushes all round the area of Thoreswood. There was even holly growing among the hawthorn in the hedge that bordered and protected the garden from the main road to Thorby at the back of their property. Loscar wood, to the east of Thoreswood along Rowle Road, was also full of holly and ivy, and a walk there with a few plastic bags could provide enough evergreen vegetation to decorate the whole house. Hazel had attended a flower-arranging course in the church rooms one autumn a few years ago, and it had culminated in the production of permanent Christmas decorations of bundles of twigs bound with seasonally coloured ribbons, and displays of dried leaves and pine cones, which had been painted red and gold. Each Christmas, she brought them out of the loft and placed them round the room: the effect was striking and tasteful. Sam remembered being quite hurt by her laughter when, one year, he had suggested making some paper chains to remind him of his childhood. They also received lots of Christmas cards, and Hazel had a way of hanging them in strings down the walls to blend in with the decorations. Sam admitted to being quite hopeless in the face of this artistry; it was another aspect of Hazel's home-making touch that he lacked.

Apart from the central focus of his home, the wrap-around

cosiness he felt as he did his last-minute Christmas shopping each year was something that Sam deliberately arranged. Present buying over, he loved to walk down the High Street in Thorby on Christmas Eve afternoon, observing the hustle and bustle whilst buying a few bits and pieces the family might need over the Christmas season. Indeed, he even thought that it was a bit better if it was wet, because then the neon lights on the shopfronts and the winking decorations were reflected on the pavements. Hazel was so busy that she really didn't have time to make mince pies and cakes and puddings, and said that, in any case, you could buy them as cheaply as you could get the ingredients these days.

So it was pies, nuts and cakes that Sam bought as he walked along the High Street on Christmas Eve. People struggled along with their parcels, head down to the wind, wrestled with self-closing doors, and called briefly to each other as they went about their business.

Sam made his way from one end of the High Street as far as the roundabout. At one end, the market square was deserted because it was not market day. It was remarkable how desolate and lifeless the whole area looked when the market was not in session. Those corrugated-iron roofs, aluminium alloy frames and bare wooden counters inspired nothing but a cold dread as they stood exposed to the elements. Put enticing produce on the counter, hang colourful cloths and trade names from the roofs and side posts, position a smiling person behind the counter, add the sound of human banter and chatter, and suddenly it would all come alive. The whole place would be full of interest, fascination, good humour, and an invitation to relate to other human beings. Warmth, happiness and satisfaction would flow.

At the side of the market-place was the town hall – large, imposing, fortress-like, with wide tiers of steps leading between colonnades to the huge oak-door entrance. Sam imagined, behind the lighted windows of the upper floors, clerks sitting at rows of desks, feverishly working out columns of figures to finish the day's work before rushing to join the festivities.

Beyond the town hall was the vibrant and pulsating heart of the commercial district. Thorby had once stood on the Great North Road, and a few heavy-beamed and low-ceilinged pubs and hotels in the town had, in past centuries, been coaching inns. For this reason, the High Street was unusually wide. Indeed, a ribbon of space between the pavement and shops on one side was now used as parking lots for shoppers. The first shop from the market end was a pharmacy, with rows of coloured bottles and advertisements covering the window-space. Next came a furniture store, which was a converted coaching inn, with an impressive stone façade. The interior was cluttered with suites, bookcases and hi-fi units, with an area for kitchen units and beds if you could see into the further recesses. Next was a frozen-food shop with tawdry stickers announcing numerous special offers and hiding the monotony of rows of freezers within. There was a multi-coloured stationer, a shoe shop and beyond a small alleyway, a branch of W.H. Smith.

There was a surging tide of people that seemed to be pressing through each door. Sam loved being a part of it, glancing around, observing people, watching the happiness bouncing from one beaming face to another. Even the old man selling his sheets of wrapping paper on the pavement by the alleyway seemed relaxed about it all.

Finally, Sam passed Marks & Spencer. It looked like some gleaming Aladdin's cave of a thousand glittering pieces, and sighed its warm breath into the raw chill of the High Street. He reached the delicatessen where he bought his mince pies and sausage rolls. Pine Properties stood at the end of the row of shops, and he looked for Hazel. She was not at one of the desks beyond the counter, but he knew she had an office right at the back. Indeed, the whole place seemed empty,

41

totally deserted in fact, but then he spotted her at the back of the large office, up to her elbows in a filing cabinet.

As the place seemed so empty, Sam pushed his way through the glass door, walked the length of the counter, which was sideways on to the front of the shop, and approached the desks and filing cabinets at the back, smiling at Hazel. She looked up, alert, thinking she had heard a customer, and Sam saw her face relax as she realised it was him.

'You're not exactly crowded out here, are you? Where is everybody?' he asked, with a grin.

'Oh, I've done my usual Christmas Eve thing, and told the staff to take the afternoon off. I do it every year, and it makes sure we all leave each other in good humour for Christmas. We don't get many applications for mortgages on Christmas Eve, although, believe it or not, I've had a steady trickle of people withdrawing and depositing.'

'I expect they're in town anyway, and think they might as well do that,' said Sam.

'Either that, or they need cash for last minute presents,' Hazel suggested. 'Are you doing our last minute shopping for pies and rolls for tomorrow?' she asked.

'Yes. I got a few extra with Mary spending the day with us tomorrow.'

Hazel's expression dropped. Sam noticed her lips tighten.

'What's the matter? Aren't you happy for her to come? You agreed to it when I phoned you from her house and asked, after I'd fixed the heating.'

'Yes. I know. What else was I supposed to say late at night with you giving me a sob story about her being on her own stuck out at Lilac Cottage?'

'I thought you'd be glad to be making her happy.'

'But it's you all over isn't it? You're so belligerent and aggressive if you're dealing with anyone in authority, or if you think things aren't quite right, but just because an old lady is on her own for one day, you come over all soppy and sentimental. There's always two sides to you.'

'Well, we've asked her now, and you agreed.'

'Yes. I know. We'll have to do it.' Sam realised how tired she looked as she swept a stray strand of hair from her forehead. 'But you'll never change. Why can't you learn? Christmas is a time for just families to be together, and only families. Like I said after the chicken hut affair, there's only us. No one else is really on your side.'

Sam shrugged and turned towards the door with a sigh. Hazel really had knocked his good humour out of him.

'Go on. Get out. I'll see you at home. I'll just wind up here and then I'll lock up and perhaps I can start my Christmas.'

Sam turned left out of the front door of Pine Properties and then he came to a roundabout. This, in effect, marked the end of the shopping area, because the two roads that led from it on the far side stopped after a few yards to allow a bypass to come across them, beyond which was the car park that Sam was heading for. Although the Great North Road had originally passed straight through it, the town now stood about three miles to the east of the A1 in South Yorkshire, just at that spot where the coalmining and steel industries in the south Pennine area gave way to the flat farmland of eastern England. Mining and steel and the heavy industry had largely gone now, and employment in Thorby was mainly located in the light industrial estates to the north of the town beyond the roundabout that Sam was approaching. They provided bases for self-employed building tradesmen, small factories for electrical goods, centres for companies using digital technology, such as those that Sam and Jack Hunt worked in.

Between the roundabout and the bypass was the biggest church in the town, very much alive on this day, its glowing interior offering a spiritual embrace to all passers-by. The stained-glass windows palpitated with the weak glow of candles from within. Sam crossed the bypass through the pedestrian tunnel, found his car and joined the flow of traffic as it ebbed from the town centre to the suburbs and beyond.

By the time Hazel arrived home and came in at the kitchen door, Sam was sitting hunched over his desk at the end of the dining-room.

'Hello. I'm home.'

No reaction. Sam did not turn round or look up. Hazel felt a pang of remorse for being a bit sour with him when he had called in at the office. She thought fleetingly of how it used to be in the Thorby house just after they were married. He always greeted her with a kiss and a smile, really glad to see her at the end of each day. Nowadays, he seemed to take her for granted, to expect her to do the cooking while he got on with whatever needed to be done in the house. Hazel admitted to herself, though, that her passion had died after those early days. Life was more like a business partnership these days. They managed the house and their shared life, and brought up Andrew to the best of their ability.

'I'll fix something to eat,' she said, her tone flatter. 'Chicken with stir-fry vegetables and rice.' She knew Sam liked that.

Still no response. She stared hard at the back of his head and hunched shoulders. How many hours, how many nights was that her view of him, as he toiled over a problem from work, or did some routine paperwork. You can send hatred towards backs and shoulders, she thought, and the person doesn't even know, and so there's no response.

Hazel turned to prepare the food. It was only a few minutes' work with the rice boiler and the wok for the chicken breasts. She could hear that Andrew's television set was on upstairs. She called him down now, and presented her husband and son with their evening meal at the round dining table. They ate mostly in silence, each absorbed in their own thoughts, each being careful not to fracture the delicate silence.

'Dave phoned a few minutes before you got home,' said Sam after they had finished. 'He asked me to go for a drink with him at the Blacksmith's Arms tonight.' Hazel was not too keen on his going out to see Dave on Christmas Eve, but murmured her agreement all the same. Dave was an old friend Sam had kept in touch with since his schooldays. All these years later, they still met at the Blacksmith's Arms almost every week, and put the world right over a pint of beer.

Andrew came down from upstairs as soon as he heard Sam go out.

'Just wanted to watch the *Sports Quiz*, Mum,' he said to Hazel, who had also come into the lounge.

'Thanks for staying quiet earlier on,' she said. 'Dad's got a lot on his mind.'

'So is drinking supposed to help?' Andrew cut straight to the point.

'No, but talking might,' said Hazel, with a shrug. 'Let's hope he talks it out.'

Much later, Andrew went to bed.

Later still, Hazel heard a car draw up on Brewster Lane. She went apprehensively to the door and opened it to find Sam and Dave walking towards it. Sam dangled the car keys towards her.

'Will you go back to the Blacksmith's with Dave and bring my car home?' he asked. 'I've had too many.'

Hazel stiffened, anxious and uncertain. Sam was smiling weakly at her, but Hazel felt that it was now safe to go on the attack.

'Disgusting!' She spat the word out with all the sneering energy she could muster. 'Pathetic!' she added, as Sam stepped inside and dropped the keys into her outstretched hand. 'Do you think that's the answer? I thought you were more grown-up than that.'

He did not retaliate. His tone was pleading.

'I'm not drunk. I'm just being sensible. I've had three pints. Dave's only had one.'

Hazel pushed past and marched to the passenger side of Dave's car. The two miles back to the Blacksmith's Arms passed quietly. Dave spoke occasionally, trying to support Sam – as he would.

'He's certainly not drunk,' said Dave. 'In fact, he's being very sensible because he knows he's over the legal limit.'

Hazel was aware of the rudeness of the grunt that was her reply. Dave, after all, was going to some trouble for a friend. At the end of the journey, she thanked Dave politely, and drove Sam's car back home, parking on the grass at the side of the house.

Sam had gone to bed but still had the bedroom light on. When Hazel went into the room, she avoided his eyes, collected her night things and made for the door to the spare bedroom. She often did this, and the bed was always made up.

'There's no need to be like that,' she heard Sam say, quietly.

'Oh yes, there is. You'll smell.'

Christmas Day was much as usual in the Dent family's house, with the addition of Mary Dyer as their guest for the day. There was no breakfast – just a sausage roll and a cup of coffee. Then there was a pause in front of those beautifully arranged parcels under the tree – coloured paper, ribbons, bows, labels, sparkling tree lights – hours of work to be ripped up in a few frantic minutes of expectation. And so the morning began with the excitement of opening presents and thanking each other, with comments by Andrew on various presents sent by distant relatives. The chaotic mound of wrapping paper grew until Sam finally waded in with a bin bag and carted off the season's rubbish.

There followed a ritual that always irritated Hazel and Andrew: Sam always insisted on buying a natural tree, scorning artificial ones and saying there was nothing like the living wood to make their decorations feel complete. The trouble was that live trees cast their pine needles over the carpet, and Sam insisted on clearing them up with his battery-operated car vacuum cleaner before he would help to get the turkey in, or do anything else.

All annual rituals over, and with Andrew absorbed in his presents – books, new software, electronic gadgets and clothes – and Hazel finishing preparation of the vegetables, Sam set off to fetch Mary.

She brought a card and apologised for having no time to buy presents. Sam and Hazel fussed over her and talked about the house and themselves and the presents Andrew had received. Mary had put on what was obviously a nearly new blue dress, wore a really beautiful mother-of-pearl necklace, had tied her hair back and had applied make-up tastefully and sparingly. Hazel noticed that she had slightly rouged her pale cheeks, and noticed with satisfaction that those cheeks became more highly coloured after two glasses of sherry, which she gladly accepted and drank with relish.

So, with everyone suitably lubricated, it was a very merry Christmas dinner that they enjoyed. The turkey had been roasting all of the morning, and during the last hour had been joined by roast potatoes, Brussels sprouts with a sprinkling of sesame seeds and bits of bacon, and then parsnips and carrots with a sprig of rosemary. It was washed down with a dry, white Australian wine, followed by plum pudding with cream.

There had been so much to eat that conversation had been only intermittent during the meal, but when Hazel and Mary lingered at the table afterwards, while Sam and Andrew removed all the dishes to the draining board, Hazel continued to enquire about Mary's home circumstances.

'Wouldn't it be more convenient for you to move into Thorby, as you have a daughter living there?' Hazel asked. 'You'd be near the shops and the doctor's, and you would be able to nip round to Bridget's any time you wanted.'

'Oh, yes,' came the reply, with a good amount of feeling. 'I like my Lilac Cottage, but I really dislike the position it's in. I've only got my neighbour and occasionally Mr Steadman to talk to, and it's always difficult when I need to go anywhere.'

'Well, how do you manage?'

'Well, Brian could come and fetch me, but never seems to want to,' she said, with the suggestion of a sigh. 'Mr Steadman is quite good, though. If he and his wife are going shopping, he sometimes asks me if I'd like a lift into Thorby and back.'

'What do you do if it's important for you to get into Thorby on a particular day?'

'There's a bus service, which will stop at the cottages if the driver sees someone waiting there. It's only once a day, though, and it takes all day to get into town and back. Mind you, I have a free pass in view of my advanced age,' she added, and the corners of her eyes creased in that engaging smile.

'But why not just move into Thorby?' persisted Hazel.

'I can't,' Mary answered rather quickly, and the gaze that met Hazel's was firm and unwavering. 'I've no money to buy anywhere in Thorby, and I have had my name down for a council house for years, but, you see, because I already have a perfectly good house to live in, I stay at the bottom of the list. I am the bottom priority. Everyone else who has nowhere to live, or who has any kind of social or financial problem, is a higher priority than I am, according to the Council, and so for years I have known that there's no chance of my moving up the list. It looks as if I am stuck out at Lilac Cottage until I get carried out. Bridget and Brian's small house is full, and they can't do anything to help me.'

'Mmm.' Hazel just made a sympathetic noise, and she silently mulled over the situation.

'What about renting somewhere privately?' suggested Hazel, after a few minutes.

'I've never really considered that,' said Mary softly, almost timidly. 'I've always had the feeling that I don't trust private landlords. You don't have any security, do you? They could turn you out if it's convenient for them to do so, couldn't they?'

'It's not quite like that these days,' said Hazel, confident now that she was on her own ground. 'Tenants have some protection in law nowadays, depending on the rental agreement and the kind of property they are in. Look, there may be more places to rent than you imagine, and we have a few at Pine every now and again. Shall I look out for a place for you?'

Mary dropped her eyes again. 'OK,' she said. 'You can let me know – but I'd want to go into full details of it all.' The look she gave Hazel was level and strong. The defensive attitude had come up like a barrier. Mary seemed to trust no one.

Usually, all the family went for a walk in the afternoon to shake the food down and make themselves feel more comfortable, but now Hazel was quick to say that she would stay in with Mary while Sam and Andrew walked. This suited them, and it gave Sam a chance to explain to Andrew who Mary Dyer was and how she had come to be invited for the day. It was getting near to four o'clock, and as dusk fell, father and son walked, not out into the countryside, which they would have done at any other season of the year, but through the village so that they could observe the lit-up Christmas trees in the windows of the houses. As they walked, they commented on the size and quality of the trees and the other features of the festive decorations displayed at each house.

They returned to find that Hazel and Mary had despatched all the debris of the huge Christmas dinner, and were now offering a light tea of cooked meats, mince pies, sausage rolls, light salad and Christmas cake. Everyone ate as little as they could decently get away with, without offending Hazel.

For half an hour or so, Andrew and Sam played with Andrew's largest present. This was a keyboard with a sight-reading course that he had asked for. He was doing very well with the simple melodies of some well-known Christmas carols. Many years ago, Sam had learnt to strum the major chords on an acoustic guitar, and so he was able to accompany Andrew in a seasonal medley, while Hazel and Mary gave encouraging comments.

Eventually, they did what they always did on Christmas evening, and got out the family's favourite game, Monopoly. All agreed that it was much better with four players than with three. Mary showed herself to be as astute as anybody in the way she played her hand and purchased property. Each move was usually preceded by a thoughtful stroking of her jaw and chin, and a soft muttering of 'Speculate to accumulate'.

Finally, it was time to finish, with cups of coffee. Hazel said that she wanted to go back to Mary's cottage with her and Sam. She had not even seen the cottage yet, and if she came, she could see that Mary was settled in comfortably. It seemed that, when Sam had fetched Mary in the morning, he had timed the heating to come on during the evening.

Mary was still bright and alert during the car ride back to Lilac Cottage. 'You've had quite a hard life one way and another, haven't you, Mary?' began Hazel.

'I suppose I have,' came a quick reply. 'The worst time was when my husband got killed. Bill, his name was, and he was killed when a gravel pit he was digging right over at the far end of the farm caved in on him. It was some minutes before anyone could get to him, and he had suffocated. I got no compensation at all, you see. Steadman wanted me to be paid because he had employer's liability insurance, but the insurance company hired a lawyer who argued that there was no negligence or blame on Steadman at all, and that it was just misadventure.'

'Wow! That was pretty rough on you,' Sam was quick to exclaim.

'Well, that's how they are,' went on Mary. 'They'll do you out of anything if you don't stand up for yourself. They're always making money out of people who don't have much. The landowners and farmers, as well as the factory bosses, they pay their workers less than they deserve for their contribution to the business that employs them.'

'Oh, you're right there, Mary,' said Sam, who was really warming to what Mary was saying, and admiring her spirit for the energy she still had after a long life of battling for her small family.

'I'll tell you something, though,' Mary continued. She sounded really fired up now. 'They're not going to exploit me any more. I keep a watch on Steadman if he suggests he's going to raise the rent, and he knows I'll take him to a tribunal if it's too much. I wrote to the pension people when they didn't pay me my winter fuel allowance on time, and I went down to see the Council when they forgot to make a reduction in my Council Tax because I don't have a street light.'

'Good for you,' enthused Sam. He kept watching her in the rear view mirror, and though the car interior was dark, he imagined a glint in her eye. 'You stand your corner, and if you want any letters typing out, I'm your man.'

'But if you got no compensation when your husband died, Mary, how did you manage with two children?' asked Hazel. She was rather irritated by Sam's tub-thumping support, and was more interested in the practical solutions to Mary's problems.

'I had a small widow's pension,' Mary answered, 'and the family allowance, as it was then. Howard was sixteen and Bridget was fourteen when Bill was killed. Howard had just left school, and went to work in the pit ten miles away. So his money and my bits and pieces kept all three of us for a while until Bridget left school. Both Howard and I wanted Bridget to stay on at school and do 'A' levels because she was very bright, but she kept asking what was the point. Then, only a year after she had left and got a job in a shop, she married Brian, who was in the army, and moved into married quarters. He got posted abroad, and she settled down to have two children. Howard worked on and studied for years at night school until he was highly qualified in mining, and eventually he got a chief engineer's job in Australia. So, you see, I've lived on my own for a long time now.'

Mary's tone subsided a little, just as they arrived at Lilac Cottage. Hazel got out and opened the rear door for her, and she waited as she unlocked the door.

'Ooh! It's lovely and warm,' Mary called over her shoulder, as she walked inside. 'The heating's obviously working well.'

'Right. I'll leave you to it if you're all right, then, Mary,' said Hazel, as lights were switched on. 'I'll be in touch again when we have something suitable at Pine Properties for you to rent.'

'Yes. OK. Thank you.' Mary's tone was very warm. 'And thank you for a lovely day today. Goodnight.'

'Goodnight.'

Hazel returned to the car. Yes. I certainly will get in touch, she thought, as Sam moved the car forward to turn round in the widened part of the road a few yards further on, and before I do, I'll make sure the heating works. Then my husband won't have to keep running out to sort it out for you because your son-in-law's too lazy.

7

The buff-coloured envelope was waiting for Sam when he arrived home from work one evening in mid-April. The public notice announcing Sam's proposed garage had originally been published in the *Thorby Recorder* just before Christmas, and then again three times in January. However, there had been a surge of applications in the New Year, and Sam had had to wait until the March meeting of the planning committee for a decision.

He arrived home tired but happy. Spring was leaping through the countryside, and the days were stretching well into the evening. He was looking forward to building his garage.

Hazel had gone to work after the morning post had arrived, but left the envelope for Sam to open. It was addressed to him as he, individually, had made the application. It had been franked by Thorby Borough Council, and Sam knew it would be news of the planning application. He snatched it up and ripped it open. The letterhead announced that it was from the Planning and Transportation Department of the Council.

He skipped past the heading announcing the proposed erection of a garage. In the second paragraph, his eyes settled briefly on the word 'refused' and he rushed on: '... within the above conservation area and the Council are of the opinion that the proposal would affect the character and appearance of the conservation area.' He read no more, but just glanced at the signature below: '*D. O'Brien.* Chief Planning Officer, Thorby Borough Council.'

Sam looked through the window. His brain felt as if seized in a clamp. His happiness vaporised and vanished. His face hardened and he felt the pressure behind the eyes that he always felt at the onset of anger. He threw the letter on to his desk.

He could not believe it. Why? What was the harm in a garage at the side of his house? Why had they done this? He picked up the letter again and read through it to find a reason, but could not: it 'would affect the character and appearance of the conservation area', and that was all it said.

Hazel came in just at that moment. One look at his face told her everything. He tossed the letter to her, and it fell on to a chair. She picked it up.

'Oh, God. No,' she murmured. 'I bet you are sick.'

Sam did not reply. He slumped into his chair and stared at the desk top while he absorbed the finality of the news.

Then his mind began to focus on the reasons. He had proposed to use the same stone that the house walls were made of. It couldn't be that. The neighbours. It must have been the objections of the neighbours. Brewster would have objected. Why? Just to be awkward, just to keep Sam in his place, just to keep control of the land that used to be his. Judith Towers would do anything to keep on his side so that she could do his wife's hair. Ray would have to do what Judith said. Sue Davies was scared of Brewster because she worked at the Council offices, and Mike would support her: he saw the whole world in terms of self-interest. Jack Hunt would not have objected. He couldn't even see the proposed garage from his house, but there was no telling with his wife, Jean: she would have applied some high moral principle to this, as to everything else.

So that was it. Without a word, they had all turned away from him just when he needed them. First it was Hazel's health and now this, just because he was trying to do something about it. Right, Sam thought. He would see about this.

He drove to his feet suddenly, and made for the door.

'Where are you going?' asked Hazel.

'Just out.'

Oh no, Hazel thought. He would brood silently now, but how deeply, and for how long?

He wouldn't talk about it until he was ready. Then he would speak as if he were wrenching the words from the depths of his soul. Hazel hated the silences. She knew how the moods ran their course, and always ended in talk, but it was the tension, the waiting and watching that stretched her patience.

Of course, he was right. He was only building the garage for her, and what was the harm in it? But, now, he couldn't do anything about the refusal, and how long would he suffer? She turned to the domestic chores, wondering how soon he would be back.

Once outside, Sam did not go for his car, but walked a mile along the Rowle Road that led to Loscar wood, to the east of Thoreswood. There was a small picnic area, and public access, but it was an extensive and beautiful wood where Sam and Hazel had often walked on summer evenings before they were married, having driven out from Thorby.

As he walked, he could feel the tightness, the tension through his whole body. He suddenly realised his fists were clenched, though he had been unaware of it. His mouth was working and his jaw muscles were hard. He walked quickly, and looked around rapidly, from point to point in the landscape. As he passed the entrance to Brewster's place, he glared with a sneering hatred at the farmhouse. All he wants is to control and dominate people, he told himself. That's why he's a councillor: all the sheep will vote for him. Well, there'll be a payback for him.

At other times, when under pressure at work, he had found that an evening walk in Loscar wood helped to dissolve his anxiety. Cords of tension loosened a little, and gnawing feelings of hatred and spite left him.

The wood was on a slight rise, and he felt a welcoming sense of familiarity as he turned left off the road and approached it. The mantle of interlaced branches and the ever-present breeze softened the heat of the falling sun, and cooled his sweaty face and neck, for he had deliberately walked very quickly. The path leading to the picnic area was barred by the speckled shade of the birches, but Sam went on into the middle of the wood where little sunlight penetrated the lattice of the hazels. In the darkest part, he sat uncomfortably on a fallen log, and tried to let the whistling innocence of birdsong soothe him. But still inside he felt a restless, rancorous, hard-driving bitterness towards Brewster, the neighbours, and all that the Council stood for. He could not rid his mind of the reason for wanting to build the garage – Hazel's lethal allergy. But no one else listened.

When Sam got up from his log to walk home, slowly and more gently now, dusk was falling. He felt a little better, but not much. The flood of outrage that swamped his mind seemed to drown out any constructive feelings. A dull, insistent thud of hatred filled him and soured him.

As he walked homeward along the road, Sam watched the cool descent of the night. He could see the stirrings of countless moths and the hesitant flutter of bats above a nearby pond and around the canopies of a cluster of oaks. Finally, the velvet dome of night swallowed all the movement, and he arrived home.

Hazel and Andrew had gone to bed, and Sam went to the spare room. Hazel expected this, and called an unanswered 'Goodnight' when she heard him about. On previous occasions when he was upset, she had pleaded with him not to take it all inside himself, and suffer so much, but talk was slow in coming.

His pillow might have been covered with fine, irritating sand for all the rest it gave him. At times it felt as bumpy as a sack of rocks. An unripe moon rose and shafted squares of pale light along the floor and on to the bed. In Sam's fitful sleep, memories of the day jostled each other for face room. In fleeting dreams, he tried to wade towards a large but distant figure, but he might have been wading through treacle for all the headway he made. Daylight came as a merciful release.

It was a silent breakfast the next morning. Hazel had told Andrew what had happened about the planning application. From time to time, they both watched Sam, but neither spoke.

'Is it any wonder that people like Mary feel as they do about councils and anyone in authority?' Sam said, suddenly.

'Keep it in perspective, Sam,' said Hazel. 'A planning refusal is nothing compared to what Mary had to put up with, what with her husband getting killed, and she got no compensation because the insurance company got a clever lawyer.'

'Yes, I suppose so,' he agreed, 'but she still has to fight to get her winter fuel payment on time and to get her Council Tax right. I agree with her attitude.'

Hazel did not want to prolong the conversation, and quiet descended.

Sam was always the first to leave for work. At the door he paused, turned and looked straight at Hazel for the first time that day.

'What you said after the chicken hut affair,' he said. 'You're right. There's only us. We're on our own.'

8

At the beginning of May, Hazel noticed that there had come on to their books at Pine Properties a flat to rent in Thorby. It had an initial six month lease, but the arrangement could become permanent with one month's notice either way if everything proved satisfactory. It was unfurnished, and Hazel thought it might suit Mary, especially as it was on the ground floor and the owner, a single man in his fifties, lived above, on the first floor.

Mary agreed to look at it, and Hazel took her there early one afternoon. It was a terraced house, with the flat consisting of three rooms and a bathroom on the ground floor. A neat arrangement of staircases leading from a shared hall and front door ensured that the flat was self-contained and private.

Sitting room accommodation was at the front of the house, and the front room was connected with a smaller, middle room by means of a sliding partition. This middle room was a kitchen-cum-dining-room and had a sash window, which faced down the short back garden. Leading from it was a bedroom of reasonable size, and opening from the back of that was a very well-appointed bathroom, which had obviously been added to the house fairly recently, probably when it was converted into flats. Having looked round and met the owner, a very pleasant man who had been very courteous and welcoming, Mary said she would think it over.

But once they had gone to sit in Hazel's car, it was a different matter.

'The trouble is, I can't see how I am going to get in the furniture that I want to keep,' she told Hazel. 'I have already asked Bridget and Brian if they will have some, and Bridget seemed willing, but Brian said it was all too old-fashioned and he would not have it in his house.

'He has always been a bit "distant" with me, you see. I think it's because he thinks I don't really approve of him and I think Bridget could have done better for herself in life. He is very close to his relatives in Thorby, you see, and he spends only a grudging amount of time coming to my house. In fact, Bridget usually comes on her own. I was afraid at one time that, because of the way he is, the grandchildren might also be a bit "distant". Kevin is, but Sarah has always visited me as often as she could. One day last August, she walked all the way from Thorby to Lilac Cottage to see me, and she has always made quite a fuss over my birthday.'

'Well, that shows how much she thinks of you,' said Hazel, realising that she would have to listen to all this chat about her family, because Mary was a customer as much as anyone else.

'There is one piece of furniture that I am keen to keep with me,' went on Mary, 'and that's my old treadle-operated Singer sewing machine. I mended all Howard's and Bridget's clothes on it as they were growing up, and I made quite a number of them on it as well. I really feel for that piece of furniture more than any other, but Brian just laughed at the idea of finding room for it in his house. Bridget had to agree because she could do nothing about it, and they would have had to hire a van to move it. So you see, I think I would rather wait for a flat where I can keep more of my furniture, for the moment, anyway, and I'll have to turn this flat down.'

'Oh, don't worry,' Hazel hastened to keep up Mary's spirits. 'We've got another flat available right now. I thought the one we've just seen would suit you better because it's on the ground floor. Would you like to see another one? We've got plenty of time.'

'Yes, please.'

Hazel drove her to the next one. The owner was a lock-smith who had a shop that fronted one of the roads leading from the centre of Thorby. His name was Ed Gleave. He lived at the rear of the shop and had a flat above the shop to let. Mary was apprehensive about always having to climb up and down stairs, but went to have a look anyway. She told herself that there would be little difference between that and climbing up and down in a house.

When she saw the premises, she was at first not at all sure. The kitchen was long and narrow, and although there was plenty of cupboard space, good work surfaces, a fridge/freezer, a good cooker, a good-sized sink and a washing machine, she couldn't eat in there. She would have to have a small dining table in the corner of the sitting room. But what was wrong with that? Now that Hazel had got her thinking about renting privately, the feeling was growing in Mary that, now that it was late spring, this would be the year when she would finally leave Lilac Cottage.

Therefore, the flat was essentially a large sitting-cum-dining-room at the front, with a narrow kitchen, a fair-sized bedroom with plenty of built-in wardrobes, and a bathroom added to the back. However, what made Mary begin to think that she would settle for something less than perfect was that out at the back there was an alleyway beyond which the locksmith had his workshop. There was a small row of old, narrow buildings, which the locksmith, who owned them all but used only one to work in, had made secure. They all had 'Ed Gleave' written above each door, as had the door to the shop on the main road, but they were not used for much except storage of bits and pieces, and Mary thought that there might be space for her to store her furniture until she could gradually dispose of it. Another feature of the accommodation was that it was not far from where Bridget worked.

After spending some time looking round and meeting Ed Gleave, Mary said that she wanted a little time to think it over. Hazel offered to take her back to her house for a meal and to spend the evening. Mary was feeling so comfortable and happy with the Dent family now that she gladly accepted.

Sam had said that he would be late, and so when Hazel, Mary and Andrew had eaten, Andrew went to his room to do some homework. When Sam came in, he was glad to see Mary, and ate his meal quickly. He seemed very relaxed in Mary's company, just as she always responded to his openness and honesty, and so the conversation went at a good pace when he joined the ladies in the lounge.

'How did you come to live out at Lilac Cottage in the first place?' he asked.

'My dad took us there after the war,' replied Mary. 'It was a matter of doing anything to find somewhere to live. Dad had not worked on a farm before the war. In fact, he had been an engineering apprentice in a car component firm when he left school. He had always quite liked gardening and the countryside, though. Mum and Dad had got married in 1936, and two years later, I arrived. After the war, Dad said he thought anyone could get used to farm work if they just used a bit of common sense.'

Sam was following this with a sympathy that he always felt when talking with Mary. 'I have read that many people wanted a change and a new beginning after the war,' he said. 'In fact, the government provided land for those who wanted to settle into smallholdings. People thought they had fought for a new world and a better world, and they were going to enjoy it.'

'It wasn't that so much,' said Mary, 'as being desperate for a house. You see, the one we lived in when Dad got called up, just outside Sheffield, was bombed.

'Oh, it was a terrible night. Dad was in the army and he had

61

been sent to North Africa, and Mum and I lived on our own. Luckily, we had gone to visit Aunt Doreen, who lived a bit nearer the city, before the air raid started. Then we couldn't get back, and I spent the night with Mum and Aunt Doreen in the Anderson shelter. Where we lived was the beginning of the open countryside, but they had put strings of lights across the open fields and lit them during raids so the Germans would think it was the built-up part where the steel furnaces and munitions factories were. Then there were searchlights around, and if a bomber got caught in a searchlight, it dropped its load. That's what happened. We just sat all night looking at each other, listening to the whistling bombs and the sickening thud of the explosions that followed, and feeling the earth shudder and shake. And in the morning, when we went home, the house just wasn't there. There was a pile of rubble and that was it. Our house was in a terrace, and the whole terrace was just a load of debris strewn along what had been a street.'

'It must have been a great shock,' said Hazel. 'What did you do?'

'Well, we did the same as everyone else was doing. We picked through the bricks and rubbish to salvage what possessions we could, and took them back to Aunt Doreen's house. But we were the lucky ones. The falling houses had killed eight people on our street that night. They had to pick the bodies out of the rubble as soon as it was light enough to see. Eight people went to bed that night, minding their own business, trying to look after their own families, and they never woke up again.'

'So how did you manage after that?'

'We lived with Aunt Doreen until near the end of the war, when her house was bombed, too. Then we had to go to the house of another one of Mum's sisters, but it was terribly crowded, and we had no proper beds to sleep in. That was where we were when Dad came home to look for us. He hadn't heard anything from my mum for two years, and thought we might be dead.'

'And then he found a job on the Steadman family's farm with a house to go with it?' Sam thought he was finishing the story.

'Well, not straight away. We didn't know what to do. They gave Dad a little money when he was "demobbed", but that was all we had.

'We tried to find another house, but what could we do? There were thousands of others in the same situation as we were in. Thousands had been bombed out with nowhere to go. Our house had been owned by the car component firm where Dad worked. The whole terrace was let to their own employees. But they were quite helpless. There were no insurance payouts, as there would be today, and no one had any compensation. The war had taken away the place where you lived, and that was that. We went to the Council offices, and they said they would put our names on the waiting list, but there were about twenty thousand people in front of us, and no houses available, not even huts or prefabs. When Dad asked what we were to do, the man just shrugged.

'You see, you young people nowadays would have no idea how we felt. We had no relatives we could move in with, and we had absolutely nowhere to go. We slept in the local park for a few nights.' Mary's eyes shone with the energy of the tale she was telling.

'And what then?' urged Hazel, being carried along with the story, as was Sam.

Mary paused for a few seconds. 'We squatted.'

Then she rushed on to explain. 'Oh, I know what people think about squatting nowadays, but at that time hundreds of people had to do it. Don't forget that there was absolutely nothing we could do about it. Nowhere to go. The alternative was just to be homeless, and live in the open air.'

'But where was there to squat?' asked Sam.

'We found some empty Nissen huts in a place the local people called the "Camp". There was running water and there were toilets, and so that was two problems solved. There was no electricity, but we just huddled together when it got dark, and prayed for the morning to come. The Salvation Army was nearby and they opened up a soup kitchen, which we used most days.'

Mary was talking with great speed and energy. These experiences had cut her deeply, and she had carried them with her throughout her life.

'Now, I've no time for these modern preachers and smug church people,' she went on, 'but I won't hear a word against the Salvation Army. They were wonderful. They really did save people's lives and asked for nothing in return.'

'How long were you in the "Camp"?'

'Probably about two or three months altogether. God knows how we survived. They connected the electricity after a while, and that made life a little more bearable. You see, not everybody was demobbed at the same time, and it was towards the end of September in forty-five by the time Dad got home and came looking for us, and we were away from the "Camp" before Christmas.'

'How did you get out?' asked Sam.

'An idea that Dad had for us to get a house. He remembered a relative of his who had lived in a tied cottage on a farm, and so he thought of a plan. One day, we took a bus out to Thorby, booked into a bed & breakfast with Dad's last remaining money, and then he just set off and walked from farm to farm, asking if anyone had a job going. He found Steadman's farm on the second afternoon, and when he came back to tell us, you would have thought he'd found a gold mine. The money ran out while we were at the bed & breakfast, and Dad had to give the landlady his watch for the last night's rent. He went back when he had got his first pay packet, paid her and got his watch back.'

Mary raised her arms and smiled at last.

'So that's how I grew up at Lilac Cottage,' she said, more gently and more quietly now. 'I won't bore you with the details of how I met Bill, but I was in my early twenties. He worked in a tomato-growing nursery just outside Thorby, but, as I had no brothers or sisters, we were able to move in with Mum and Dad when we got married. Very soon after that, Dad retired and my parents went to live in a cottage on the Rowle estate, because Dad had always done some part-time gamekeeping for the Rowlinson family.

'Bill took Dad's job in the early nineteen sixties, and the house went with it. As you know, I had Howard and then Bridget, and each year I did some seasonal work on the farm, pea-picking and potato-picking, but that's all I could manage.'

Mary was speaking more quietly and calmly as she talked about her life in Lilac Cottage after the war. Once Bill had settled into her father's job, Mary got the cottage the way she wanted it. Life became a steady rhythm, and there was nothing to fire her with such passion as the recounting of her wartime experiences had done.

Hazel wanted to move the conversation on. She asked how long Mary would need to make up her mind about the flat, but she did not hesitate at all.

'I think I'll have that one,' she said, 'as long as Mr Gleave will let me use one of those storage areas next to the workshop for my spare furniture, that is. There's no question of a lease, it seems, and so I would just have to pay the rent by the month. I could be in before the end of this month.'

'Right. I'll sort out the agreement in the morning,' said Hazel, quite pleased.

'I'll help you to move with a hired van if you like,' Sam offered, 'unless Bridget and Brian want to see to that.'

'I don't think so.' Mary smiled her gratitude. 'I doubt if Brian would take a day off for me. Thank you, Sam.'

'It will be quite a wrench leaving Lilac Cottage after all these years,' Sam remarked, and was surprised when Mary's face became darker and more severe.

'I suppose it will be a wrench, yes,' she said, 'and there have been happy times, but there's been a lot of sadness, too.' Hazel and Sam both suspected that she was about to embark on another passionate narrative, and did not encourage her, but that was what she wanted.

'The worst time was when Bill was killed,' she began, 'but when I was in my teens we had the most enormous rows in our small family, and many's the time I've cried myself to sleep. Dad was always trying to restrict what I did, always criticising if I wore make-up, always asking hundreds of questions if I wanted to go anywhere. Mum made most of my clothes, and there was some terrible shouting in our house if they were too low-cut or too short. We often had to conspire together and hide things from him.'

Mary smiled as she said this, and Sam and Hazel smiled, too, and exchanged glances, but they did not expect what came next.

'The worst time was when I was sixteen and Dad made me leave school. It was awful, terrible, and at one point Mum told me she would have left him if she could, but it was just impossible. We couldn't go into her parents' cottage and there was nowhere else to go, and no way to earn money.' Mary paused, feeling the tears pricking the backs of her eyes as she looked away.

'You don't have to talk about it if you don't want to,' said Hazel, as gently as possible.

'It's all right.' Mary swallowed and controlled her tears. 'You might as well know, and then you'll understand why I feel about Sarah as I do.'

Another pause, another swallow.

'I was one of the first kids to take the eleven plus test in the forties,' she said, 'and I passed to go to Thorby Grammar

School, as it was then. I was a bit bothered before I went, in the summer when Mum was getting my new uniform and all that, but I needn't have worried. I loved it, every minute of it. I had to go on the bus every day, and I met a really good friend called Laura. She lived even further out than I did, near Rowle Abbey. We were both really good at what they called the "literary" subjects, English and History, and especially languages. We had to do Latin, of course, which I did not much like, but I loved French and German. Laura and I got top marks all the time, and when we took GCE, we both got Grade 1s – we didn't have all this A, B and C in those days – in every subject except Science. Laura was staying on into the sixth form to take 'A' levels and go to university, and I desperately wanted to do that, too, but Dad said we couldn't afford it and I had to leave school and get a job.

'Mum secretly told me that we could afford it if we really tried, as I was the only one. Laura's dad only worked on the Rowlinson estate, and she said we could get grants if our parents couldn't afford higher education, but Dad asked what did a girl want with education. She was supposed to get a job for a few years, and then look around for a nice lad.

'I just wept and wept and cried myself to sleep the night he said that. Then he repeated it the next day. Mum protested and that's the only time I saw him hit Mum. It was a good job she had plenty of hair over her ears because that's where he hit her. He sort of took a sideways swipe, and she kind of staggered back through the doorway, her eyes nearly popping out with astonishment and her mouth hanging open.

'I nearly choked with crying, and I just couldn't speak for ages. It hurt more than I've ever been hurt and I've never forgotten it. I can still see it and hear it.

'It was very quiet in the house for a week or two, and that's when Mum told me that she would leave him if she could, but she couldn't. And at school when the teachers started asking questions about what we were going to do, I just couldn't say anything. I would go away and sob in the toilets, and usually Laura came and found me. In the end, the teachers got the idea, and I left, got a job as a typist and eventually I met Bill.'

There was a heavy silence, and Sam and Hazel sat, rather awkwardly, embarrassed at this outpouring. Hazel was just about to suggest a cup of coffee before Sam ran Mary home, but then Mary prolonged things a little further.

'Laura's got a top job in Brussels now, of course, and I can hardly afford the rent on an old flat.' Mary paused just long enough to draw breath. 'Bridget insisted on leaving school because she took her 'O' levels soon after Bill died, and at that time we really could afford nothing.'

Then, through tightened lips, she said, with a controlled passion: 'The same thing is not going to happen to Sarah, though. Oh, no! Sarah's as good as I was at languages, and I'm going to see to it that she goes to university. She's doing her 'A' levels this year, and then she's going to university. I didn't tell you, did I? Just after Christmas she heard she had got a provisional place at Cambridge. Newnham College she'll be going to – provided she gets all 'A's in her 'A' levels, of course, but she'll do that. As long as they let her study and revise properly at home, she'll do that.'

Mary's eyes filled with tears. 'She is really bubbling with it when she talks to me, but she says that at home they have put a real dampener on it. Brian says that he can hardly afford the important things in life, let alone Sarah faffing about with books for another three years or more. But Sarah really wants to go, and we have had some sessions of tears already. The trouble is that Bridget stays quiet, a bit afraid of Brian, and she made the decision the other way round when she was leaving school. Sarah says Kevin just makes fun of her, but he's too young to really know what it's all about. I think Brian is a bit like my own dad was, and Bridget a bit like my mum.

'But just think of what's nearly in her grasp. It's absolutely unbelievable: someone from our family at Cambridge!'

She gripped each cuff of her cardigan so fiercely that her knuckles showed white.

9

It was Jack Hunt who, a few days later, told Sam what had happened before the planning committee meeting that decided he could not build a garage. He phoned to ask him to come to his house for a drink, as he sometimes did. Jack always drank at home rather than go to the Blacksmith's Arms, and he was not the most sociable of people, though he was a good friend to Sam. His wife always seemed to be working. Jack was one of those self-contained people who liked their own company, and yet were never bored. He travelled abroad a lot, and didn't have a great deal of leisure time, or at least not leisure time at home.

Charles Brewster had phoned Jack some weeks ago, Jack said. He said that he was going to object to the building of the garage and was asking whether he, Jack, felt the same way. Jack said he had told him to get lost, though not before Brewster had told him that the Davies and Towers families were going to object on the grounds that it spoilt the view and the character of the area.

'He doesn't need to threaten or pressure them,' said Sam. 'He only needs to speak to Judith and Sue in a certain way, and they soon get the message. As a councillor, he would know Don O'Brien, the planning officer, and he wouldn't say anything to him in public, either. Never mind about allergies and illnesses, never mind about doctors and your representatives on the Council: nothing is as important as who you know.'

At least, Jack had loosened Sam up a bit, and he was talking quite freely when he returned to Hazel that evening. She wished that Jack had distracted Sam from the thing that was filling his mind the whole time, drowning out more normal thoughts and activities. He spoke about little other than Charles Brewster and the Council.

Sam and Hazel did not sit down to discuss the entire thing. Hazel would have been happy to do that, but it was not Sam's way. Ideas and plans formed slowly in his mind, and Hazel got to know what he was thinking by comments and opinions that he let out casually. This might occur during a conversation about something else, or they might be blurted out on their own, triggered by something on television or in a newspaper, or something that had happened at work.

At the moment, Hazel was getting a bit alarmed by some of these blurted-out comments. They ranged from a muttered 'Like Brewster' or 'Just like the Council', to threats of what he was going to do to either of them. When the threats increased and became dangerous or, in her opinion, just silly, Hazel decided she would have to say something. It seemed that Sam would not give up. He would not get it into his head that they couldn't do anything about the planning decision, and she would just park her car on the grass and forget it. He would not let it rest. His obsession was getting dangerous and poisonous and sometimes just plain childish.

One time, Sam suggested he could poison Brewster's Labrador dogs, or his hundreds of sheep.

'Don't be so utterly stupid,' snapped Hazel. 'What would be the point of that? Only the animals would suffer, not Brewster.' She was really annoyed. She had shouted the words. Her neck reddened, and her hands gripped the sides of the chair she was sitting in.

Another time, he suggested he could put boulders just inside the gate of Brewster's drive when his car was out, so that he wouldn't see them on the homeward journey until too late, as he turned into his drive at speed.

'Oh, for heaven's sake, grow up!' Hazel spat the words out. 'Kids do that sort of thing. Someone will see you, and what if you get caught?' Again, she lost her patience with him.

'Don't care,' he muttered. Hazel looked sharply at him. She wondered if he really was losing his sanity. She could not believe he was serious.

The muttered threats and sour mood went on for a few days, with Hazel getting more impatient. There came a time when she could take no more, and really thought Sam was losing his mind. She had never known him to be as bad as this. He was becoming irrational.

Sam came home late one night without phoning to tell his wife, as he usually did. Hazel had prepared the evening meal, and they were most of the way through it when she asked why he had worked late. Sam explained that he had not worked late but had gone looking for Charles Brewster's car.

'What did you want to find Brewster's car for?' Hazel asked sharply, the pitch of her voice raised, with a little tension in the air.

'Well, he doesn't park in the Council car park, but in side streets nearby.'

'What's that got to do with you?'

'I want to know where he parks so I can fix his car for him.'

'You what?' Hazel's voice rose further, in pitch and volume.

Sam went on in the same tone. It was as if he had prepared an explanation.

'I've decided to fix his car to get back at him. I can easily get his filler cap off, and then I'm going to pour some fine-grained sand down where the petrol goes. That'll fix his engine well and good. It'll get into the carburettor and through into the cylinder heads. It'll deposit itself in all sorts of places and do all kinds of damage. The garage will be weeks sorting it out, and it will serve him right.'

'Are you completely mad?' Hazel was nearly screaming. The skin round her eyes was screwed up with an intensity that was frightening to see. Andrew, who always ate quickly, had finished his meal and decided to leave the table and go up to his room. He could see a gigantic row starting. Hazel got up, walked round and stood over Sam, glowering down.

'Are you seriously saying you're going to do that to his car? That's criminal. If you're found out, you could be arrested, you fool!'

'But he parks in a side street. I could do it all in half a minute, and no one would see.'

'But what's the point?' Hazel was shrieking. She clenched both fists and shook them at him. 'If you're seen, you'll get arrested. If you're not seen, he'll never know who's done it, and there's no point. He'll think some yobbo in town did it.'

'The point is,' said Sam, still surprisingly calm, 'I will have the satisfaction of knowing that I've got back at him.'

'You're completely mad.' Hazel had totally lost any sense of respect for him, or any intention of rational talk. 'You're off your head, out of your mind, screwball.' She paced up and down the dining area, glaring at Sam. 'This is a criminal act you're talking about. You'll be seen. The police will be round here to arrest you. What about me? What about Andrew? We're your family, and you'll drag the whole family into this stupid, this utterly stupid, this utterly crazy game you're playing.' She breathed for the first time. 'For God's sake, think a bit. Forget the garage. You can't do anything about it. You hadn't bought any of the stuff for it. I already park on the grass, anyway. Forget it!'

Sam sat and watched and waited. Then he went on: 'I don't see why people like Brewster should just do anything they want, and get clean away with it. He can just do anything, and everybody fits in with what he wants.'

73

Hazel sat down at the table again. She put her head in her hands, looked down and said nothing.

'It goes on all the time,' continued Sam, 'and this time he thinks he's won, over us. What's the garage to him? Nothing. He just wants to stop it because he thinks he still owns the land and all the people who live on it. Well, I'm going to kick back.'

'You're crazy,' said Hazel, in a low tone. She had regained her composure, but was close to despair at Sam's attitude.

'Oh.' Sam intended to finish his speech. Now that his plan was out, he could talk freely. 'Well, I tried to do something about the chicken huts because I got scared that afternoon at the hospital. We lost because no one would back us up. I wanted to build a garage for the same reason, for you.'

There was no response from Hazel. Sam raised his voice for the first time, and banged the table with the flat of his hand.

'For you!' he shouted.

The rest of the food had gone cold, and Hazel decided the best thing was to collect all the dishes and the uneaten food, and take them over to the draining board. Her hands shook. Her legs felt weak. She cleared away doggedly until she had finished. Sam watched. Neither spoke.

Hazel felt fragile because of the nervous tension of the argument, but she was not in the least afraid. They had had rows before, and she knew Sam could be a passionate man when arguing, but she always felt absolutely safe. She was as certain as she could be of anything that he would never hurt her, never touch her in anger. It was simply not part of his nature.

Eventually, Sam got up, got his coat, walked to the door, and said, 'I'm going to the Blacksmith's Arms with Dave.' As he put his coat on, Hazel noticed that he constantly jerked his right arm through the sleeve, as if punching a hole through it. A stranger would have thought he was adjusting his arm inside the sleeve, but Hazel had seen this gesture before, and knew it was a sign of the most aggressive mood of all.

'If you're going through with this crazy idea,' Hazel shot back at him, 'you can get away from me. Get out, and don't drag me and Andrew into it. I'm having nothing to do with it.'

The door slammed.

The following evening, Hazel arrived home at her normal time. As usual, Andrew had got the school bus home and had been in the house nearly two hours. There was nothing unusual in the fact that Sam was not yet back. Most days, he was the first out in the morning and the last back in the evening.

Hazel came in through the kitchen door, and as she moved through into the dining area, she noticed a white envelope lying in the middle of the dining table. She put down her bag, coat and car keys, and scooped up the envelope.

It had just 'Hazel' written across the front and was sealed. Puzzled, she tore it open. There was one sheet of duplicating paper, covered in Sam's handwriting.

Dear Hazel,

Forgive me for just leaving this letter, and not discussing this with you, but it seemed the best thing to do.

You were right yesterday. I have got obsessed with Brewster and the Council, and I shouldn't drag you and Andrew into it.

I was doing it all for you, but it's me that's got this obsession. As usual, you are the logical one, but I hope you can understand how utterly frustrated I am.

Twice now the Council has just swept us aside as if we don't matter, and I'm sure that it was because of Brewster's influence both times. When we needed our neighbours, they joined Brewster and all of them just turned away.

I don't know how much more serious it could be. You could have died that afternoon we went to the hospital, and yet when we try to do something about it, the Council, because of Brewster, the Council – elected by us – just pushes us away. We are of no account, nothing. You could die for all they care. What do individual people matter?

How could I do nothing? That amounts to saying that they can do anything to us, anything, and we will not even protest. Is it any wonder that people like Brewster are as arrogant as they are? They can just behave like that all the time, and nothing ever happens to them.

You are better at handling problems than I am, Hazel. You could write letters and consult expensive lawyers, but I know it would change nothing.

What am I? Am I a man? What do you want me to be? How can I not do anything? Every part of me is shouting out to do something. I've never felt such pressure inside.

So I'm going away to sort myself out. I'm not sure what I'll do, but I'm sure I don't want you and Andrew to get into any trouble because of me. You are the two most important people in my life, and you nearly died. I keep telling myself that you nearly died and what am I going to do about it?

I couldn't get any work done at TCS today. I just couldn't concentrate, so I came home at lunchtime, got a few things together, wrote this, and now I'm going away for a while. I feel dreadful, and I'm so sorry.

I want it to be as easy on you as I can make it, so I'll tell you I'm not far away. Dave lives on his own since his wife left him, and he said I can stay at his house until I get my mind sorted out. So if you need me for anything urgent, his number is in our address book.

Please do not ring to ask me to come back to discuss this. I am just not worth living with at the moment. This way, I am sure that you and Andrew won't get hurt. It's only to protect both of you that I'm going.

I feel so strange and it's all so horrible. Whatever happens, please remember that I love you both very much, more than anything in the world.

All my love to you both.

I'll see you again soon, I hope.

Sam.

Hazel's eyes just raced over the page, and then she felt as if she was collapsing inside. She felt a little weak, and sat down at the table. She put her head in her hands as the tears came.

'Oh, God. Has it come to this?'

She sat and cried softly for a while. She felt very alone. She could see how it would be: no one to reach out to for reassurance, to discuss anything with, to argue against. It didn't seem real. This was something that happened to other people. Could this really be happening to us?

Then, saddest of all, she noticed Andrew. He had come silently into the dining room, and stood watching.

'What's the matter?'

Hazel couldn't answer him. She couldn't speak. Her throat hurt. She looked at him, red-eyed, through tears. She blew her nose, and then covered her face with her handkerchief.

Andrew guessed the worst: 'Has Dad gone?'

Hazel nodded. Andrew stood still. His face creased around his mouth. His chin trembled slightly. His soft brown eyes were shattered, like pools whipped up by the wind, and the water spilled.

Hazel reached out her arms, and he went to her. She held him fiercely, and for a long time they were locked in the embrace, rocking very gently, and each drawing some strength.

Much later, after they had eaten a little, and after Hazel had let Andrew read the letter, they went to bed. Hazel did not expect to sleep. She lay, sometimes with a curiously empty mind, telling herself she did not care any more, and at times going over recent events, as if from a distance, knowing how things had worked out. She knew that she would go through the mechanics of daily routines, and felt she didn't care what would develop.

Towards dawn, she drifted into a shallow sleep. Shadowy images chased each other down echoing halls of her memory. Then a fog closed in.

Finally, dawn came as a friend, and she got up to meet the day.

10

'Are you coming to the Blacksmith's, then?' Dave asked.

'No. You go. I got things to do.'

'What things? Leave 'em. What's the good of being free if you don't enjoy yourself?'

'I don't feel free,' said Sam, with some impatience. 'I didn't come here for that. I came here to protect Hazel and Andrew.'

Sam had lived with Dave for only just over a week, but he felt it was a strain. He enjoyed Dave's company when he saw him in the pub once a week: men's talk; sport and work; people they knew; places they'd been. It was a 'matey' comfort.

Up to now, Sam had then liked to go home to Hazel. He felt that life with her was a complete life, a home and family. But he found that Dave wanted to continue this 'matey' kind of life all the time.

Dave didn't seem to care about anything. Sam couldn't decide whether he was naturally like that, or whether he was putting it on. People behaved so differently in public and in private, thought Sam.

The house was a mess. Dave went out for many of his meals. When he ate at home, it was because he brought a 'takeaway' in, or he phoned for a pizza to be delivered. He had arranged for a lady who lived nearby to come and clean the house once a week: tidying, vacuum-cleaning, washing down surfaces. Then he arranged for her to come for another half-day per week to do the ironing. He could just about manage to operate the washing machine himself, and had a drier, but he couldn't be bothered with the ironing.

Sam found all this rather strange. He kept all his personal possessions in one room, his bedroom. This was always tidy, and he insisted on cleaning it himself. He also insisted on doing his own washing and ironing, separately from Dave. He was ironing now, as Dave tried to entice him out.

'I want to get all this ironing done,' he said. 'It mounts up if you don't keep on top of it.'

'Oh, you worry too much,' said Dave. 'I didn't realise you were such a worry-guts. Anyway, it's women's work. Put it with mine, and let Mrs Eccles do it.'

'No, thank you,' said Sam, with some force, once again getting a bit impatient. 'I don't want anyone else looking after my stuff. I'll do my own. It's not women's work. It's just work. Anyone can do it.'

'Well, I think it's women's work,' went on Dave. 'They like to feel in charge of all that kind of stuff. They'd think a man was a pansy if he did it. They want a man to watch football and go to the pub and be a man.'

Sam did not reply. After all, this was Dave's house. He didn't want to get into any kind of argument, though he was increasingly irritated by what he saw as Dave's narrow-mindedness. Football and the pub: is that all there was? And he seemed to think women liked it that way.

'OK, then. Suit yourself.' Dave interrupted Sam's thoughts and slammed out of the back door.

Sam didn't know how long he would keep up this single-man's life – until he had fixed Brewster's car, he supposed. He knew where he could get the fine-grained sand he wanted, but he was still observing Brewster's driving and parking habits. When he had done it he would lie low, and no one knew his address except Hazel, although the police, if it came to that, could always contact him at TCS because plenty of people knew he worked there. He supposed that the longer life went on like this, the less likely Hazel would be to have him back, but he quickly dismissed such thoughts. He really could not contemplate never going back to Hazel and living with her and Andrew as a family again. What he was doing was only temporary, to save them getting hurt if his plans for Brewster went wrong. It never occurred to Sam to question what he was doing. He just assumed his wife and son still believed in him. It was impossible for it to be any other way.

After ironing, he drove to the all-night supermarket, the one he shopped at on Saturday. He hoped and prayed Hazel would not be there. He bought bread, butter, milk, some vegetables and the smallest piece of liver he could find. There were also a few pre-cooked convenience foods, things he could heat in the microwave oven.

He felt so empty as he made his way out to the car. He hated shopping like this, just for himself. On Saturdays, he always tried to bear in mind the things everybody liked, and always bought favourite nibbles for Hazel and Andrew. What he had bought this time he would eat on his own, in silence. He asked himself why he was doing this, and then told himself it would not be for long. Once he had got this senseless feeling for revenge out of his system, he could get back to normal. He knew it was senseless, but he felt somehow he had to do it. He couldn't take the unspoken insults, the being trampled on by the likes of Charles Brewster, his neighbours turning away when he most needed them, the high-handed ways of the Council.

After loading his goods into the car, Sam returned his trolley to its park. He pushed through scores of other people hurrying to and fro, into the supermarket and out of it. It was the middle of May now, and not dark yet, but the shop lights and the high overhead car park lights were on, and the gentle light touched all the scurrying figures and upturned faces with a soft glow. Sam saw no one he knew, and felt pangs of loneliness. Voices seemed everywhere: mothers called to children, friends met each other and chatted and laughed, elderly couples murmured quietly to each other as they moved into and out of the shop, holding each other for support.

Sam responded to no one, and had no one to respond to him. The connections that feed the spirit had been severed. Many people, he knew, liked the independence of being alone; they sought it and thrived on it. He thought they were stronger people than he was. He needed to connect, to bounce off others, to be warmed by others' closeness and interest. To lose all this made him feel strained and anxious. He returned to the car and drove back to a cheerless, empty house.

A few days later, on Sunday afternoon, Sam was resting for a while after he had been mowing the lawn. Dave kept the garden more tidy than the house and, especially in summer, worked hard to make it a garden to be proud of: flowering borders, tightly clipped shrubs, rose bushes and weed-free pathways. Roses were Sam's favourite flower: tough and adaptable to any soil and any weather, and yet tender and soft in their beauty, the eye of an observer always being drawn from the ragged outer edge of the bloom in towards the ever-receding and secretive heart.

As Sam rested from his exertions in the garden, the phone rang and startled him. He thought it would be a message for Dave, who was out, but he was surprised to hear Hazel's voice – quiet and calm, steady and confident.

'Sam, will you come, please? Andrew has some strange pains in his chest. I think I'll have to call the doctor out. He's upset, and said he wished you were here.'

The simple request was like a kick to the heart.

'Of course,' he said. 'I'm on my way.'

A scribbled note to Dave, a quick whizz round to gather up his clothes and some possessions, a dash to the car, and he was gone – driving hard, straight to where he belonged.

A few minutes later, Sam swung into Brewster Lane at speed, braked and turned left to park beside the house, next to Hazel's car, without bothering to go down to the barn.

Hazel had been watching from the window, and felt her body relax as she saw him. She watched him spring from the car and come towards the front door. When she saw the strength in his stride, she knew why she wanted him back and why Andrew had asked for him. It was him they wanted to lean on. No matter what was said about being independent, going in their own direction, he was their strength; they needed him. Hazel was not ashamed to admit she wanted to lean on someone, to be enfolded by a strength that was not hers.

Once inside, Sam asked briskly, with an urgent edge, 'How is he?'

'He's feeling better now. He's resting. He says the pain goes off when he keeps still.'

Hazel noticed Sam let his shoulders sag a little, and knew that the fear and tension were leaving him. Andrew was feeling better, and that was all that mattered for the moment.

What mattered for Hazel was that Sam was back. She threw herself against him and wrapped her arms around him until she touched his shoulder blades and then pulled him into her body. Her mouth reached for his, and as they kissed she moved one arm up until she touched the hair at the back of his head and drew him harder into the kiss. She had not done that since before they were married, when they knew that dizzy onrush of passion as each wanted to engulf the other. Relief flooded through every part of Hazel's body. She held her softness limply against his hard body, and briefly had that childhood feeling that everything would be all right now that everyone was together.

They seemed to stay in the embrace for a long time,

though Hazel realised that it was only a few seconds before she felt Sam gently detaching himself from her. She stepped back so that he could go through into the lounge to see Andrew, who was lying on the settee. Andrew looked up slowly as Sam crouched in front of him.

'OK, son? Where's the pain?'

'Well,' he answered quietly and without moving, 'early in the afternoon, I had this sudden pain round my ribs, low down, on the left. I was going for my bike to go round to my friend's house, but by the time I got to the bike, the pain seemed to have gone inside my ribs, and every time I moved, it hurt more. I thought it must be my heart. I did everything slowly. The pain always started up again when I moved. If I leaned forward or tried to bend down it was agony, and I couldn't do it. I daren't even get on the bike to ride it, and so I came back in and told Mum.'

'And it still hurts when you move?'

'Yeah, but I can breathe all right. Do you think it's my heart?'

'I don't know,' said Sam. 'It seems very strange. I wouldn't have thought it was heart trouble at your age, and with you being a bit of an athlete. Has Mum sent for the doctor?'

'Yes,' cut in Hazel, standing behind Sam. 'She grumbled about coming out on a Sunday, but after I had described everything, she agreed to come – I think, because she was a bit puzzled. We're still waiting.'

Dr McCurrach arrived soon after that. She asked questions, felt around Andrew's chest, measured his pulse and blood pressure. She said everything seemed normal, and she was sure there was no heart problem. She listened to his chest with the stethoscope and said there was no infection, no sounds of wheeziness or difficult breathing. Andrew continued to do everything slowly, very much afraid of starting up the pain. The doctor suggested the possibility of chronic wind, for which there was no cure, but to wait for it to go away. Finally, she advised Andrew to rest, and asked Hazel to ring her again if it got any worse.

'She needn't tell me to rest,' said Andrew, quite uncharacteristically, after she had gone. 'I'm not leaving this settee except to go to the toilet. I'm not even sure I want to go to bed tonight. It comes on worse again if I try to lie down.'

Somehow, they got through the rest of the afternoon and evening, and all went to bed. Andrew read for a long time until, finally, his mind surrendered to the night. In his dreams, he floated constantly over a brightly lit landscape and no one could pull him down to earth, where he wanted to be.

Next morning, everyone woke early. It was Monday. Normally, tension rose a little as each person went out to meet their new week. There was a quietness about this Monday morning. Everything seemed to move slowly. All three had slept lightly and fitfully. Though they were in separate rooms, it was as if they had been connected by an anxiety and restlessness. With the dawn came a feeling that they could get up and get on with things.

Andrew just grunted when Hazel looked in to ask if he was all right, but when he had heard both his parents go downstairs, he got up, each movement having a measured slowness. The pain was still there. He felt it each time he moved. He took care not to lean forward. He went downstairs slowly, carefully, not wanting to jar his chest. He felt a little more like speaking when he went into the kitchen/dining area and caught the smell of breakfast.

'How are you today?' It was Sam.

'The pain's still there.'

'Same as yesterday?'

'Yeah. It comes on when I move.'

'Well, you're not going to school.'

'I know that.'

This was unusual. Andrew hated staying off school, getting out of the routine.

'And I'm staying here with you.' Sam spoke quietly, but firmly. Hazel glanced sharply at him. That was unusual, too. The routine of work meant a lot to Sam. But she also noticed that Andrew did not protest. In fact, he didn't say anything, but continued eating. He had not lost his appetite.

'What about you?' asked Sam. The whole conversation was in short, sudden bursts. Hazel knew this was coming, but had not quite made up her mind.

'I've got some clients booked in,' she said, weakly. She noticed the sour look from Sam, but nothing more was said until they had all finished eating.

Before they moved away from the table, Sam spoke quickly, and strongly: 'I don't believe this thing about wind. It would have moved, or it would have changed in the night. It's not wind. I'm worried.' All three looked at each other. Uncertainty hung between them. 'In fact, I don't believe the doctor,' he continued. 'There's no rush, but I'm taking you to the hospital.' He looked hard at Andrew, but Andrew did not respond; he just sat. Sam decided to make it easy for Hazel.

'You go to work. I'll take him, and we can keep in touch if you'll keep your mobile switched on.'

'Yes. OK,' said Hazel quickly, grateful for Sam's lead. Fleetingly, she wondered what she would have done if he hadn't come back. 'We're supposed to keep them switched off in the office, but I don't care today. I'll keep it on.'

'Right. That's settled, then,' said Sam. 'As I say, there's no rush, but we won't hang about, either. I'll just ring them at TCS.'

Sam drove quickly and smoothly through the morning traffic to Thorby General Hospital. After Sam had registered Andrew at the A & E department, and they had been seen by the triage nurse, they had to wait only about forty-five minutes. There had been a road accident earlier, but apart from that, it was a fairly quiet time.

When they had been ushered into the cubicle, the doctor asked Andrew to lie on the bed. Sam intervened and carefully explained that Andrew would much rather sit in the chair, and would be more comfortable there, if it was possible to examine him in a sitting position.

The doctor paused briefly as if puzzled, but agreed to this, and there followed the same examination by stethoscope that Dr McCurrach had carried out the day before. There were many questions about the pain in his chest, when it occurred and what was happening at the time, and whether it had moved or increased since then.

After much note-taking, the doctor arranged an X-ray, and then there was a long wait in a small ante-room. Finally, another doctor arrived.

'We'll have to admit him, Mr Dent,' he said. Then he smiled at Andrew. 'The doctors will have to keep a close eye on you,' he said, with warmth in his voice. His manner was gentle and reassuring.

Sam was not at all surprised, and had packed a bag for Andrew before they had set off from home. He hadn't even left the bag in the car, but had brought it in with them. 'I've brought him a bag, and he's ready right away,' he said.

Andrew smiled across the small table towards his dad. How glad he was he had come back. He knew he could trust him, whatever happened, to do the right thing. He was just as glad as was his mum to have his dad around when there was any trouble. It looked as if he had been proved right this morning. Andrew was so relieved that something was being done; he just knew that something serious was going on.

'What you have done is that you have torn a bit of your lung,' the doctor was saying, still smiling, still reassuring. 'There's no need for alarm, and it will probably heal itself, but we must keep a careful watch. We call it a "spontaneous pneumothorax" and what has happened is this: at the end of all the airways in your lungs are tiny little air sacs called alveoli. Quite a number of these have burst in an area low down in your left lung. The X-ray shows where. That is why there are no sounds of breathing in that part of your chest, and the pain is caused by the escaped air filling the cavity lining. This is fairly common in young athletes, and you may not have been doing anything strenuous at the time. It just happens.

'Normally, it will heal itself,' he went on, the unwavering gaze of father and son telling him that they were seizing upon every word, 'but we must keep watching you closely. If the air pressure in the small cavity won't let the lung tissue grow again, we may have to take some of the air off, but let's hope it doesn't come to that.

'What you need to do is to stay quiet, stay still and rest in bed. Then leave the rest to us. OK?'

Sam and Andrew nodded at the same time. There were no questions. Now they had been told, it all made sense.

'Right, then. We'll take you to Ward 3B and hand you over to the sister. Don't forget, gently and quietly does it.'

There was an even bigger smile, and Andrew hung his head in sheer relief. He was almost happy, he was so relieved.

In the next half-hour, the formalities were completed and, at about lunchtime, Sam left the ward, telling Andrew he would be back to see him, with his mum, in the evening.

After telephoning Hazel, Sam did not go straight home. He drove over to Dave's house to collect the rest of his gear and to leave a note thanking him for the stay and explaining what had happened.

Then it was Sam's turn to surrender to relief as he moved back home. Why had he ever left? What a fool he could be sometimes. This was where he belonged – for ever. He put away his things, lay on the bed, closed his eyes and found a kind of peace.

Sam and Hazel were in touch with each other by telephone just after Sam had left the hospital, and then again later in the afternoon. In the early evening, Hazel went straight to the hospital from work and met Sam there.

Hazel did not like hospitals. There was something about the general smell of disinfectant, and echoing voices in shiny corridors, that made her cringe a little, though she tried not to let it show.

She remembered her last visit a few months ago. She had been barely conscious. Her head felt the size of a football, and she had vague memories of strong hands guiding her into a chair, and a doctor giving injections. Later, when the swelling had subsided and Sam was allowed to take her home, she had felt empty of all feelings.

This time, she felt quite relaxed as they walked towards the wards, for she was just as relieved as Sam that they had quickly discovered what was wrong with Andrew, and seemed confident that his chest would soon heal. Nevertheless, as they approached the wards, the sight of people who were ill brought on strong feelings. There was a little fear, of course, but also a feeling of helplessness, of sympathising and wanting to do something but knowing that she had to keep her distance and leave things to those who knew about them. Her usual drive slackened and her daytime energy drained away.

Hazel explained to Sam that she had promised to call on a colleague at work who had had a breakdown and was in Ward 2A. She had heard that she was in a really bad state, and was not looking forward to seeing her, but she had promised everyone at work that tomorrow she would tell them how Susan was getting on.

Sam waited some distance away, and Hazel had difficulty in finding and recognising her colleague. As she looked down at Susan, who only six months ago had been on everyone's invitation list, she saw a ruin of a young woman – thin, wasted, obviously sedated. Her damp eyes stared, and her thin face showed in outline the bones of her skull. 'I tried to do some knitting,' she said, painfully forcing a smile. She took it from the top of her locker, and as she briefly answered Hazel's questions, she pulled at the knitting, tugged at it, wrenched it into strange shapes, and twisted it into knots.

'I'm a bit better now, though,' she said, and turned her head on the pillow, afraid to meet Hazel's eyes. Tears began to run. Hazel swallowed. Her mouth was dry. Her throat hurt.

'You'd better leave her now,' whispered a nurse at her elbow. Hazel nodded, unable to speak. She felt as if her heart would dry up.

Unspeaking, she rejoined Sam and found Ward 3B. Sam's heart gave a lurch when he saw there were screens round the bed where he had left Andrew. The sister noticed his reaction.

'Don't worry, Mr Dent,' she explained. 'Dr Cameron has been examining Andrew, and he has a few students listening to his chest. We don't have many such cases, and he wants his students to understand what's going on. Andrew is quite OK.'

She smiled, a smile of reassurance and apology.

Returning her smile, Hazel and Sam accepted the chairs she offered. It was a children's ward, and Hazel's attention was caught by a young nurse, barely eighteen it seemed, and surely only a trainee.

She was helping a young girl playing at fitting pegs into a board. The girl was heavily bandaged round her body. She had obviously been in a fire. Wads of foam were wrapped round her arms. Her hair was straw-coloured and seemed to stand out from her head in tufts. It looked brittle. The skin of her face was shrivelled and wrinkled in some places, and stretched tight over the bone in others. There were strange little lumps and bumps on her forehead and cheeks. There were no eyebrows. She concentrated on her game with the pegs. The young nurse constantly chatted and smiled encouragement.

She'll have to go through most of her life with that face, thought Hazel. And that young nurse – she treats her so naturally. I couldn't do her job.

At that moment, the ward sister called the nurse by her name. She leaned towards the girl and her lips brushed the shrivelled cheek – the merest touch. 'I've got to go now,' she said, softly. 'See you tomorrow.' She kissed her again. 'You are beautiful,' she said.

Hazel watched entranced. She was awe-struck. She felt privileged to watch and wanted to shrink until she was invisible.

'Andrew is free now,' said the sister.

So engrossed had Hazel and Sam been that they had not noticed that the screens had been withdrawn from around Andrew, and the doctor and students had gone. As his parents approached, Andrew smiled.

Hazel could see only her son as she rushed towards him. She had a vague feeling that she would embarrass him, but she couldn't help herself. She put her arms gently round his neck. 'Oh, I'm so happy,' she breathed, as she kissed him. 'Thank God you're OK.'

Andrew came home in less than a week. Dr Cameron had said that he was pleased with his progress. The sounds of breathing were coming back, and a further X-ray had shown that Andrew's lung was slowly expanding to fill the cavity and resume its normal shape.

Andrew, for his part, said that the pain was much better, and so, with many warnings not to rush about, and to take everything gently and slowly and steadily, the hospital had allowed Andrew to complete his recovery at home.

With his return, peace settled on the family home. His parents were delighted to have him back, and went round the house beaming their pleasure. Sam had been heard singing in the bathroom. Hazel just didn't want to think about garages or planning applications or environmental health. She was so glad to have the family whole again. Nothing else mattered.

'Sam,' she said, the night after Andrew had come home, 'what about us all going down to Burnham for the Spring bank holiday week? I know it's short notice, but surely we'll be able to book up somewhere.'

'Good idea,' said Sam. 'I think we could all do with a bit of a break, and I should think some gentle walking about in the sea air would do Andrew's chest a power of good. I'll ring Mrs Ellis.'

Two weeks later, the family made their way southwards along the A1 in Sam's car. Hazel looked rather vacantly at the passing countryside. This, the east, was the quiet side of England – gently undulating, an unbroken patchwork of arable farms, various shades of yellow, brown and green. Occasionally, the road skirted round a town, where were visible a few church steeples, a power station, blocks of flats and offices, and on the outskirts, the fraying edge of industry, factories whose chimneys pointed skywards, rigid, dumb and black.

Clusters of partridges, or lone whirring pheasants, spurted out from the hedge bottoms as they sped by. They passed the occasional kestrel hovering above the roadside verge, its wings trembling. As she looked ahead, it seemed to Hazel that the road was sucked towards and under the car. She was fascinated by the approach of traffic on the other carriageway, especially the motorbikes, whose hum as they grew from a speck and were thrown towards them from a distance exploded to a roar as they drew level, and droned as they receded behind them.

Sam turned, and headed directly eastwards and after half an hour or so, the land became flatter, a perfectly level, almost treeless landscape, the soil dark and rich. This was fenland. It had its own beauty: vast, open skies and a desolation like that of the sea. Agricultural machines prowled the huge prairie fields. Tractors went on their coughing, lurching patrol, ushered slowly forward by diving circles of gulls. The simplicity and bleakness gave a kind of peace.

After another two hours, they arrived in Burnham and were greeted, as they had been on numerous holidays through Andrew's childhood, by a beaming Mrs Ellis.

A gentle, simple, peaceful week followed. They just walked about and looked at a world full of harmless pleasures: people fishing, swimming, sailing and messing about in boats. They sat on wide, sandy beaches, drove through little knapped flint villages, drank coffee in low-ceilinged, stone-built cafes and visited friendly market towns full of the slow throb of small-scale commerce.

Just to look at those wide, distant, flat horizons brought a feeling of serenity and stillness. The sense of freedom seemed without limits. It seemed to flood through body and soul, driving out tension and anxiety. As they walked in the small resort, the old, haphazard, but strongly constructed buildings gave a sense of firmness and permanence, which was a million miles away from the transient world of electronic communication and fluctuating commerce, of phones, computers, emails and Excel files, which they had left at home. Here, no personal relationships were based on pecking orders of threat and menace. The very names of places – Jolly Sailor's Yard, the Old Custom House, the smoking shed, the whelk house – took a person back to a safe and solid world where the pace of life was slow and sure, and where life depended on the elemental forces of wind, tide and sea.

One particular evening, towards the end of the week, Hazel and Andrew said that they were tired and wanted to get back early to the cottage. Sam continued an evening walk alone. He walked past the small yacht basin where the masts nodded and kissed and crossed, and along the salt-marsh and mud flats where the crooked fingers of small streams touched the sea across the sodden land. He passed by the grey, brown, soft-green coastal vegetation, gently topped by a purple mist of sea lavender. Finally, he reached the desolate flatness of the shore, where gulls and terns wheeled and screamed, and waders picked their way through the tidal pools. He heard the sea ease back and forth. His lone state engulfed him, but not with sadness. He let the peace of the moment wash over him, and as he watched the sea melt away from him, he felt the gnawing acid of life in Thorby and Thoreswood leaving him.

He turned and walked back to the cottage along a path at the back of the salt-marsh. The marsh faced north, and the sun was dying in the west after a cloudless day. Now the low sun spilled gold across the rippling creeks, the still pools became copper, and everywhere birds twisted, turned and called in this in-between world of land and water. Sam was overwhelmed by a sense of beauty, and a feeling of peace, harmony and profound happiness filled him and warmed him.

Back in Thoreswood, the telephone rang and rang. Mary needed him urgently.

11

'Well, you see, Sam,' said Mary, when Sam rang her back, 'Mr Gleave has said I can move into the flat straight away, tomorrow if I can arrange it. There are still a few days of May left, but he says it doesn't matter. As soon as I can manage it, I can move in. I can't wait.' She was full of excitement.

Sam, Hazel and Andrew had only just got back from the holiday, and, while Hazel sorted out the post, Sam was dealing with the phone messages.

'What's the big rush, Mary?' asked Sam, hoping he could calm her down.

'I can hardly believe this, but when I told Bridget what Mr Gleave had said, she said Brian would take a day off so, as you have offered to hire a van to move me, the two of you could do the job.'

'OK,' said Sam, casting his mind through the week ahead. 'We'll see when we can do it.'

'And that's not all,' Mary raced on breathlessly – she could hardly contain herself – 'I can hardly believe this, either, but Brian has also said that for the period of the exams, Sarah can stay with me if it'll make it any easier for her. That's why I can't wait, Sam. It'll make all the difference, her being with me, where no one will bother her and it's quiet. She's got her first exam in two weeks' time, and so the sooner she moves in, the better. I told you she had to get all 'A's in her exams.'

'OK, then, Mary, I'll see what I can do and we'll arrange it with Bridget.'

Before she had gone on holiday, Hazel had had written into the tenancy agreement, at no extra charge, the use of a storage area next to the locksmith's workshop. Mary had decided that she would have to store all her surplus furniture there and then slowly dispose of it. She reasoned with herself that if she didn't do it now, someone else would do it eventually, and not be so careful about what happened to it. The tenancy was to run from the beginning of June, which was a week before her month's notice to Mr Steadman expired.

Sam took a day off work in the middle of the following week and Brian hired a van. Between them, they moved all the furniture, most into the flat and some into storage. It was half-day closing at the shop where Bridget worked, and so she was on hand to settle Mary into her new home and to make a final visit to Lilac Cottage.

There was a time when Sam was resting after all the moving had been done. Mary was making the first pot of tea in her new flat, and Brian and Bridget had set off for Lilac Cottage. Mary gave Sam a cup of tea as he sat at the small dining table in the corner of the sitting room, and then she sat down opposite him. When he looked up, she was looking steadily at him, and Sam knew she was about to say something serious.

'Sam, I would like to thank you and Hazel for being so good to me over the last few months. You and I only met because I didn't know where the church rooms were for the History Society open day and then I ran out of the exhibition and forgot my bag. Yet you had me round at your house on Christmas Day and once or twice since then. You've fixed my heating for me, Hazel has helped me an awful lot with the flat, and now you have taken a day off so that you and Brian could move me in. Thank you so much, Sam. Please thank Hazel for me. Now I can be near the shops, be closer to

Bridget, and can keep an eye on Sarah. She'll be moving in here soon.'

She smiled and patted Sam's arm as she said this last part, and then she became serious again. 'I want you to know how grateful I am,' she said, 'and I hope we can keep in touch. You certainly know the address!' There was a squeezing of the wrinkles round the eyes as she smiled.

'That's OK, Mary,' said Sam, with a deprecating gesture of his hands. 'I feel I have got to know you well, and I would like you to know how much I admire your spirit. You have told us some of the things you have been through, and what I most like about you is the way you are determined never to be trampled on, never to be put down by those in authority.

'I have the same kind of feelings that you have, and I have been like that all my life. This last year, I have been incensed by a number of things. Hazel nearly died because of an allergy, and the Environmental Health people would not prohibit the source of the trouble because none of our neighbours would support us. Then, we were refused planning permission for a garage to get Hazel's car away from the source of the allergy. Some influential people blocked the application – not so that you would notice, but I am convinced that they did.

'You, though, Mary, you seem to trust no-one and are determined to get what you have a right to and what you think you deserve.'

'Oh, but I've come to trust you now, Sam,' went on Mary, 'and as for being determined to get what I want, that's what I want to talk to you about.'

She reached below the table into the pocket of the cardigan she was wearing.

'Do you remember this?' She put on the table a little leather pouch, which reminded Sam of the tobacco pouch carried by people who roll their own cigarettes. He quickly surmised that she might have got it from her father. Then she took out of it the golden artefact that she had begun to show to Geoff Lowis back in November at the History Society exhibition.

Mary put the pouch on the table and placed the object on top of it. For a short time, Sam looked at it with a mixture of perplexity and awe. He remembered the effect it had had on Geoff Lowis, and that Geoff had been quite sure it was a valuable piece of gold.

'What is it, Mary?' he asked, at last.

'I don't really know what it is,' she replied, 'but I do know that it's very old and I think it's very valuable.' Sam just nodded. He was not quite sure what to say, or what Mary expected him to do.

'Shall I tell you how I got it?' Mary asked.

Sam just nodded and grunted, very curious about what she was going to say.

'It's been handed down in my family for two hundred and fifty years,' she began, 'but it must be a good deal older than that. My mother gave it to me after my father died, and made me swear to keep it secretly and to hand it on to one of my children unless I needed it in an emergency. She said that even my father didn't know she had got it, and if he had, he would have sold it at the end of the war. She herself had come close to selling it then, just as I nearly sold it when Bill died.

'She also gave me a diagram of a family tree, which traced our ancestors back for two hundred and fifty years. This thing has been handed down and kept secretly by one person in each generation all that time, and for the same reasons, for its value and because no one else knows where it is, or even that that person has got it.

'My great, great, great grandfather found it at Rowle Abbey in 1746, and all the generations of our family have lived round here ever since.'

'Well, how did he find it?' asked Sam, marvelling at this incredible story. 'Was it just lying on the ground?'

'Oh, no,' explained Mary. 'It was hidden in a recess in a stone wall. He saw it, realised it was valuable and secretly took it home. He was working at the Abbey, you see, but he seems to have taken great care not to tell anyone else that he had found it. He certainly did not tell the man who was employing him at the Abbey at that time.'

'Wouldn't that have been the Rowlinson family?' asked Sam, impulsively interrupting Mary's flow.

'Oh, no,' she said, with a slow smile of triumph. There was a short pause while she enjoyed the dramatic effect of her story.

'Who then?' asked Sam.

'None other than Capability Brown,' Mary announced emphatically.

'What?' Sam could hardly believe his ears. 'The famous Capability Brown?'

'Yes, him.'

'Come on, then,' said Sam, a little impatient at the air of theatricality that Mary had assumed. 'Tell me how he came to be working for Capability Brown.'

Mary made a rather impatient gesture with her hands, as if, now that she was beginning to tell Sam the important facts, she wanted to get the story over with quickly.

'Well, the Rowlinson family at that time,' she said, 'in the middle of the eighteenth century, wanted the Rowle Hall estate landscaped. Like just about every other wealthy landowner in the country, they sent for Capability Brown, and he decided that, to give the best aspect of the parkland, he would leave the end wall of the Abbey standing, to give a rather grand effect, but he demolished all the other walls, leaving about a foot of wall to show the layout and foundations. That's why it looks like that today. The Abbey, at that time, was just as it had been left after the dissolution of the monasteries by Henry VIII, two hundred years earlier. It would have been in a bad state of repair, but the walls would have gone up to the roof at a great height, because Rowle was a Cistercian abbey.'

'It was a very big job to knock it all down and cart the stone away, then,' commented Sam, as Mary paused for breath.

'Yes, but it seems that's what he did,' said Mary. 'Of course, as with all of Brown's other grand designs, he had to employ an army of local people to do the labouring work. They weren't all on display at the History Society's exhibition, but I have seen lots of other accounts of payments made to labourers by the Rowle estate at that time, and my ancestor, Jack Drakes, is in them. James Brindley employed hundreds of local people when he brought the canal through on the other side of Thorby just after that. They called the men "navvies" then. Jack's name is in his accounts, as well.'

'I didn't know you had such a detailed knowledge of local history,' remarked Sam. 'How did you come to know all this?' This amazing account of things had revived him from his tiredness at the end of the day.

'Oh, many times during the school holidays I went to Thorby public library with Sarah,' she explained, 'and while she did her studying, I did my own research in their archives. Don't forget, I was no slouch at academic work when I was younger.

'Anyway, this demolition of most of the Abbey took nearly a year, and in the course of it, Jack Drakes found and kept this golden thing. The story is that he had originally kept it in a small box, because there is still a piece of old brown paper with it, on which he wrote where and when he found it. He also asked each keeper of it to write their name at the bottom of the paper, which they have all done, and now mine is there, too.

'There is a piece of writing where he says that he wants his descendants to keep it secretly, one for each generation, so that its value will increase and increase. He says that if it is not kept in a bank, and if there is no written record or account of it, except his piece of paper which stays with it, then no one knows you've got it, and it can't be taxed or examined or anything else. He gives his opinion that that is the way the lords and landowners keep their wealth. They don't work for money. They own things that get more and more valuable each year, and that's how they stay rich and the workers stay poor. At the end, he writes that this is a small and portable thing for our family that will get more and more valuable until someone really needs it. As I told you, my mother said that she almost sold it at the end of the war, but then my dad got a job, along with Lilac Cottage, in the nick of time.'

'Hmm. Quite the economist, your ancestor, Jack, wasn't he?' said Sam. 'A bit like you,' he added, smiling at Mary. 'A socialist who has kept a secret little bit of capital to watch it grow.'

'Maybe so,' resumed Mary, without returning the smile. 'Don't forget what a hard life the workers had in those days. Anyway, let's get to the point of why I am telling you all this. I have decided that the time to get the value out of this thing is now.'

She paused and looked at Sam to see if there was any reaction, but Sam just nodded for her to go on.

'I expect you can guess who it's for – it's Sarah. I've already told you she's got an offer of a provisional place at Cambridge University, depending on how she does in her 'A' levels this summer, and I know she'll do it.

'One of the reasons I have moved into Thorby is to give Sarah somewhere to run to, and now, soon, she can move in. When I was her age, I never had anywhere to go, or anyone on my side, but I'm right behind her now. I'm sure she's as clever as I was, and I really, really want her to go to Cambridge. Then someone in our family will be able to read the important books and know the law. She needn't be trampled on by those with the best education. I was trampled on because I was a girl, but she can do it. She can go all the way.'

Sam smiled. Mary had already told him and Hazel about this all-consuming ambition of hers for Sarah to go to Cambridge, and now he could see that she was in full flow again. He did not want to interrupt.

'But you know how it is nowadays,' went on Mary. 'This damned government makes you pay your own fees, and you have to be going about in rags even to get a grant. Brian can't pay, and I have nothing to sell except this, and at my age I can't think of any other way of getting money.'

The passion was rising. Both fists were clenched as they rested on the table. Her mouth and lips were tight, and her bloodshot eyes bulged with a shining intensity. Her voice, though, was quieter, and her manner calm, as she finished.

'So I'm asking you to help me, Sam. I don't trust anyone else, not even those people at the History Society. You've been so good to me, and I'm asking you for just one more thing.'

She lowered her head a little, but her eyes seemed to bore straight through the eyes of Sam, right to the back of his head. He knew she wanted this like she had wanted nothing else since she was sixteen.

'Well, I'll see what I can do. I'll have to think about it, Mary.' His main feeling was one of humility, of being trusted with something so precious that had been passed down through so many generations, and Mary also wanted to trust him with Sarah's future.

'Do you want me to take this?' he asked, again unsure of what she expected of him.

'Yes,' she said. 'Please see what you can do for me.' By now, they were both standing up, and the slam of a car door told them that Brian and Bridget were returning. Mary again gazed hard into his eyes. 'Please don't tell anyone else in the family that you've got it.'

'I'll see what I can do,' he promised again. He heard footsteps on the stairs, and in his haste he fumbled, as he replaced the object into the pouch. Quickly, he moved round so that his back was towards the door and he was shielding the pouch. The door opened just as he slid it into his coat pocket. Then he turned. Bridget and Brian were smiling. He didn't think they had noticed anything. He returned their smile and headed for the door at the top of the stairs, nodding to Mary.

'I'll see you soon,' he said.

12

Sam reflected on these things that Mary had told him as he drove home to Thoreswood. He thought it was amazing. He had had no idea that all this had been behind the things that Mary had told him and that she had been planning. There was her relationship with Sarah, who was very good at languages, as her mother and grandmother had been, and Mary's own family history, with her unhappy experiences with her father when she had wanted to stay on at school. There was also her frustrated ambition and her determination to realise it through Sarah, her moving house to be near Bridget's family and to provide a bolt-hole and other support for Sarah. And all the time she had had her own secret weapon, which dated back to her great, great, great grandfather and Capability Brown himself, and possibly even to the time of Henry VIII, when the monasteries were dissolved and robbed.

Sam wondered at the way it all fitted together, and he wondered even more at the controlled planning of Mary, and her intelligence and knowledge. After her mother had given her the golden artefact, she must have researched the history of the Abbey and the accounts of Rowle Hall. She must have had all that in mind when she was telling Sam and Hazel those things on Christmas Day and a few weeks ago, after tea at their house. He thought that if she was going to intervene and make university possible for Sarah, she had timed it exactly right. Now he, Sam, had to play his part with that bit of gold.

He was not quite sure where to start, whether to go straight to a jeweller, who might give him a valuation, or to a museum, which might tell him what it was, and its value. A third possibility was to have a word with Geoff Lowis. He thought he'd better stick with the person he knew for the moment, although perhaps he had better not tell Hazel the whole story just now. It would seem a bit like betraying Mary's trust.

One aspect of all this that Sam really liked was the way Mary, by keeping it secret, kept her own power. No one could do anything about it. Its value was not in any account; it could not be traced or confiscated. It was an asset that could not be frozen. It was something that she could release and bargain with whenever she wanted. Sam felt a part of this power, now that she had confided in him. He must not let her down.

When he reached home, Sam gave Hazel an account of the day's removal operations, and of how Mary was now settled into the flat with her own furniture and the rest of the furniture in store.

After Hazel had gone up to bed early, Sam took the golden artefact out of his coat pocket to have a good look at it.

It was heavy, being made of gold. It was about three inches tall, with a loop at the top, which was not big enough for a finger to be inserted, and Sam guessed that it was so that it could be suspended by a cord. The main part was cylindrical, about an inch across, although tapered slightly towards the top, and it was about an inch and a half wide at the bottom. There were three decorative rings around this cylinder, near the loop at the top, but otherwise the column was plain and unremarkable.

It was when Sam looked at the base that he had a big surprise – the surface on which the whole thing stood. This was a circle about an inch and a half in diameter, and it consisted of a raised diagram, in very clear relief, of a coat of arms with the letters H R above it, occupying the top arc of the circle. Underneath these letters was a shield with fleur-de-lys at the top left and bottom right quarters, and lions in the top right and bottom left quarters. Underneath, a ribbon bore the words, '*Dieu et mon droict*'. Sam noticed the spelling of '*droict*', which, he knew, was normally '*droit*'. What surprised him was how very clear and intricate the whole design was, and it seemed curious that it should occupy the surface that the object stood on, so that it would be hidden from view if this was an ornament of some kind.

He turned it over and over in his hands and marvelled at the brightness and clarity of it. He took a few minutes just to admire it, before returning it to the pouch and hiding the pouch behind books in a drawer of his desk at the end of the dining room.

Then he went to bed after a tiring day, and dreamed of labourers digging canals which were already filled with water, the water showing stone monuments just below the surface.

Sam was busy at work, and had to work late for the next two nights, and so it was the Monday of the following week before he could give Geoff Lowis a call from work.

'You remember Mary Dyer, the old lady who ran out of your exhibition last November?' asked Sam.

'Sure, I remember,' came the reply.

'She had just shown you that piece of gold,' Sam prompted.

'Yes. I've often thought about that. I'm puzzled over it, what it might be.'

'Well, when you guessed that she might be short of money and wanted it valued so that she could trade it in, you were not far wrong. Hazel and I have kept in touch with her since that time, and she has told me that what you thought is true. Now, she has given it to me to see what I can do for her. Do you think I could come round and show it to you so that you can tell me what you think?' Sam was sure Geoff would not be able to resist.

'Certainly. Do you mean here, while we are in town?'

'Yes,' replied Sam, with some relief.

'OK. Drop in any time this afternoon. I'm free and I'll be in my office. Tell any of the staff you have an appointment with me, and they'll show you up.'

Geoff managed a branch of a well-known bookshop in town, and Sam thought that was probably the most private place possible to let Geoff have a sight of it. He would act on his advice and really get things moving. Sam had brought the object to work with him, and in spite of the weight, had kept it in the pouch in his jacket pocket so that he always knew exactly where it was.

Sam called round at the shop in the early afternoon. He was soon in Geoff's office and, after some quick pleasantries, he took the object from the pouch and placed it on the blotter on Geoff's desk. Geoff looked at it for a few seconds, picked it up and frowned as he inspected the loop, and then turned it over to look at the bottom.

He looked quickly at Sam, and then back at the bottom of the object, but did not speak. His mouth opened slightly, just as it had that November afternoon in the church rooms.

Then he spoke softly – 'Wow!' – and this was followed by more silence. Finally, he looked up at Sam.

'Good grief,' he murmured feebly, as if he was recovering from a profound shock. Then he seemed to gather his thoughts, and spoke softly, but said each word slowly and deliberately. 'I've never handled one of these before,' he said, at last, 'but I think I know what it is. I can tell you that it is incredibly valuable and has enormous significance, depending on where it was found. Do you know how she came by it?'

Sam thought that it was probably best not to release any information at the moment.

'I've no idea,' was his bland reply.

'Well, I repeat, it's incredibly valuable, and it's very old, and if "HR" means what I think it means, this is like finding the crown jewels!'

Sam was uncertain what to say for the best.

'Where do I go from here?' He tried to give the appearance of being unimpressed by Geoff's enthusiasm, but his brain was churning.

'You'll have to tell a person at the Council offices called the "Finds Officer".' Now that Geoff was over his initial shock, he was the authoritative businessman giving orders. 'That is a lady called Elaine Disbrey in the case of Thorby. You will have to give it to her, and she will eventually give it to the museum. First, though, she will probably have to report it to the coroner and have it identified by the MLA – Museums, Libraries and Archives Council – at the British Museum in London.'

'The coroner? But what on earth is it?' This was so far-fetched that Sam was becoming alarmed.

'I think' – and Geoff chopped his hand on the desk for emphasis – 'I think it's what is called a seal-matrix. I also think it's made of almost pure gold. I'm certain it is old enough to be treasure, which is why you'll have to give it to Elaine Disbrey.'

'And if I don't?' Sam told himself to keep calm in order to manage the situation.

'If you don't' – Geoff was again at his most authoritative – 'you'll commit an offence under the Treasure Act of 1997.'

'An offence? Under an Act of Parliament?' In spite of his attempt to keep calm, Sam was losing his coolness. 'Why is it all so serious?'

'Well, we don't know where Mrs Dyer got it from,' explained Geoff, 'but it came from somewhere, and by law you can't just do what you want with a piece of treasure you find.'

Sam pursed his lips. He really was a bit annoyed that it would not be a matter of a straightforward valuation.

'And another thing,' continued Geoff, 'because I've seen it, I'll have to report it, and if I don't, I'll be committing an offence under the Dealing in Cultural Objects Act, 2003.' He leaned towards Sam and tried to sound more confidential and friendly: 'If you don't, Sam, you'll have the police after you. This is a very valuable object, and there's no doubt in my mind that it's treasure.'

'And what about money?'

'That depends on how she came by it. If that is straightforward, she could get the full value of it from the museum service because it is in such good condition, but if it was ever taken without the landowner's permission, she won't get anywhere near the value. In fact, she could get nothing at all.'

Sam blew out his lips in a sigh of exasperation. His fingers fumbled as he took possession of the object again, and his hands trembled as he replaced it in the pouch and returned it to his pocket. He stood up. He made a resolve to keep his thoughts to himself, especially about the landowner's permission, but he had to find out as much information as he could before leaving Geoff.

'What did you say made it like finding the crown jewels?' he asked, carefully trying to steady his voice.

'Those letters, HR.'

'What do they stand for?'

Geoff looked away, and then back at Sam, and then there was a long pause before he replied: 'The implications of what they could stand for are so absolutely staggering that I am not going to tell you what I think they could be. It would be such a let-down if I was wrong, so let's leave it at that, Sam. You tell the Finds Officer at the Council, so that she can take it from you and report it to the coroner.'

He said this with a finality that told Sam that he wanted

him to leave. Sam himself could not wait to get outside, breathe some fresh air, and think about what he had heard.

'Bye.'

'Bye.'

Once outside, Sam breathed deeply. What now? Talk of the British Museum, Acts of Parliament, the coroner and the police seemed a bit frightening. One thing was certain. He would have to work out his next step on his own. For a while, he must not show this object to anyone else or tell anyone else about it.

Later that evening, Sam sat at his desk running through in his mind Geoff's reaction to the seal, which was what he thought it to be, what he had said about its importance and the different Acts of Parliament that seemed to relate to it. He had replaced the pouch behind his books at the back of the desk without Hazel noticing. She was engrossed in a drama on TV at the moment, and he was ostensibly working on the summer edition of the village newsletter, but in reality he wanted some time to himself to decide what to do about the seal.

He reflected that on his way back from Mary's last week, he had decided to start with the person he knew best. Although that had given him a good amount of information, and had made him even more excited about the seal, it had not solved anything for him. Something at the back of his mind made him not want to do what Geoff had told him to do, go straight to the Finds Officer. This may have been because of Mary's position regarding how it had been found and handed down. Mary was surrendering a most precious and valuable heirloom for one reason only – to get money to help Sarah to get to university. He shrank from the notion of meekly handing it in, probably getting a lot less than it was worth, or even nothing at all, and possibly incriminating Mary. But he could not just do nothing.

In the end, what he decided to do was to consult all the

people who could help, beginning with the weakest, the least involved, and work up to the Finds Officer. He realized he would have to be careful how much information he revealed to each person. It was the best plan he could think of, and there was no time to lose.

Accordingly, he took the seal to work the next day, and towards the late afternoon, he nipped out to Wehrle's, a long-established and well-respected jeweller and watchmaker in Thorby High Street. When he told the assistant what he wanted, she said she would have to fetch Mr Wehrle himself. When he appeared, he motioned Sam through into his workshop at the back of the shop, and lifted a lid in the counter to allow him to pass through.

Mr Wehrle was a short, fat man who wheezed every time he breathed and who trundled around his premises with little short steps, which seemed like kicks at the carpet, rather than at a normal walking pace. Once inside the workshop, he kicked his way across to a cluttered desk, and did not seem to lose much height as he squatted on to a rotating chair with a very dirty and frayed seat. He was fat enough to appear quite round underneath his waistcoat at the front. He was bald except for a fringe of hair at the sides and back of his head, and about half a dozen strands of long hair which were brought over from above his left ear, crossed an expanse of smooth, shiny skin and came to rest somewhere near his right temple. Sam momentarily wondered what was the point of those hairs, and decided that he would have cut them short if he had been Mr Wehrle.

'What have we got, then?' he wheezed as he spun round to face Sam, whom he had left standing. Sam, without comment, took the seal from the pouch and handed it to him. Mr Wehrle turned it over in his hands, pulled at the loop, looked at the bottom, and placed it carefully on the desk. He looked up at Sam, and then down again at the seal. He breathed at it, with a loud sussing noise, and then stuck what looked like an eggcup with a glass bottom under his eyebrow, and proceeded to scrutinise in detail every part of the object, while Sam watched in silence. He sussed at it again and looked up at Sam.

'What do you want to know?' he asked.

'Can you give me some idea of the value?' asked Sam, noting the harshness and directness of Mr Wehrle's manner.

There came the sussing again as he slid to his feet, shuffled over to a small, square table at the end of the desk and placed the seal in one pan of a set of scales. A number of brass weights was put into the opposite pan until a balance was achieved. The sussing and wheezing gave way to a meditative 'Hmm'.

'This is rare,' he said, at last. There was a long pause. 'And it's almost pure.'

He unloaded the scales, shuffled back to his seat and looked up at Sam.

'Is it yours?' he asked, and the question surprised Sam.

'It belongs to a friend,' said Sam.

'Hmm.' He looked away, and something about the impatient turn of his head made Sam think he did not believe him.

'How much is it worth?' Sam attempted the same harshness as had been in Mr Wehrle's tone.

'The price is fluctuating a bit at the moment,' he replied, 'and I don't want to commit myself precisely.' Then he looked steadily at Sam: 'But it will be five figures.'

Sam raised his eyebrows and blew softly to express surprise and to try to show Mr Wehrle that he was pleased. He was vague, as Mr Wehrle had been vague.

'So that's at least ten thousand pounds?' asked Sam, with an expressionless face and voice.

Mr Wehrle gave a short nod. 'Gold is about £300 an ounce at the moment,' he said.

'Do you know what it is?' he asked abruptly.

'I haven't the faintest idea,' replied Sam. There was a coldness between them that did not invite honesty, but in any case, Sam was determined not to reveal any more information than was necessary.

'Do you want to trade it?' There was the same cold and clinical detachment.

'I'll have to see what the owner says,' said Sam, cagily.

'Well, could I point out, so that you can bear it in mind when consulting the owner' – the tone was now the exaggerated courtesy that anyone might use when explaining a problem to a child, and Sam was sure that he still did not believe him – 'that I will need a bill of sale or a receipt that shows precisely where it was obtained.'

'Oh, certainly,' said Sam, in the same icy tones, having already decided that he was never going to do business with this man. He approached the desk suddenly, scooped up the seal and had it in the pouch in an instant.

'Thank you, Mr Wehrle. I'll be in touch,' he said.

After making his way through the shop with a formal politeness, Sam, once in the street outside, gripped the pouch in his pocket very tightly.

13

The next day, Sam went to the Municipal Museum of Thorby in his lunch hour. He expected that this would be a rather longer interview than with Geoff Lowis or Mr Wehrle, and he did not want to take any official time off work.

A slim young man representing the curator sat just inside the entrance at a small desk displaying the notice, 'Enquiries'.

' I wonder if there's anyone who can help me identify this and assess its value for me,' said Sam, quietly and politely. 'I do not necessarily want to give it to the museum.'

The young man took the seal when Sam offered it, looked at it quickly, turned it round and raised his eyebrows with a rather blank expression.

'I think you'll need to see Mr Nethercott, and I'll just check whether he is back from lunch yet.' He spoke into a telephone by his left elbow and then replaced it smartly. He sprang to his feet. 'Would you come this way, please, sir? What did you say your name was?'

'Dent.' Sam was impressed by the energetic efficiency.

The young man led Sam to a large, oak-panelled door at the side of the main room, which Sam noticed had an enormously high ceiling with a domed skylight. He knocked briskly on the door and then put his ear to the wood. Sam heard no reply, but the handle was turned and the door was pushed heavily open.

Having been announced by name, Sam walked across a

very wide space towards a solid, spacious mahogany desk, the door gently clunking shut behind him. A tall man with frizzy, pewter-coloured hair took off his reading glasses as he rose to his feet and offered his hand across the desk.

'Gavin Nethercott,' he said, clearly, in a smooth tenor voice.

'Sam Dent.'

Gavin sat down and looked expectantly towards Sam. Sam had kept the seal out of its pouch and had kept hold of it when the young man had returned it to him, and now he offered it across the desk.

He was getting used to people turning the object over as they looked at it, feeling the loop, stroking their fingers down the column, and then the intense frown of concentration as they peered at the design on the bottom. Mr Nethercott replaced his reading glasses before making his detailed inspection, which Sam estimated lasted a full two minutes, punctuated by a 'Good Lord!' in the middle. Finally, he placed it carefully on the desk and looked up at Sam, who had sat, without invitation, in the chair facing the desk and then had waited patiently.

'Good heavens! This is a rarity,' he said, looking steadfastly at Sam. 'Do you know what it is?' The gaze was unwavering.

'I think it's a seal,' Sam replied readily. He thought there was no harm in giving away the fact that he knew that.

'Yes, it is. How did you know that?'

'Geoff Lowis told me.'

Mr Nethercott wasted no time in enquiring how Geoff Lowis had got involved in looking at it, and it was clear that he knew him.

'Hmm.' Mr Nethercott put his hands together with his elbows resting on the desk, and raised his hands in front of his face with the fingertips touching, so that they formed a sort of steeple. He seemed very calm and thoughtful, and looked past his hands at Sam.

'It's also treasure,' he said, 'because I'm sure it will be well over three hundred years old. In fact, it's one of the best pieces of treasure I've ever seen. It's almost pure gold and is in perfect condition.' He now cradled his hands in front of him, and then rubbed the knuckle of his right thumb across his front teeth.

'It's very rare to find an old seal-matrix at all,' he went on, 'but the condition of this one will make it very valuable in itself. It's solid, as I expect you can tell by the weight. But the most amazing thing of all is what is on the bottom. Do you know what that design is?'

Sam shook his head. It was the bottom that had amazed Geoff Lowis.

'It's a royal coat of arms. I won't go into detail, but you can tell that by the various features of it. Just excuse me one moment.'

He got up from his desk, crossed to a bookcase at the door side of the room, took out a large, leather-bound book and carried it back to the desk. Standing at the end of the desk, he flipped open the cover, rapidly consulted an index and then fingered through some pages about a quarter of the way through the book. Then he moved sideways to his chair, reached for the seal, examined the bottom and compared it with a coloured design, which occupied half a page of his book. He sat in his chair again and looked back at Sam, the book lying open on his desk and the seal standing on it.

'It's more than amazing,' he continued. 'What makes this quite astounding is that it is a seal of Henry VIII. That will make it nearly five hundred years old. "*Dieu et mon droict*" it says on the bottom, and that spelling of "*droict*" alone dates it to the sixteenth century, that is, the time of Henry VIII. Now the excellent condition of this object caused me to suspect for a minute that it might be an elaborate hoax, but I don't think so. Not only would it have to have been made by a highly-skilled goldsmith, but he would also have had to be a very knowledgeable scholar to know about that archaic spelling of "*droict*".'

Then Gavin Nethercott leaned back in his chair. This was an unusual case for him, but he was used to this situation in general. He was confident and knowledgeable and anyone who came for a valuation, or to offer an object to the museum, always suffered from the disadvantage that they were not knowledgeable and usually not confident. He was well aware of his own advantages, and knew that his manner was authoritative.

'The questions are: where did you get it? and where has it been until now?' he said, with all the aplomb and panache that he knew he possessed.

'It belongs to a friend of mine,' Sam said, evasively, and Nethercott knew that he was evading him.

'And could you tell me this friend's name?' The tone was gentle and encouraging.

'She wants to remain anonymous,' was the reply.

'Oh, it's a lady,' said Nethercott quickly, and Sam winced at his mistake.

'Could you tell me how long she has possessed it?'

'It was found two hundred and fifty years ago and has been passed down through generations of the same family.' Having thought about this since seeing Geoff Lowis, Sam had decided that this put Mary in the best, most innocent light, and his release of this information was quite deliberate.

'Ah!' Mr Nethercott was clearly grateful for that. He replaced his elbows on the desk and leaned forward.

'You see, those initials, HR, also suggest it was a personal seal that King Henry would have carried about with him, and if he lost it somewhere, then that is proof enough that he had passed that way: no one else could use his seal. Plenty is known about Henry's affairs in London, his quarrels with the Pope and the Roman Catholic Church, and his battles abroad, but not a great deal is known about how much he travelled around England. He stole the money, property and lands of all the abbeys and monasteries, but he always got his henchmen to organise what went on: Cranmer, Cromwell and people. The Pilgrimage of Grace occurred in this area in 1536, but there is no evidence that Henry himself came to deal with it. Do you know where this seal was originally found?' he asked eagerly, leaning towards Sam again.

'Not exactly.' Sam was wary.

'Well, do you know if it was found locally?' Sam could tell that this was important to Nethercott and to the importance of the seal.

'Yes. I think so,' Sam conceded. In view of what he had said about it being handed down, that seemed pretty consistent.

'Oh. That could be vitally important to the significance of this seal,' went on Nethercott smoothly, as if explaining a perfectly ordinary fact of history. Sam was relieved that he didn't threaten him, or try to bully him in any way.

'Look,' he said, raising his hands slightly in an apparently friendly gesture, and as if he was giving advice in confidence, 'you will have to give the name of your friend eventually, because this seal will have to go down to the British Museum to be investigated and assessed by the Museums, Libraries and Archives Council. I'm afraid it's the law – the Treasure Act, 1997, which contains a Code of Practice, and the Dealing in Cultural Objects Act of 2003.'

Mr Nethercott paused, but, in the absence of any response from Sam, he continued in his advisory tone: 'You will have to tell our Finds Officer, Elaine Disbrey, in the Council offices. She will report it to the coroner and tell you what to do next. As I say, eventually it will go down to London, but first you must take it to Elaine.'

Now that he was coming to the legal advice that Geoff Lowis had already given him, Sam became alert to the impulse that he wanted to keep possession of the seal.

Suddenly, and without speaking, he stood up, reached across the desk and took it from where it stood on the open book. Mr Nethercott was quite surprised and almost imperceptibly started forward a tiny amount. Sam realised that he could have waited for him to give it back, and he had no intention of refusing to let Sam have it.

'As I was saying,' he continued, 'you will have to take it to Elaine Disbrey and let her have it for a while. What eventually happens to it is up to her and, particularly, the MLA. I'll tell her if you like.' He gave a slow, reassuring, and what Sam thought was quite a charming smile. 'I think she needs some warning about this. Another thing is that you will have to tell her the name of the owner.'

Sam could tell that Mr Nethercott was trying to bring the interview to an end, but he had gone on the defensive again.

'What about the value?' he asked tersely.

There was a non-committal shake of the head.

'If it was found locally,' said Gavin Nethercott, 'and especially if it was found on the site of an old abbey or monastery, then from my point of view I would say it is priceless, but you don't seem to know much about that, or at least you're not telling me' – yes, Sam was sure that he was a bit suspicious about the existence of the friend and the plea for anonymity – 'but it really is up to the MLA. What I'm most interested in is whether I will ever see it again or have it in this museum.'

Mr Nethercott could tell that Sam was a little strained and edgy, and tried to calm him.

'Don't worry,' he said. 'If you, or your friend, can't have it back, you will be paid the value of it, probably the full value in view of its excellent condition.' Again, there was the smile, but he added, as an afterthought, 'What you get paid also depends on how it was originally found, though.'

Sam knew that he had now got as much information as possible, and still had got possession of the seal. Mr

119

Nethercott had confirmed, and added to, all that Geoff Lowis had said.

'Thank you very much,' he said, as he replaced seal and pouch in his pocket and made for the door. Mr Nethercott came round the desk very briskly and, such was the distance involved, beat Sam to the door in order to open it for him, as goodbyes were exchanged. Sam also realised that he stood at the door and watched him go all the way past the receptionist's desk and out of the main door.

It had been a rewarding interview for Mr Nethercott, but it left Sam with the same problems.

He marched vigorously back to work. Because he had not had to wait, he was still well within his lunch hour. He bought a sandwich on the way and ate it in his car before returning to his desk.

His thoughts remained focused on how he could help Mary in this situation and what to do for the best. He wondered about one of Mr Nethercott's closing remarks about an old abbey or a monastery. Was he fishing for a reply? Sam could tell that Nethercott knew that he had not told him all the details. Was it just an intelligent guess, a shot in the dark, or had Sam given away something, or made a hint that had led him to identify Rowle Abbey?

That did not really affect Sam's problems about what he had to do next. He now had nowhere to go except to the Finds Officer. That was the only way that he could make progress. No one else seemed to want to take the seal from him; indeed, they said they could not. Neither could they really estimate the value or offer him hard cash. Money was what he wanted – it was just that he wanted as much as possible for Mary.

One problem was that this seal seemed to have more value than just its financial worth. What Geoff had suggested about its historical significance had been more than confirmed by Gavin Nethercott, who, though a discreet and urbane civil servant, had not been able to conceal his excitement and enthusiasm.

Another problem, as Sam saw it, was the way it had been originally found by Mary's ancestor. The authorities – that is, this MLA body in London – might decide that he had taken it unlawfully, and that it has belonged legally to the Rowlinson family all this time. In that case, Mary might get nothing. But a problem overshadowing these two, was the fact that it looked inevitable that Sam would have to surrender the object to other people in order to make any progress at all, and nothing would happen until he did that.

He really did not like to lose possession of the seal. Mary trusted him with it, and instinctively he knew that she would not want him to do that. She had a deeply embedded feeling that possession was an advantage over everything else, and once it was lost, all bargaining power had gone. Sam shared this gut feeling, and at the same time he knew its futility. It led nowhere. The only value that possession had was possession itself. Mary couldn't very well pay Sarah's fees with a lump of gold.

It was perhaps fortunate that Sam's work that afternoon was largely a mechanical exercise. He was transcribing on to a new document of his own some selective conclusions about a data collection exercise carried out for a corporate client of TCS. As he did this, more slowly than usual, he kept turning these problems over in his mind. Logically, his next move was inevitable, and yet he shrank from it. At the same time, he was being driven by an anxiety: he could help Mary only by taking action of some kind, and there was no point in delay, for the sooner he took the next step the better.

Towards the end of the afternoon, Sam began to get annoyed with himself. He realised he was feeling weighed down and depressed. The only way to cut through that was to take action. He would have to take the next step.

He logged off and shut down his computer at about four

o'clock, looked up the Council's general enquiries number in his telephone directory, went out to his car and phoned Elaine Disbrey on his mobile phone. He had decided to do this as carefully as possible, and he would make it clear that his co-operation with the official procedures was reluctant. Even if the call was traced to his mobile, he could not hand in the seal if he was not physically in the Council building.

Sam was surprised at the speed with which he was put through to Elaine Disbrey's office. It might well be late on Wednesday afternoon, but her voice sounded brisk and efficient. He had decided to begin the conversation by saying that he was asking for some advice about what he thought was a valuable object that he had in his possession.

His attempt to fend off Elaine Disbrey lasted only seconds. When she asked his name, he refused to give it, saying that the object in question belonged to a friend of his. However, when, at her request, he began to describe it, she cut in after two sentences.

'I think you are Mr Sam Dent. Am I right?'

Sam felt his resolve collapse inside. Mr Nethercott must have already told her. It would seem childish to deny it.

'That's right,' he said, with flat resignation in his voice, and immediately he said it, he realised, with a little leap of energy, that he had a tactical advantage. Neither Geoff Lowis nor Gavin Nethercott knew that Mary Dyer didn't live at Lilac Cottage any more. Therefore, Elaine Disbrey did not know, and Sam would certainly tell no one her new address.

'Well, let me explain,' continued Elaine Disbrey, smoothly and fluently, quite unaware of the impact she was having on her caller. 'Mr Nethercott, at the museum, has told me all about you and the object. He thinks it is a seal-matrix in excellent condition. Mr Nethercott is a very knowledgeable man, and I have no reason to doubt his judgement. If all that he has told me is true, then that seal-matrix that you have in your possession, Mr Dent, is a very valuable object. Mr Dent? Are you there, Mr Dent?'

'Yes,' in a terse, unfriendly tone.

'It is my duty to explain to you, Mr Dent, that, valuable an object as that may be in financial terms, it seems that it has an historical worth far beyond what can be calculated in economic value. It sounds, from what Mr Nethercott has told me, and has told you, that it is treasure under the terms of the Treasure Act, 1997. Are you still there, Mr Dent?'

'Yes.'

'Did Mr Nethercott tell you that this seal would be treasure under the terms of the Treasure Act of 1997?'

'Yes. He did.'

'That means, Mr Dent, that you will have to bring it to me and that I will have to report it to the coroner. I will also have to have possession of it so that I can send it to the Museums, Libraries and Archives Council in London, which will value it. They will also decide whether it can be given to our municipal museum here in Thorby, and they will assess what reward you, or your friend, will receive.'

There was a short silence.

'Did you follow all that, Mr Dent?'

'Oh, yes.'

'So when can I expect you to bring it into my office?' She obviously had no thoughts other than to drive directly towards what had to be done next.

'Well, I can't get into Thorby at the moment,' Sam said, vaguely. As he was using a mobile phone, Elaine Disbrey had no way of knowing where he was. 'In fact, I think you'll have to give me a few days so that I can find an opportunity to come in and see you.'

'But don't you work at TCS?'

This felt like a slap in the face again. That must be Geoff Lowis once more. Was there anything he hadn't told her?

'Hello? Are you there, Mr Dent?'

'Yes. I do, but I'm working at home at the moment.' It was all he could think of on the spur of the moment.

'And home will be Number One, Brewster Lane, Rowle Road, Thoreswood. Yes?'

'Yes.' Sam reflected that these people knew absolutely every detail about him. He felt an anger towards Geoff Lowis and Elaine Disbrey rising inside him, but knew he must control it.

'Well, you must bring it in as soon as possible,' replied Elaine Disbrey, in the same mildly threatening, but brisk and clear tone she had used all through the conversation. 'I'll wait for you, then. I must say,' she added, and Sam detected slightly more rise and fall in her voice, as if she were trying to be more personal in her tone, 'I'm really looking forward to meeting you and seeing the seal.'

'Yes. Thank you.' Sam closed the call abruptly. He thought to himself, I bet you can't wait to see it, but there's someone else I need to see before I see you.

Sam had already decided what he must do next. Before he surrendered the seal, he would have to go and tell Mary all that he had found out. As it was hers and she needed the money, Sam would have to explain that there was no way to get the money without letting the seal go. But Mary should decide whether he did that, and when.

Because he was a little angry, and because his brain was churning after the conversation with Elaine Disbrey, Sam decided he couldn't settle to work for the little part of the day that remained.

He did, though, leave his car and return to his desk in order to send the document he was working on back to his own home computer as an attachment to an email, and he picked up the data collection document itself, which was in paper form. He did this because he had a feeling he might not be at his desk the next day.

*　*　*

As he drove home that Wednesday evening, the mild anger, which had been simmering at the end of the conversation with Elaine, was still there. He felt annoyed about people he had met giving information about him to other people in the Council offices. He didn't blame Gavin Nethercott for reporting the facts to Elaine Disbrey straight away, for that was central to his work and in the line of duty. But he couldn't believe how much personal information Geoff Lowis had given her. He had given her his name and address and where he worked, and he had described the seal.

Sam also reflected that, if he decided not to co-operate with the normal procedures he had been told about, Geoff Lowis had said that Elaine Disbrey could ask the police to track him down. If the police wanted to get after him, they knew where he lived and worked, and therefore could get the telephone numbers at both places, and would also be able to trace his car registration number.

He had already decided to go and see Mary the next day. Because he could not get his mind off the seal and everything it involved, he took the seal into the lounge to show Hazel that evening. He had not had a good talk with her about it since he had helped Mary to move into her new flat last week.

As soon as he showed her the seal, Hazel's eyes widened with surprise, and then she went through the same routine as Geoff Lowis, Mr Wehrle and Gavin Nethercott had done. She stroked the column, felt the loop and examined the bottom with wonder.

She listened with silent interest as Sam told her Mary's story, and descriptions of his meetings with Lowis, Wehrle and Nethercott. He also gave her a word-by-word account of his telephone call to Elaine Disbrey.

Hazel interrupted him when he was talking about Sarah and how good she was at languages.

'Well, I've never heard of her,' she said, 'and I've been really involved with the PTA ever since Andrew started at the High School. We had a money-raising effort for furniture for the sixth form common room last year, and worked with the students, but I don't remember Sarah. What's her surname?'

'I've no idea. It'll be Brian's family name. I don't know what that is.'

Suddenly, the explanation struck Sam. 'Anyway, she won't go to Thorby High School, because that takes all the pupils from the villages to the south of the town, which is why Andrew goes there. Sarah's family lives pretty well in the middle of town, which is the catchment area for Thorby Academy.'

'Oh, so it is.' Hazel put her hands to her face, slightly bashful about her mistake. 'They are a specialist languages school, apparently. I suppose that's why they chose the name "Academy". It's a lot better than the "John Reed Comprehensive School", which is what it used to be. It sounds a bit more academic, and a bit less technical. That'll go down well at Cambridge.'

Sam glanced briefly at Hazel. It seemed to him that Hazel was not totally in sympathy with Sarah, as he was.

Hazel also interrupted when Sam was complaining about how Geoff Lowis had taken it upon himself to phone Elaine Disbrey about what he had been told, and about all the details he had given her. Sam saw it as a betrayal of confidence.

Hazel laughed an impatient laugh, and shook her head.

'Your job doesn't bring you face to face with the public.' She had told Sam that before. 'If it did, you would know that the top management watches you like a hawk. If there were the slightest whiff of Geoff being associated with anything a little shady, anything that had the slightest suggestion of something that did not play precisely according to the rule book, he'd be out on his ear, or at least demoted. He might get away with a parking ticket, but anything to do with putting a foot wrong in legal procedures, and that's it.' Hazel made a cutting motion across her throat, and said the words with feeling.

'OK, OK.' Sam sighed. He had had that lecture before. He resumed his account until he came to the end.

'So when are you taking it and giving it to her?' Hazel asked.

'Well, I thought I had better see Mary and tell her all about it first,' said Sam. 'I don't think she has much idea of its historical importance. When she talks about the value of it, I am sure she means just the financial value.'

'Yes. It might be a good idea to tell her everything, and let her see it for the last time before you have to hand it in.'

Sam began to indulge in one of his devious and rather sly habits, which seemed to have developed more in recent months, that of not telling Hazel everything that he was thinking, only so much as he wanted her to know. He wasn't sure what Mary's reaction would be, or whether he would hand the seal over to Elaine Disbrey straight away.

Hazel noticed that he did not reply, and turned sharply to look at him as they sat side by side. 'Don't you think?' she asked sharply.

'Oh, yes,' replied Sam suddenly, as if starting out of a reverie.

He put the seal back in its pouch and took the pouch and put it in its hiding place at the back of his desk.

He was quite unsure of what was going to happen tomorrow. Would he be able to soften the blow for Mary? Would he be able to keep Mary's best interests as his top priority? Would he be able to keep his nerve, whatever happened, after he had been to see her?

14

Next morning after breakfast, and after Hazel and Andrew had set off – Hazel, as often happened nowadays, giving Andrew a lift into school instead of his catching the school bus – Sam phoned his line manager at TCS, one of the directors, to say that he did not feel very well and was going to work at home. He received the customary grunt in reply. He was trusted at TCS.

He drove into Thorby and parked in a residential street some distance away from Mary's flat. He soon found the alleyway between the locksmith's shop and the workshop. There was an external door behind which was a covered stairway to the flat, so that whoever lived in it had private access, separate from the shop and separate from Ed Gleave's flat on the ground floor. After ringing the bell, and while he was listening to Mary slowly and awkwardly clunking down the stairs, he noticed that Ed Gleave was in his workshop, while a junior minded the shop. Ed had a view from his window by his bench straight down the little alleyway and so was able to see anything that was going on.

Soon the door was tugged open, but was still on a chain. Mary's face appeared round the edge, the skin tightly drawn with anxiety as she peered out.

'Oh! It's you.' The skin noticeably softened as she unhooked the chain. 'Come on up.'

At the top of the stairs, Mary was panting quite heavily, but she turned left into the lounge and shuffled across to the small table and chairs. She motioned to Sam to sit opposite her. She fiddled in the pocket of her cardigan and took out the yale key with which she had just opened the outside door. Sam had not replaced the chain when he pushed it shut behind him.

'Look,' said Mary as she regained her breath. 'You have this key to keep. I expect I'll be seeing you plenty of times before we've sorted out my little piece of gold. I've got three spare keys, and I'm going to give one to Bridget, one to Sarah and one to you. It'll be safe enough to leave the chain off the outside door. It seems a very stout door with a good, strong lock.'

'Are you sure?' said Sam, a little surprised.

'Yes. Go on.' Mary was a little impatient. 'Those stairs take more out of me than I thought they would, and I don't want to be up and down them too many times. I don't suppose many people apart from you three will be coming up here. Anyway, if I'm at all bothered about who's rung the bell, I can look out of the bedroom window and see who's at the door. They won't see me from there, especially at night, but I can even call to them through the window if I want, although I don't expect I will.

'Anyway,' she resumed, after more heavy intakes of breath, 'what brings you here so early in the day? I haven't been up long. Would you like some tea? There's half a pot left from breakfast.'

Sam accepted a mug of tea, and smiled his happiness as he settled into the warm and homely atmosphere Mary had already created. She seemed to generate it so naturally and easily in everything she did.

He was soon repeating the same descriptions he had given Hazel the night before: his meetings with Geoff Lowis, Mr Wehrle and Gavin Nethercott. Sam had brought the seal with him, carefully pouched in his pocket, and it stood on the table between them as he talked. He explained to Mary exactly what it was. Then, during his account of what Geoff Lowis had said about the historical significance and value of the seal, he noticed the effect on Mary. She became excited. There had been a tiredness on her face when she first showed Sam into the lounge. Now it lifted from her. The creases round her eyes lost their darkness, and the eyes themselves began to shine. She picked up the seal and peered intently at the coat of arms design on the bottom.

'Well, who would have thought that?' she asked. Her mouth sagged open a little, and as Sam continued, the rest of what he said was interrupted every so often with 'Good heavens', 'Well, I never' and 'Well, I had no idea.'

Finally, his long narrative came to an end.

'That's a lot to take in!' exclaimed Mary. 'I think I'll have to have some more tea.'

Sam sat patiently and silently while she went back into the kitchen and bustled and fussed around. Soon, he had another mug of much hotter tea in front of him. Mary was speechless and somewhat breathless as she sat down again.

'You see, Mary,' began Sam, 'I can't be sure how much money you're going to get at the end of all this. What all the official people have told me is that I should hand it in to Elaine Disbrey. She will then send it to the Museums, Libraries and Archives Council in London to have it valued and to decide where it's going to go. It seems that it is so valuable that we won't be able to have it back and it will have to go to some museum somewhere. It's treasure, you see.'

Sam paused, watching carefully for any effect on Mary. She was sitting very still. Her eyes still shone, looking steadily and without blinking at Sam, but the creases had darkened and her mouth was tightly shut.

'But I'll get the value,' she blurted out, suddenly.

Sam raised his eyebrows and sighed. He told himself to stay patient and calm. He decided that he had better make sure Mary understood all the aspects of the situation while he was with her to explain them. He tightened his lips as he prepared for the next step.

'According to the condition of the object, yes,' he said, stepping carefully from word to word, 'but what's a little vague is how it was found and who it really belongs to.'

'I told you. Jack Drakes found it and the family has had it ever since.' Mary spoke with some force and had obviously got her fighting strength back. Sam noticed that her stiff old hands had become clenched, with the knuckles white and the blue veins showing.

'But it was not on his land and he was working indirectly for the Rowlinson family, who did own the land.' Sam spoke as softly and calmly as he could manage.

'But does that mean they'll get the value? Have they owned it all along?' The words rapped out of Mary's mouth, pushed by a new surge of emotion.

'I think it's for that MLA lot in London to decide,' Sam said quickly, 'but you didn't take it yourself, and they may take that into account.'

Sam had been afraid of how this situation would strike Mary, and he watched with some anxiety to see how she would ride the blow and absorb the possibility that she might lose everything.

She lowered her forehead on to the knobbly backs of her hands and sat silently and still for a long time. The old, weak chair back creaked once, loudly. Then the room was oppressively quiet. Sam felt as if the stillness was pressing down on both of them, as if he could have reached out and touched it.

When Mary lifted her face again, her eyes were brimming with tears. From the depths of her throat came a low groan. Slowly, this took form: 'Oh, no!' she moaned. 'It can't be like that.' There was another pause. Sam watched, wordlessly.

'Oh, no,' she repeated slowly. 'All those years Jack Drakes laboured, and how all the others worked and toiled down the years, and all the time they had this one thing' – her clenched hands now shook, her shoulders shuddered, her voice trembled – 'this one thing that they could use to fight against those who owned everything, when they had nothing.' She put the backs of her hands to her eyes again, and dampened the cuffs of her cardigan. 'And all the time they thought it was theirs.'

Sam thought it best not to say anything, and they both sat for a long time in the stillness. Sam collected both mugs, emptied the dregs and poured two more teas. He sipped his tea – too noisily, he thought – but Mary ignored hers. She seemed so unhappy. She sat with her head bowed. Sam couldn't leave her. He thought that perhaps just his presence would help her and reassure her. It had been such a blow.

'Let's go and sit in the armchairs,' she said, after a while, and got slowly and painfully to her feet. Sam followed her meekly across the room. She eased herself into her favourite armchair. Sam sat, too. There didn't seem to be anything to do except sit and show sympathy.

Then Mary began to cry, softly and quietly. The tears fell slowly. Her nose began to run and she stifled it on her cardigan sleeve.

'We'll just have to wait for news from London.' Sam tried to break the silence gently. Mary nodded, and the tears came again. Sobs began to shake her frail frame. She snatched short breaths between the sobs. Sam walked over and put his hand on her thin, bony shoulder. As he looked down, he was brimming over with compassion.

He thought about how much she had endured at the end of the war, sleeping in the open and then squatting in unfurnished and unheated huts. She must have been hungry as well as cold on many nights. She passed the eleven plus, and competed against privileged children in the grammar school, and then her father smashed her dreams and crushed her spirit by denying her any more education. So, she lived for her children and then her grandchildren, and now her life had come to this.

She had worn herself out in the service of her family. Sam wondered how she had struggled to feed and clothe two teenage children after her husband had been killed. What an isolated and lonely life she must have led out at Lilac Cottage for all those years. But her spirit would not be snuffed out, and now again her hopes lived in Sarah. She had so carefully guarded her secret, and now Sam had to bring her mixed news such as this.

Soon, the sobs weakened, she shook less and she constantly dabbed at her eyes. She clutched her own arms, seeking comfort. Half the morning had gone.

'Can I get you anything?' asked Sam, who had gone back to his seat now that the worst effects of the shock had passed.

'No. I'll have to calm down and think what to do.' She sighed an enormous sigh and smiled weakly at Sam. 'Thanks for staying with me.'

She seemed to collect herself. 'But if we give it up, we've lost everything,' she said, a little more strongly, and Sam was relieved to see some energy rising.

'Unless we give it up, we can get nothing,' he said, and spread his hands in a gesture of helplessness. 'It looks like we've nowhere to go. We'll just have to wait and see what they give you.'

'It could be nothing,' murmured Mary, and sank into the chair again.

Then she looked up quickly and fixed her reddened eyes on Sam.

'But what about' – she paused and looked at Sam for several seconds, as if deciding whether to go on – 'what about if we took it to someone who could melt it down?' Another pause. 'Then the ancient artefact has gone, but the value of the metal is still there.'

Sam thought for a moment. 'It would still be treasure,' he

said, 'because whether it's treasure is determined by the percentage of gold in it, and its age – over three hundred years.'

'But we would have the value because it's just gold,' persisted Mary. 'No one in the metals business would know where it came from.' She had revived now, thinking she had thought of a way out.

'People know we've got it, and I would be prosecuted,' Sam continued thoughtfully.

'Who knows?'

'Geoff Lowis and Gavin Nethercott have seen it, and Elaine Disbrey knows of it.' He paused. 'Of course, they couldn't do anything about it except prosecute me, and they might prosecute you as well. There would still be an argument over the ownership of the gold, though, and I suppose they would have no sympathy if we had done that.'

Another silence descended, in which the two of them thought their own thoughts.

'I don't suppose anyone's ever done that with an ancient artefact,' added Sam, and he lapsed into thoughtfulness. On impulse, his compassion for Mary turned into generosity.

'Look, I'll tell you what, Mary. What you want is money to make sure Sarah goes to university.' Mary didn't even nod. She just sat quietly looking at Sam, wondering what was coming next.

'Right?' Sam asked, looking for reassurance. Then she nodded.

'Well, what about if I lend you five thousand pounds? Then we could take our time with the seal, and eventually find out how much we could get.'

'But supposing we got nothing. How could I repay the loan?' Mary asked, reasonably.

'Oh, let's meet that when we come to it. The fees wouldn't take all that money, and I could just pay what it costs. I could afford it. What do you say?'

134

Mary looked down and studied her hands resting in her lap for a while.

'I don't know what to say,' she said, at last. 'If you really mean it, that would get Sarah to start at Cambridge, and we could see how things went on.'

'Right,' said Sam decisively. 'We'll do that to begin with, and then I could have another chat with Elaine Disbrey, without necessarily handing over the seal.'

'We'll have to decide what to do sooner or later,' Mary protested feebly, 'and the sooner the better.'

'But for the moment, Sarah wants the money up front to pay fees in advance and for accommodation.'

'We've got until October, but that's right,' said Mary with a calmness that belied her growing excitement as she realised that, in this casual way, and out of the generosity of this young man, her dreams for Sarah were about to come true.

'Well, then, shall we do it?' Sam was as eager as Mary was excited.

'OK,' she said.

'That's that, then.' Sam stood up and put his hands into his pockets, as if he expected to find the money there. 'Now, obviously I don't carry that amount of money around with me. My debit card is no good to you, so I'll have to go home and get my cheque book. I'll pay a cheque into your account if you can't get out to do it, although you're not far from the bank here.'

'I don't know what to say,' said Mary once again. 'This really is very, very kind of you. You keep the seal for now, and I'll tell Sarah and Bridget once we've paid the money in. Thank you very much, though "Thank you" doesn't seem much to say for all that money.' The eyes that gazed into Sam's were full of feeling. She was obviously so grateful that Sam began to feel embarrassed.

'Right then,' he said. 'I'll let myself out now, and I have the key you gave me to let myself in again. I won't come back today. I'll see you tomorrow morning.'

'Thank you again.'

Sam felt so good about himself that he bounded down the stairs three at a time.

15

With his spirits buoyed up by this new plan to help Mary, Sam settled to work at home that afternoon, as he had told his manager at TCS that he would. He had already emailed his work home the previous afternoon.

Thursday afternoon was not a busy time for Hazel. She got away immediately the Pine Properties branch closed at five o'clock, and was home by five-thirty.

'Wow! You're home early,' she called, as she came in the kitchen door and saw Sam at his computer at the end of the dining-room.

'Yes.' He saved his work and shut down the computer. 'I sent some work home to do it, and I've been to tell Mary how far I've got with the seal.'

Hazel dumped her bag on one of the work surfaces and began to open the fridge and other units, ready to prepare their evening meal.

'What did she say about it?'

'She was pretty upset.'

'Upset? Why?'

'Upset at the fact that we'll have to give up the seal, and upset that she might not get the full value of it, or any money at all if it is decided that it's the Rowlinsons' property. I had to spend some time consoling her. She even suggested getting it melted down and trading it in just as gold.'

'That's pretty stupid,' cut in Hazel, sharply.

'Yeah.'

There didn't seem to be an easy or smooth way of leading on to the rest of what Sam wanted to say. He had decided that he must tell Hazel because he might have to go and stay at Dave's house again in case Elaine Disbrey sent the police after him about the seal. Geoff Lowis had told him that that could happen, and for the time being he was refusing to give up the seal. So Sam just let it spill out, suddenly.

'What I've done is I've promised to pay her the value now, so that we needn't hand in the seal just yet and can take our time finding out how much we can get for it.'

There was a slight bang as Hazel put down a dish into which she had been putting some ingredients for a pudding.

'You've done what?' The words ripped through the air, a slight pause behind each. Hazel whipped round to face him.

Sam stayed calm and looked steadily back at Hazel. 'I've offered her the money because she needs it for Sarah when she starts in October, and we'll see how much value we can get for the seal in due course.'

'But the only person who can get you money for the seal is the Finds Officer person at the Council. People have told you that.' Hazel was speaking loudly, and with some force. Sam had expected to spark a fiery response, but this looked really menacing.

'Yes,' he replied quickly.

'So that's what you do.' Hazel's eyes were wide. There was no relenting.

'Look, she was really upset.' Sam was still steady. He thought it best to cajole Hazel. 'It's been her life's ambition to get Sarah to university, and she thinks she's got the means, so I thought I'd lend her some of my spare money so she can do that, and I'll get repaid when we hand in the seal.'

'You must be out of your mind,' Hazel continued in the same high pitch, the same peevish tone. She noticed, out of the corner of her eye, Andrew peep in through the doorway, and then he quickly withdrew. She realised that the television was on. He had not gone up to his room to do his homework. 'You don't know how much you're going to get for the seal, and could I remind you that it's "our" money, not "your" money? It is a joint account, you know.'

'I just thought I could help.' Sam's tone had a pleading edge to it now. 'If only you could have seen her. You would have thought her whole world had collapsed around her. Don't you feel any sympathy for her?'

'Of course I do, but I don't go doing daft things like giving her our money. You want to help her, so you hand in the seal to the proper person. Then she'll get what she's due.' Hazel was on fire; she was talking very fast.

'She has this fear that if she gives up the seal, she's lost what she's got to bargain with. She's lost what all her ancestors had been toiling for all those years to pass on.' Even as he said it, Sam had a feeling Hazel was stiffening herself against any argument.

'Oh, so that's it!' Hazel's lip curled and she turned on him with a snarl. 'The two of you have ganged up to have your little fight against authority. You've got something that they can't get at, that they can't do anything about, so you want to play your little game. Oh, of course, we must bring all our fine feelings into it, mustn't we? We're just helping an old lady. We're feeling sympathy for her. We're full of compassion for her. But really you want to play your little game, have your little rebellion against authority. Well,' and now she banged the dining table with her bare hand, 'not with our money. How many times have we said "Only us"? You soon forget. Get it into your skull, will you? It's only us.'

Hazel was now nearly screaming, her eyes blazing. She nearly choked, and with a swift energy, she grabbed a beaker, splashed in some cold water and quickly gulped at it before continuing.

'Anyway, didn't Geoff Lowis say that it was illegal not to

hand it in when you knew it was treasure, and that you could have the police after you if you don't hand it in?'

'Yes,' replied Sam, with a sigh. He knew now that he wouldn't win. Hazel knew him too well, and he would have to take the inevitable last step. 'I thought I'd go and stay at Dave's again for a short time – just so that you and Andrew aren't involved.'

'Oh, here we go again!' He had really roused Hazel to fever pitch. 'All your little rebellions collapse in the end. Haven't you learnt that yet? And what about me and Andrew? We've got to carry on living our lives while you play your silly little games. The trouble with you is you've never grown up from being a student, have you? Students are forever wanting to put the world right, to fight against injustice, to stand up for the poor, to protest and march and carry on.' Each phrase was accompanied by a sneering gesture. Hazel now gasped for breath, but her eyes were flashing and her colour was high. Sam knew she would not pause now, and he would have to ride it out.

'Well, it's all very well for students.' She continued her headlong rush. 'They have no responsibilities. They have only to think of themselves and their precious morals, but when you grow up and get married, you make all sorts of commitments, all sorts of connections. You can't just act on your own any more. You're part of a whole network. Are you so selfish you can't see that? What about me and Andrew? Everything you do affects us. You married me. Haven't you learnt yet that that makes us one person? I know everything about you, how you think, what you believe, the pace you live at. You've grown into me and I should think I've grown into you. You are nearly forty years old, you know. You're not some spotty student with a great big moral conscience. Grow up. Grow up, why don't you?'

Sam thought she had finished, and he opened his mouth to draw breath and reply, but the torrent continued.

'Oh, yes. You go off and stay with Dave. You two are a good pair together. Really two of the boys, aren't you? Well, I'll tell you something.' Now she came near him and put her face six inches away from his. Eyeballs bored into each other. 'Most of the boys grow up to become men. Except for a few, that is. You and Dave. And I'll tell you something else.' She had withdrawn slightly, but now she thrust her face right into his again. 'You think when you've played your little game, you'll be able to come creeping back here and I'll be waiting for you. You can settle into your comfy life again. Well, not this time.'

Hazel flung her arm towards the kitchen door and pointed at it. 'You walk out of that door and you do not come back in. That's it. Finished. And I'll tell you a third thing, too. If the police come round here, I'll tell them exactly where you are, address and telephone number. I'll tell them where you work, and anything else they want to know about you. I just don't care any more and I've had enough. I'm not getting on the wrong side of the law, not for you or anybody else. It is up to you whether you go out of that door, but if you do, you stay out. I'm not doing this again.'

Finally, Hazel stopped. She was breathless. She kept taking great gulps of air until her breathing steadied. She was determined she would not get upset like the last time Sam went to Dave's. Now, she was dry-eyed and burning. She could feel the pressure behind her eyes. She knew her cheeks would be scarlet, as she glared at Sam. She slumped into a kitchen chair. She heard a movement from inside the lounge – Andrew, probably going up to his room.

Sam said nothing. He knew Hazel as well as she knew him. They were passionately in love once, and Sam thought she didn't really mean half the things she had just said, but to stay in the house tonight now, after that, would be unbearable. The tension in each room would be so thick that they couldn't escape. It would sit between them like a great, dense fog.

Sam got up from his chair in silence. He got together a few papers, reached for the seal in its pouch from behind some of the books on his desk, and, without a word, went up to the bedroom, while Hazel sat and glared. She had regained her breath and had slightly cooled. She heard Sam speaking into his mobile phone.

A few minutes later, he reappeared and crossed the dining-room, morose, sullen, sour. He carried a bag, which was obviously full of clothes.

'See you again soon,' he muttered, as he opened the door, went through, clumsily banging the bag, and closed it firmly behind him. Hazel said nothing. She just sat and stared at the door. She couldn't believe he had gone, after what she had said. She wondered why it was that people have a great urge to do things in spite of all logic. All their friends and family are telling them not to do something, and they know they shouldn't, and yet they do it. She reflected that he must have thought she didn't mean it. Well, she thought, we'll see.

She went to the sink and drank another glass of cold water. Then she went through the lounge and slowly climbed the stairs, knocked on Andrew's door and went in without invitation. Andrew was at his desk and looked up, wide-eyed, expectant, mouth slightly open.

'I'm sorry, love.' Hazel put her hand on his shoulder. 'Your dad's being absolutely stupid again. He's been going on about that old lady, Mrs Dyer, and it seems that she's given him a valuable possession of hers for safe keeping.'

Andrew looked down at his desk. His face crumpled and he screwed up his eyes very tightly.

'We've had a great row and now he's gone off to his friend Dave's house,' Hazel was saying. 'He says it's so we don't get involved. He says it's to protect us. We wouldn't need any protection if he weren't so damned stupid in the first place. I'm not sure I believe all this about protecting us. He said that last time. He's mostly gone because he knows I'll keep giving him hell until he does the right thing. That's how much he really cares for us, just leaves us on our own.' She paused for breath. 'I've had enough this time, though. I told him I wouldn't let him back. We can't go on like this.' For Andrew, it was as if a leaden cloud had descended. He rose from his chair and put his arms round Hazel. He drew her to him and buried his face in her bosom.

'Oh, no,' he moaned. 'Why do you have to row?'

Hazel thought she would be strong. She started to argue her case.

'Well, do you know what he's done? He's only given away thousands of pounds of our money to Mrs Dyer for her granddaughter, and now he's playing silly buggers …'

She broke off suddenly, as Andrew pulled away from her.

'Stop it!' he yelled. He looked at her through reddened eyes, and now the tears were running.

'But can't you see what he's doing? If he takes that cheque book, I'll ring the bank and tell them to stop all cheques. It's a joint account, and they can insist on having both signatures for a large amount.'

Andrew covered his face.

'I don't care.' He spoke slowly, from a deep, dark despair, and shook his head as he wiped the sleeve of his jumper across his eyes. Then he cut Hazel short before she could launch into a speech.

'I just want you two here, now, together. I don't care about anything else.' He pumped his fists up and down in exasperation. Hazel could see he was not going to listen. There was no point in explaining. Whatever the arguments, he just blindly wanted his dad. He had needs deeper than logic, deeper than rights and wrongs. She was just thankful that he wanted her, too.

There was nothing more Hazel could say. She reached out and drew him to her, hard, tight, and they stayed in the embrace for a long time, until the hurt eased a little.

Eventually, she loosened her hold and Andrew slumped down on to his chair.

'I'll cook some chips and burgers when you feel like coming down,' she said quietly, and left him.

A long time later, they ate a simple meal in silence, avoiding each other's eyes.

When they went to bed, each of them had damp eyes and an aching throat, and they slept only fitfully.

16

Dave had received Sam in his normal loud, affable way when he had arrived on Thursday evening. He soon suggested that they should go to the Blacksmith's Arms for the evening, and Sam succumbed without comment. He was glad it was a fairly quiet evening.

He had only shallow, short stretches of sleep during the night. He was capable of a logical appraisal of any personal situation in which he found himself, but at important crises he also trusted irrational feelings that surfaced in his mind. Now, one thought that nagged at him and would not go away was Mary's idea that her position would weaken once the seal was handed over. The feeling of guarding a secret that had been passed down through the generations was as much a legacy to Mary as was the object itself. Sam sympathised with Mary because of his deeply buried distrust of people in control. It was something that he shared with her, and probably accounted for the compassion that he felt for her, in view of the difficult life she had led.

Dave had set off early for work on Friday morning, and as Sam took his time in munching through some of Dave's breakfast cereals, drinking his coffee and eating his toast, his mind had not really settled on what to do next. If Elaine Disbrey really did alert the police, as Geoff Lowis had said she could, although she herself had not made the threat, then they knew his address and Hazel had said she would soon tell them where Dave lived. They also knew where he worked, and he thought it might be only a matter of time before they found out Mary's new address. Therefore, he reasoned, if he was going to act on this feeling that he and Mary shared, he would have to fall back on the most basic tactic of all. He would have to hide the seal in another place, a place that nobody could know about or identify, except himself.

Sam phoned TCS to say that he would be working at home again that day. He used his mobile phone so that the call could be traced only to him. He drove to Loscar wood and parked near the picnic area that the Council had established on the south side of the wood.

There were always people around the area who liked to enjoy the countryside and the fresh air, and so he knew he would not be conspicuous as he walked slowly through the wood and out on to the north side. Very few of the dog walkers and other strollers went beyond the northern edge, because the terrain soon became rather bland and productive farmland. Sam behaved like any other walker as he made slow progress along a narrow track until he came to a wire fence that ran from east to west. He knew very well that this was the farm next to Brewster's, and that the fence had been erected only a short time ago to restrict grazing cattle. This meant that the earth around each of the wooden posts had recently been disturbed and lay in rough form where the workmen had shovelled it.

Sam set off along the line of the fence and counted seven posts to the east. At the post, he looked back towards the wood for any sign of movement or human activity, and he also looked quickly round in every direction. He was sure there was nobody about. He had brought a small trowel from Dave's garden shed and now he made swift and deft use of it as he dug a hole two feet to the east of the post, and two feet deep. He placed the seal in its pouch at the bottom, and then refilled the hole. Quickly, he pocketed the trowel and retraced his steps to the wood. He waited around for a few minutes, still looking in all directions, until he was quite sure he had not been seen. He looked for some time and with some feeling at the spot he had selected, dwelling in his thoughts on what it contained beneath the surface, before he turned and walked briskly back to the car.

He returned to Dave's house and carefully replaced the trowel exactly in the spot where he had found it, and then set off to visit Mary again, this time carrying his cheque book.

He parked a few streets away and walked quickly to the flat. It was now mid-morning, and he did not expect this visit to take long, although he realised that he might have to go to the bank for Mary before he returned to his car. He then intended to go back to Dave's house and to work on his laptop computer for the rest of the day. He was not sure how long he would stay at Dave's.

Sam noticed that Ed Gleave was not in his workshop as he took the few steps down the alleyway to Mary's door. That meant that he was in the shop at the front. As he put his key into the lock, he half expected that Mary would have absent-mindedly replaced the chain the night before, but she hadn't, and he was able to walk straight up the stairs. Towards the top of the stairway, he called out 'Hello Mary', so that it was not too much of a shock or surprise as he entered. He called quite loudly, because, for all he knew, she might be in the bathroom or even the bedroom.

There was no reply, and everything seemed still and silent. He noticed that one of the small work surfaces in the kitchen seemed set out for Mary's breakfast, and there was a cereal bowl with the contents half-eaten. She obviously ate there rather than in the corner of the sitting room. He stood in the kitchen for a moment or two, wondering which room to look in. He called again and listened, but there was no reply.

He pushed open the door into the sitting room, and looked round quickly: everything seemed neatly in order and the small dining table had not been used. Back in the kitchen, he thought that perhaps she had gone out, and wondered whether to wait for her to come back, or to leave the cheque near the breakfast things, where she would be sure to see it.

Then, for the first time, an uneasy feeling struck him. He thought that she might have been taken ill, and so perhaps he had better look into each room before he left.

The bathroom door was shut, and he knocked on it gently. There was no answer, and so he turned the handle. It opened with a slight squeak, but there was obviously nobody in the bathroom. He thought that if Mary was still in bed, she must surely have heard him by now. Still, he had better look in. In any case, the door was slightly ajar. He took four quick steps towards it and pushed it open.

What he saw turned his heart to ice.

The bed was in line with the door, with the bed head furthest away, against the far wall. And on the bed lay Mary, fully clothed. She was absolutely still, her eyes closed, and she was mostly on her back, but slightly turned to her left side.

Sam stood motionless and silent.

Then he found his voice. 'Oh, no,' he said aloud, but quietly. Instinctively, he moved round the bed to where Mary was. Her right hand seemed to trail over her right hip at a rather awkward angle.

He leaned across and took the hand. The skin felt cool, but it was not stone cold. Sam fumbled for the pulse. Nothing. He put the hand back so that it wrapped slightly round her waist. He was sure she was dead, but obviously she had not yet gone stiff. Then timidly, gently, he touched her face. That was very cool. It was a pale, creamy colour.

'Oh, no.' Sam's voice was a breathy whisper this time.

He straightened up and quickly looked round the room. Mary seemed beyond help. He would need to phone the ambulance and the police. He realised that it might seem odd that it was he who had found her after letting himself into the flat with his own key. He called the ambulance on his mobile phone, but was not sure about the police. This was not, after all, an emergency, and he didn't know the local number. He thought perhaps it was best to get the owner of the flat to come and see how he had found Mary. As a well-known locksmith, he was bound to know the number of the local police.

Sam left everything undisturbed and went back through the kitchen to the stairs. He wondered why there was a half-eaten breakfast, when Mary was lying on the bed. As he went down the stairs, gripping the handrail very tightly, he realised his legs were shaking. It was many years since he had felt fear and shock through his legs – not since he was a child, in fact.

As he came out of the external door, he was relieved to see that Ed Gleave was now in his workshop. It would not be necessary to disturb him in the shop, with customers waiting. As he pushed through the workshop door, he noticed that Ed was working at a small lathe with his back to the door. There was some noise, and he didn't notice Sam until he walked up to stand beside him, and then he switched off the lathe. He gave Sam a blank, questioning look.

'I've just found Mary Dyer upstairs,' began Sam.

'What of it? She lives there.' Ed still looked blank.

'I've phoned for an ambulance, but I'm sure she's dead.'

'What?' The blankness turned to shock and a frown.

'How do you mean?' Ed looked bewildered. 'I've seen her go in and out since she's lived here, and she has seemed perfectly fit.'

'Well, will you come and look where I found her?' said Sam, with some urgency. 'As I said, the ambulance is on its way.'

Ed walked to the wall and threw an 'Off' switch before following Sam out of the workshop, across the alley, through Mary's door and up the stairs. He spoke as they climbed.

'Didn't I see you here yesterday?'

149

'Yes. I visited Mary yesterday. She seemed in good health.'

'I've seen you somewhere before, though,' Ed persisted. He was still rather taken aback by this sudden interruption to his work.

'Oh, yes. I helped her move in,' replied Sam, as they reached the top of the stairs.

'Yes. That's it,' said Ed, with a flick of the fingers.

'Through here.' Sam led the way through the kitchen to the bedroom. Just after he had pushed the door open and entered, he turned to watch Ed's reaction. There was a quick, slight intake of breath as he took in the sight of Mary.

'Yes, she certainly looks dead,' he said, as he also made his way along the side of the bed and touched the same hand that Sam had touched. He snatched his hand away rather quickly, and Sam guessed that he was surprised at the coolness of the skin.

'I wonder what caused it?' he said. 'There's no sign that she was in any distress.'

Sam thought how serene and peaceful she looked, after the passions he had witnessed the day before.

'A heart attack, probably,' Sam surmised. 'Shall we call the police?'

'Oh, yes.' Ed nodded. 'A sudden death like this: they'll have to be called.' Immediately, he took his phone from his pocket and pressed the buttons. Sam noticed that the police number was already programmed into his phone.

'I'll go and wait for the ambulance.' Sam headed for the stairs, and as he started down, he heard Ed speaking into his phone.

The paramedics, when they arrived, leapt up the stairs three at a time, and were already at work on Mary by the time Sam arrived in the bedroom. They felt for a pulse at the side of the neck, under the jaw and in the wrist. The older one pressed his ear against her heart and then straightened up and looked hopelessly towards the younger man.

'Resuscitation?' he asked, but without eagerness. The other shook his head, slowly and sadly.

'She's been gone far too long.' He turned to Sam. 'We can't take her just like this,' he said. 'We'll have to summon a doctor.'

'The police said to leave the body just as it is until they get here,' interrupted Ed. 'They're on their way.'

The police arrived within five minutes, a sergeant and a young constable. They immediately took in the situation, and accepted the opinion of the paramedics that nothing could be done to revive Mary. Then the sergeant questioned Sam in the sitting room, while the constable asked Ed what role he had played, and when he had last seen her alive.

Once the doctor had arrived, examined the body and stated that Mary was dead, the paramedics asked his permission to remove the body to the hospital in the ambulance. The sergeant asked the doctor for his initial opinion, and the doctor said that he thought it might have been a heart attack. The fact that she was dressed probably meant that she had felt ill while eating her breakfast and had gone to lie down on the bed, when the fatal attack had occurred. He said that he would have to inform the coroner, because he had not been attending the lady, and he expected that there would be a post-mortem examination.

'Normally,' he said, 'the coroner asks the police to attend the scene and investigate, but in this case,' he added with a smile, 'events have moved rather more quickly.'

With that, the doctor left. The sergeant told Sam and Ed that they were free to leave, and he would be in touch if he needed to speak to them later. Meanwhile, he would have to look for the name, address and telephone number of the next of kin.

After the doctor had duly reported Mrs Dyer's death to the coroner in the late morning, the coroner, as was normal procedure, telephoned the duty sergeant at Thorby Central Police Station.

'I've had the sudden death of an elderly lady, Mrs Mary Dyer, reported to me by Dr Furnell a few minutes ago,' came his august and dignified tones, 'and now I must formally ask you to investigate: Flat B, Number 36, Oxford Road.'

'We are already attending the scene, sir,' replied the sergeant, 'and two witnesses have been interviewed: the man who found her, and the owner of the flat, Gleave the Locksmith, on Oxford Road. There seem not to be any suspicious circumstances. Can you tell me if there will be a post-mortem, sir?'

'Oh, yes. She does not seem to have been attended by a doctor recently, and certainly not by Dr Furnell.'

'We'll wait for that to establish the cause of death, then,' continued the sergeant, 'and depending on the cause, there may be no need for an inquest, though you will decide that, and then we can close the file.'

'There's one interesting fact of which I feel I should inform you,' the serene and composed voice of the coroner continued, 'because there is probably no way that you would discover this in the normal course of your enquiries. Yesterday morning, this same lady, Mrs Mary Dyer, was reported to me by an officer of the Council to be in possession of a very valuable item of treasure. I might add that the address I was given is different from the address at which she died today. I was given the address of Lilac Cottage, Rowle Road, Thoreswood.'

'Are you suggesting that there is a connection between the item of treasure and the death of the old lady, sir?' asked a surprised and puzzled sergeant.

'It is not up to me to suspect or to suggest such a thing, as you well know.' The sergeant detected a rather more imperious tone in the coroner's voice now. 'I merely provide you with the facts of a situation and commission you to investigate them. As my public duty also includes the recording of finds of treasure, I am in the unique position of being able to point out to you the coincidence of these two reports concerning this lady on two successive days. In my capacity, I make no connection. In your capacity, you might. Could I just say that I would be very interested in anything unusual that you might find if you search the two premises at which Mrs Dyer seems to have lived.'

'Very good, sir,' said the sergeant, somewhat tersely. 'Will that be all?' After a positive reply, he put the phone down. He was always irritated by officials who spoke to him in a slightly haughty manner, especially when his own tone had been friendly, and as informal as he could make it.

However, the call made him pause for thought. What the coroner had said seemed to turn a routine enquiry into the non-suspicious death of an old lady into the possibility of something more. He decided that it was impossible not to act, because if anything developed later, he would not have a leg to stand on if the coroner accused him of neglecting his duty. He picked up his phone again and pressed one digit.

'Is Stuart Cooke there, please?' There was a pause of a few seconds. 'Would you come to the desk as soon as you can, Stuart? There's something I'd like you to handle.'

Almost immediately, the door behind the sergeant opened, and in breezed a cheerful-looking young man in his early thirties, dressed in a dark brown suit, a light brown striped tie, and a pale fawn shirt. 'What can I do for you, John?'

The sergeant gave a slight snuffle before he began to speak. 'I've just had the coroner on the phone. An old lady died in the flat above Gleave the locksmith's shop this morning. It seemed like a perfectly routine enquiry. Sergeant Parry and Constable Eves went round. In fact, they are still there, tidying up, and Parry has already radioed in to say that there are no suspicious circumstances. But the coroner has noticed that the old lady seemed to live at two addresses, and he's had it reported to him that she's got some valuable item of treasure. He says he'd be interested if we found anything. I've written the two addresses and the lady's name on this bit of paper.'

Stuart studied the paper with a ponderous 'Hmm,' and then he fired into life again. 'You want me to take it?'

'I haven't got the manpower,' said the sergeant, with a shrug.

'OK. I'd better get warrants for these two places in case the owners prove not to be co-operative,' Stuart said, brightly, 'but first I'd better get down to the Council offices before they all go off for the weekend, and find out about a certain bit of treasure.' He shook his head briefly. 'Just when I thought I could put my feet up for the afternoon and slide off early for the weekend.'

17

Stuart Cooke sat down at his desk at the end of Friday. He had had a busy afternoon, getting two search warrants and interviewing Elaine Disbrey and Gavin Nethercott. He now felt that he knew most of the facts about this situation, but he was not sure they were leading anywhere in particular. After the long talks in Elaine Disbrey's office and at the museum with Mr Nethercott, he felt that he was at the end of an educational course.

He had also spoken to Sergeant Parry and PC Eves, who said they had seen nothing unusual or suspicious in Mrs Dyer's flat. They had, however, come across the Lilac Cottage address a few times, and they had deduced that she must have moved from there within the last few days. They also gave Stuart the address of Mrs Dyer's daughter, Bridget, who was next of kin and whom they had visited at lunchtime to give her the sad news. Indeed, they had taken her for the formal identification in the afternoon.

'I want you to help me on a new one, Kevin,' he called across to a young man writing a report at a nearby desk. 'I don't think this one will move very fast, and you can have your weekend off. On second thoughts, give me half your Saturday morning tomorrow. We may be doing two or three searches next week, but they can wait. I just want to make a few calls along the High Street tomorrow morning, while memories are still fresh.'

There were three shops that sold watches and jewellery in

Thorby. Two of them were local branches of a national chain of jewellers, but the third one was the last that Kevin visited on Saturday morning, and it was Wehrle's, a local and well-respected firm with a long tradition as watchmakers and jewellers in the town.

Here, Kevin discovered that Sam had visited Mr Wehrle towards the end of Tuesday afternoon. He noticed the same rather distant and fairly hostile manner with which Sam had also been treated. Mr Wehrle was well familiar with people wanting to have valued and then to trade in objects made of precious metal, which had been found in lofts or inherited from relatives. It was necessary to treat everyone with a degree of clinical detachment, especially as in recent times many claimed to have bought such objects from Sunday market stalls or various other traders who visited sites only for one day or even half a day. He had also, many times in his professional life, had visits such as this from police officers, but he knew, and Kevin knew, that his business affairs had never attracted the slightest suspicion of any illegal conduct.

Sitting at the same desk as he had done on Tuesday afternoon, Mr Wehrle wheezed through a summary of Sam's visit.

'I gave the young man a very vague valuation,' he concluded, with a noisy sigh. 'I must admit, though, that I'm always suspicious of people who insist that the object they are offering does not belong to them, but to a friend, and that was so in this case. He didn't have a receipt or any other evidence of where it had been obtained – at least, not one that he showed me.'

Back at the station, Kevin wrote a short account of his morning's work, and left it with Stuart, who told him to go away and enjoy his weekend.

Stuart, meanwhile, began to worry about the fruit of his own morning's work, which had consisted of a visit to Bridget. Something was prodding his instinct that everything was not quite right about this case. It was that Bridget had no knowledge at all of her mother's owning a valuable object of some historical significance. Stuart knew that her expression of bewilderment was genuine by the eager and energetic way in which she came back at him with many hard and direct questions.

She knew all about Sam and who he was. Indeed, she conceded that her mother spoke highly of him and had done ever since she seemed to have met him around last Christmas time.

'But,' she argued, with considerable passion, 'I'm sure my mum would not confide in someone she's only known for six months, and leave me out of it. Mum wasn't secretive like that.'

'Did you get on OK with your mum?' Stuart asked, with a directness that slightly shocked Bridget.

'I resent that question,' she said, glaring at Stuart. 'Mum got on OK with me and all my family, and always did all she could to help us. In fact, she had just moved into Thorby to be nearer to us.'

'We have to consider all aspects of a situation,' said Stuart quietly, in an attempt to mollify her.

The more he thought about them, the more Stuart was disturbed by these two new facts: Sam's visit to the jeweller and Bridget's ignorance of the existence of the seal. He suddenly had the feeling that he would be spending a long weekend working.

He knew about Sam. But why had Sam taken the seal to have it valued without telling anyone else? Why did Bridget not know about the seal, and why had Sam not discussed it with her? It was he, after all, who had found Mrs Dyer, although he had done so after letting himself into the flat with a key that he told Sergeant Parry she had given him the day before. He had a key, and yet had known Mrs Dyer only about five or six months. And why had he visited her the day before her death? Why wasn't the door secured by a chain? Most old ladies living on their own did this. This line of thought prompted him to decide that his next move would be to visit the flat, not only to check on the existence of a chain, but also to search the flat himself. He had to find the answers to all these questions. He wanted to proceed with safe, careful steps.

Stuart decided to have a snack at about midday on Saturday, so that he was left with a lengthy afternoon in which he guessed he might be busy. It was true that he had sent Kevin off for the weekend, but he could always contact him should he need him again.

Ed Gleave's shop was closed for lunch when Stuart arrived, but when he went round to the back alleyway, he could see a light in the workshop.

'Come in,' called Ed, in response to Stuart's knock.

'Good afternoon.' Stuart was quite brisk. 'I'm enquiring about the death of the old lady in the flat above your shop yesterday morning. Was it you that found her?' It was always a part of Stuart's technique, when weighing up a witness, to begin by asking questions to which he already knew the answers.

'No. It was some young chap she knows who had helped her move in a few days ago,' said Ed. 'He came here to tell me about it just after ten. Then we went up to the flat together.' Ed took a bite out of the sandwich he was eating, but was keen to continue: 'I must say that the lady seemed perfectly fit and healthy to me, and every time I saw her in the few days since she'd moved in she was quite happy. There was one thing that I've been thinking about, though,' and here Ed waved his sandwich at Stuart and began to spit crumbs in his excitement, 'I wonder why he visited her for over two hours on Thursday morning.'

'Visited her?'

'Yes. I saw him ring the bell on her outside door just after nine and she let him in. Then I saw him come out about two hours later. She certainly didn't show him out, and he came out all in a rush – just pulled the door behind him.'

'Oh, thank you,' said Stuart, slowly, lost in thought for a moment. 'Thank you. That's very interesting.'

Ed lent Stuart the key that Sam had given him, and so he was able to carry out a thorough search of the flat himself. He had the notes from Sergeant Parry and Constable Eves, but he could not be sure how thorough they had been with the search of the flat or with the interviews, and so he was very keen to cover this ground again himself.

As he let himself in through the outside door, he noticed a security chain hanging from the doorpost. He spent over two hours doing a very thorough search of the flat, but did not uncover any information that moved his enquiry forward. Mary Dyer had a small medicine cabinet, but all she kept in it were the usual painkillers for headaches, indigestion tablets and the mineral and vitamin supplements that many old people took nowadays. He found many references to Mary's son, Howard, and his wife, Joyce, and daughter, Maria, and there were letters from them and photographs of them. There were also many documents, letters and photographs referring to Bridget, Brian, Kevin and Sarah. He found a copy of Mary's will, which rather surprised him, as he thought that most old people left this with their solicitor. He also found references to Sam and Hazel in a diary Mary had kept, but he found no trace of what he was really looking for, the seal, or any reference to it.

Just as he was finishing, Bridget arrived and explained that this was the first opportunity she had had to visit the flat and sort a few things out. Stuart indicated where he had found some significant documents, and then left, returning the key to Ed.

He had decided that his next important step was to talk at

159

length to Sam, and to discover whether he actually had the seal at the moment.

Hazel had finished the afternoon shopping and was at home when Stuart called at No. 1, Brewster Lane. Saturday mornings were usually busy at Pine Property services and everyone was expected to work, but the afternoons were slack, and only one in three of the staff worked, on a rota basis.

As Stuart was not in uniform, Hazel looked at him rather anxiously until he announced that he was Detective Inspector Cooke, and showed his identification. That made her even more anxious, and then she became annoyed. She pursed her lips and deliberately showed exaggerated signs of impatience as she stepped aside and motioned him to come inside.

She was polite and hospitable, and offered Stuart tea or coffee, which he declined. He was anxious to get on with his questions, and to see Sam in private as soon as possible.

In answer to his first question, he was surprised to hear that Sam was not at home and indeed was not living there at present.

'He just does that every so often,' Hazel hastened to add, by way of explanation. 'He goes off and lives elsewhere when he gets fed up with living with us.' That was not true, and was an over-simplification, but Hazel decided that it was more plausible than the truth. Still wanting to be co-operative, however, she rushed on: 'But at present, I think I know where he is. I think he's gone to stay with his friend, Dave, and I'll give you the address and telephone number.' She grabbed a pad of post-its from a work surface in the kitchen, quickly wrote on it, and handed the first one to Stuart.

'Thank you,' said Stuart, quickly taking in this information. 'How long do you think he's been there?'

'Since Thursday night.' Hazel rapped out the answer. She

was determined to give the police all the information it suited her to give.

'Since Thursday night?' repeated Stuart slowly, while he thought carefully. He had already decided that if he spoke to Hazel alone, he would confine his questions to the seal, which he thought she was bound to know about, and not to mention Mary's death, on the off-chance that she did not know. 'Do you know if he went to work at the usual time on Friday morning?' he asked in a casual, conversational tone.

'Well, I've just told you he wasn't here,' Hazel replied sharply. 'As far as I know he went to work as normal yesterday morning, but, of course, I can never be certain what he's doing.' She really felt this tone of sarcastic indifference towards Sam, and did not care about communicating it to Stuart.

'Hmmm.' That was all Stuart wanted to know. Then he went on to ask Hazel about the seal, and she readily told him all she knew, including a detailed description, which tallied with those of Gavin Nethercott and Elaine Disbrey.

'The fact is, Mrs Dent,' said Stuart when she had finished, 'it is the seal that I am most interested in. Do you know if he has left it in the house?'

'Oh! Good heavens, no,' she said, again with a show of impulsive impatience. 'I saw him take it out with him, but I'll show you where he kept it, so you can check.'

Hazel led the way to his desk and pulled out the books behind which he had kept it. Then she waved her arms, the palms of her hands upwards, in a gesture of emptiness.

'Do you mind if I look around for a few minutes?' asked Stuart, to Hazel's surprise.

Her lips tightened, and she became more defensive. 'Have you got a warrant?'

'No,' said Stuart, calmly and evenly, 'but I could get one if you insist. It really will be more convenient for both of us if you allow me to look round quickly for a few minutes without my having to get a warrant.'

'Huh!' she snorted. 'It seems as if you won't take my word for it that he's taken it with him.' Then she paused. She did not want to change her co-operative manner and to appear to withdraw her goodwill. 'Oh. All right, then.'

Stuart turned back to the desk, indifferent to her change of mood. He briskly shuffled through various papers that lay on the surface, pulled out handfuls of books and replaced them, and then got to work on the two drawers. What was in the drawers was not tidily arranged, and so he had to lift various layers of papers and thin folders with the back of his hand until he was satisfied that he had cast an eye over everything.

Hazel stood without moving, looking hard, her eyes boring into the back of his head and shoulders. He was aware of the silent hostility behind him, but ignored it and was deft and efficient in his search. She wanted very much to let him know that she was not pleased at his not taking her word for where the seal was.

'And could I just have a look in the bedroom?' he asked, as he turned to face her, wearing his professional smile.

Hazel made a deliberately noisy and exasperated sigh as she beckoned him to follow her. They had to go through the lounge to the stairs, and Andrew was now in the lounge watching Saturday afternoon sport on television. He turned round to Hazel, puzzled, a little alarmed. Their eyes met, and Hazel looked up at the ceiling to show Andrew her annoyance.

Stuart made for the wardrobe once he had been shown into the bedroom, and he spent some time flicking shirts, coats, skirts, blouses and fleeces backwards and forwards. He looked carefully around the floor of the wardrobe. It was fitted along one length of the room, and so there was no top to examine, but only an inside top shelf. The divan double bed did not allow any space underneath, but he searched two sets of drawers. Hazel again treated him to a long, cold, relentless stare.

He asked to see the other bedrooms, and although he was quick and perfunctory as far as Andrew's room was concerned, the spare bedroom again had the wardrobe and drawers searched. The bed in this room was slightly raised on casters, and Stuart got down on his knees to peer underneath. Hazel stifled an urge to giggle and to tell him that they had no chamber pots.

Finally, he followed Hazel down to the lounge and into the kitchen, where he apologised for taking up her time, and left.

Hazel couldn't wait to get back into the lounge and to unload her pent-up feelings on to Andrew. He had switched off the television.

'The idiot!' She split the quiet of the room with all the force she could muster. 'Look what he's done! He's not handed in that seal, which is a criminal offence. I bet he's been back to see Mary Dyer, and then he's not handed it in because she doesn't want him to, although it's the only way to get money for her. Oh, sorry, love, you don't know about the seal, do you?'

Hazel stopped herself in mid-flight, and took a long, deep breath, before explaining to Andrew as much as he needed to know. 'Mary Dyer gave Dad a valuable, golden object, which was a king's seal, after he had helped her to move. That was the valuable possession I told you she had given to him for safe keeping. It's been in her family for generations and originally came from Rowle Abbey. She wanted him to trade it in and give her the money for her granddaughter to go to Cambridge University because she's very clever. He's shown it to the museum and phoned someone at the Council offices who deals with these things, and they say he's got to hand it in, by law. The silly fool is not doing so, for one of his crazy reasons, and they've sent the police after him.' She paused for breath. Her eyes were wide and shining, her fists clenched, her whole body rigid.

'Why?' she shouted at the room. 'Why does he do such irrational things? Everybody he knows is telling him not to keep it to himself. Everybody, all the experts, are telling him what to do. We're his family, and we're telling him just to do the right thing and not go following some crack-brained idea. But no! He has to know better. He has to defy everyone, everything he's told, and do something stupid.'

Hazel's energy was winding down, and she fixed her attention on Andrew, as she said, more coolly, 'I tell you, Andrew, I'm not letting him back in this time. When he went off before, I was upset. All I knew was I wanted him back. I didn't want to carry on without him. This time it's different. I've had enough of his messing about, of doing stupid things. There's no telling what he might get up to, and I can get along without him.'

Although in a lower tone, Hazel had gathered momentum again and was unburdening herself to Andrew. It was the first time she had told him what she had been thinking. She stopped abruptly as she saw him put his hands over his ears. He was closing his eyes and grimacing. He had been attentive when Hazel was explaining about the seal, but his unhappiness had started when she had begun her diatribe against Sam.

'Are you listening to me?'

Andrew had heard every word, but did not reply. He just screwed up his eyes more tightly. He could not take things in and sort them out in the face of this barrage. Just as had happened two days before, on Thursday night, feelings had flooded his mind and blocked out all logic. He took his hands away from his ears, but bowed his head and kept his eyes closed.

Hazel wanted him to open up a little. 'Come on. I've told you what I think. You tell me what you think.' But she did not want to be unkind. She waited. She waited so long, in silence and without coming near him, that Andrew had to face the fact that it was his move.

Finally, through a throat that was beginning to hurt, he managed to mumble, 'He's my dad and I want him back.' He pressed the heel of his right hand against his forehead.

Then Hazel approached him. Her spite evaporated, and compassion for Andrew took its place. She could see how much he was hurting. He was still sitting on the settee. She put her hands on his shoulders as she stood in front of him. Then she took away one hand and gently held the top of his head.

'OK, love. We'll leave it for now,' she said.

Later that afternoon, Stuart Cooke did not want to waste time driving back to his office in Thorby in order to sort out the many factors in this case. The feeling that he had had at the end of the morning, that things were developing in a suspicious direction, was becoming stronger.

It was true that when Mary had been found initially, the police and the doctor did not see anything unusual about her death, and there had been no direct evidence of anything suspicious since. However, the coroner had asked the police to investigate what he thought was a strange coincidence of events, and so they had to do as he asked, and certainly Stuart was beginning to have suspicions now.

Meanwhile, Hazel had given him the address where she said Sam would be, and Stuart thought that his meeting with him had better take place as soon as possible. Once someone had run from one place, they were likely to keep on running.

Stuart drove to Loscar wood and parked on the approach to it. There was nobody about. He wanted to look through his notebook and plan his next moves.

He took stock of what he knew.

An apparently fit and happy elderly lady had been found dead yesterday morning in the flat in which she lived alone, with no sign of anything untoward except an unfinished breakfast.

She had been found by a young man, whom she had known for about six months. This same man had taken a very valuable item that the lady possessed to a jeweller to have it valued two and a half days before. That same man had also taken it to the museum two days before she died. He had been seen to visit her on Thursday, the day before she died, for over two hours. On the morning she died, he had let himself into her flat with a key he said she had given him the day before. That morning, the door chain had conveniently not been on the door.

The old lady's daughter knew nothing about the valuable piece of gold. The man who had found her and had tried to have the golden object valued, had suddenly, the night before her death, left his home, wife and family.

All this might be circumstantial, thought Stuart, but the circumstances had an element of suspicion and so he decided he had better meet Mr Sam Dent as soon as possible. Mr Dent knew that he had already committed a criminal offence by not surrendering an item of treasure after being told three days ago to do so. Therefore, reasoned Stuart, he could arrest him and charge him with that, so that he could hold him while he questioned him about the old lady's death. Yes. He was satisfied that that was the safest and best plan of action. What he actually did would depend on what happened when he asked about the seal. If Sam simply admitted that he'd got it and handed it over, then most of the suspicion would disappear, although there were still questions to be answered, such as why he had had it valued, why her daughter had never heard of it, and why he had suddenly left home.

A brief phone call to Bridget established that all keys for Lilac Cottage had been handed back to the farmer, Mr Steadman, and so Stuart would have to go to the farm for them. Before he set off, Stuart phoned Kevin to meet him at Lilac Cottage. He was slightly worried about the possibility of other tenants moving in before the cottage had been searched. The cottage itself wouldn't take long to search if it was still empty, but it might be as well to have a witness when he met Sam Dent.

Lilac Cottage was still unoccupied and Stuart, accompanied by Mr Steadman, who had brought the keys, carried out a quick inspection of all the bare rooms and any likely cubby-holes and hiding places.

Kevin arrived just as Stuart was leaving the cottage and thanking Mr Steadman for his help. Stuart gave Kevin a quick summary of what he knew so far and of his present plan. He gave him Dave's address, and they set off.

Dave himself was out when they called, and so, once Stuart had said who they were and produced identification, Sam invited them in. He was not at all co-operative when Stuart asked him about the seal. He answered in short, terse sentences in a very stiff and formal way. A thick tension filled the room.

'So where is this seal, then?' Stuart asked, wanting to get to the point of his visit.

'I'm not telling you,' Sam replied bluntly.

'Why not?' Stuart's voice was loud and menacing.

'Because Mary Dyer has trusted me to get as much money as possible for it, and that is what I still intend to do.' Sam did not sound nervous. His voice was clear and steady. 'I can assure you, for what it's worth, that it's not in this house or in my house in Brewster Lane.'

Stuart was now getting very impatient with this unco-operative, awkward and apparently perverse man.

'Do you know that this seal is treasure?' he asked, emphasising every word.

'It may be treasure. It's not for you or me to decide whether it is or not,' Sam replied in acid tones.

'Well, are you aware that it is a criminal offence not to hand in the seal to the Finds Officer if it's probably treasure?' Stuart matched Sam's sourness.

'I've had it in my possession for only a few days, and in any case, it is not mine.' Sam was not going to be beaten verbally.

'I think a night in the cells will do you some good.' Stuart delivered this with a sneer, and it was a threat he often made to awkward customers.

Sam stayed silent.

'I think I'll search this place first.' Stuart turned away suddenly.

The search took quite a long time, with Sam sitting sullenly in the lounge, as if detached from it all. There was none of the courtesy and care with which the Brewster Lane house had been searched. Sets of drawers were examined from the bottom drawer up, not pushed back in, and deliberately left in a dishevelled state. Coats, shirts, fleeces and hanging trousers were roughly pushed about in the wardrobes, and the sliding doors were slammed. Dirty washing was tipped about and left where it lay. Every cupboard and every container was looked into, including the oven, refrigerator, freezer, crockery and saucepans. Things were banged about.

Dave arrived home as they finished, having not found what they were looking for. He was totally bewildered, and Sam quickly explained. His polite request for everything to be tidied back to a state in which it was found was just ignored.

After the search was over, Stuart turned again to Sam.

'Right, then,' he said. 'You have had some time to think things over. I'll ask you again. Where is the seal Mrs Dyer gave you?'

Still, Sam stayed silent.

Stuart had had enough.

'Mr Samuel Dent, I am arresting you for failing to surrender to the Finds Officer an object likely to be treasure, in contravention of the Treasure Act, 1997. You do not have to say anything, but if you do not mention anything that you later rely on for your defence, it will be prejudicial against you.'

Silence from Sam.

Stuart had now taken such a dislike to Sam and his aloof, arrogant attitude, that he insisted on handcuffing him and having Kevin ride in the back seat of his car for the drive back to the station in Thorby. A patrol car brought Kevin back to his own car, so that he could go off and enjoy his interrupted Saturday evening.

When they were back at police headquarters in Thorby, Stuart made preparations formally to interview Sam who, at Stuart's invitation, used the phone to ask a solicitor to be present during his recorded interview. He did not have any particular relationship with any solicitor, but Hosking and Newberry had handled the conveyancing of both the houses he had bought since he had been married, and so he phoned Jim Hosking to ask if he would come or to arrange for someone else.

It was just seven o'clock, and Jim said that he was going out later but would come for an hour or so. He arrived twenty minutes later, dressed for his evening out.

During the lengthy interview, Sam explained from the beginning his relationship with Mary Dyer, so that both Stuart and Jim Hosking could understand how the seal came into his possession. He went right back to the History Society exhibition in November and covered his initial meeting with Mary when he switched on her heating system for her, and the way in which he and Hazel had looked after her on Christmas Day. He gave an account of the search for rented property in Thorby, in which Hazel had played the major part. He explained how he had helped with her move to the flat, and that it was after this that Mary had told him about the seal. She had given it to him with a request to trade it for as much money as he could get, so that she could help Sarah go to university. He even explained the story of her early life and frustrated educational ambitions, and then gave detailed accounts of his meetings with Geoff Lowis, Mr Wehrle and Gavin Nethercott. He said that he had explained all this to Mary on Thursday morning.

Because she had become so upset, he had suggested lending her the money to look after Sarah's interests while he continued to explore ways of getting the best value for the seal. It was as he went home to fetch his cheque book that he had had an enormous row with Hazel, and had left to live for a while with his friend, Dave.

Stuart, of course, knew everything that had happened from Friday morning. Now that he had the full picture, he could understand why Sam had visited the jeweller, why Bridget knew nothing about the seal, and how it came about that Sam had a key to the flat.

Stuart, at each stage of the story, had to decide whether it was plausible, but all his experienced observation of Sam's manner of speech and gestures, and his new outburst of candour now that he was in custody, made him think that all this was genuine.

'You have admitted to contravening the Treasure Act of 1997, because you have now had the seal for eleven days, since a week last Wednesday, the day you and Brian moved house for Mary.'

'I didn't get the seal until late Wednesday afternoon,' butted in Sam, 'so you can't count Wednesday as a whole day. Ten days.'

'OK, ten days,' agreed Stuart, 'but it is now five full days since Geoff Lowis explained to you the consequences of not handing it in, and then Gavin Nethercott and Elaine Disbrey both reinforced that.'

Jim Hosking listened attentively to all this, for he had to learn the situation very rapidly.

'Let me point out,' he said eagerly to Stuart, for now was

the first chance he had had of catching up with the situation, 'that the coroner knew of the seal on Wednesday, if not before.'

'That will be true,' Stuart came back at him, 'but only because other people had told him, officially or unofficially. Sam has done nothing about handing it to Elaine Disbrey or reporting it to the coroner. And yet it's Sam who's actually got it.'

'But Sam does not own it,' Jim said rather forcefully, getting into his stride.

Stuart realised he now had to battle against both of them on the other side of the table round which they sat.

'It is very much a debatable point, who legally owns that seal,' he replied. Then, coldly and with heavy sarcasm, he continued, 'The point at issue is Sam's undoubted knowledge about the seal and his refusal to go through the normal procedures of which he is fully aware.'

'Let me assure you again,' said Sam, 'that the seal is not at Dave's house or Lilac Cottage or Mary Dyer's flat or the Brewster Lane house, but I have not given it to anyone else and it is safe and undamaged.'

This did little to ease the strained and hostile atmosphere.

'So you keep saying,' Stuart burst out with some petulance, 'but I'll ask you again in Mr Hosking's presence. Where is the seal?'

Sam sat silently.

'Will you tell me?' asked Jim.

Sam shook his head.

Jim Hosking was almost as annoyed as Stuart was. He looked daggers at Sam. He drummed his fingers on the table. Then he made no comment or attempt to intervene when Stuart charged Sam with the offence under the Treasure Act. Stuart also said that he would hold Sam until he disclosed the whereabouts of the seal, thinking that, if released, he might recover it and run.

'Oh, no, you don't,' Jim shot back at him, stung into action now that Stuart had overstepped the mark. 'Forty-eight hours, and I'll be back tomorrow anyway.'

'Yes. Forty-eight hours. Magistrates' court on Monday.'

Stuart looked like thunder as he led Sam away to the cells.

18

Jim Hosking was back at the police station by mid-morning on Sunday, demanding to see his client and Detective Inspector Cooke. He had to wait some time before Stuart arrived from home, and again he complained in icy tones to Sam that he made matters worse by refusing to say where the seal was.

Sam had spent a sleepless night constantly asking himself what was the point in remaining secretive about the seal now that Mary was dead. He might as well hand it in to Elaine Disbrey or go and give it to Bridget now that at least three people knew the full story and three more knew the legal bits that mattered. And yet he had such a stubborn feeling deep within himself that he wanted to keep the advantage of possessing it for a while longer. He knew it was this feeling that infuriated Hazel, puzzled Jim Hosking and made Stuart Cooke still suspicious that there was something that he didn't know about. He still felt that, in memory of Mary, he would try a little longer for a valuation so that he could hand over to Bridget a specific sum that was for Sarah's education and only for that. That's what brave Mary would have wanted.

In spite of his coolness towards Sam, Jim stated that he had studied in detail the terms of the 1997 Treasure Act, and had discovered that under the law Sam had fourteen days to report the existence of his item of treasure to the coroner, and that gave him until Tuesday or, strictly speaking, until mid-afternoon on Wednesday.

Stuart left the room to check on this legal fact and also to decide what to do with Sam if it were true and Hosking insisted that he was released. There was something about Sam's stubbornness and awkwardness, about his refusal to produce the seal, that made him suspect that there was something strange about this whole matter. Stuart knew that his doubts would be resolved when the results of the post-mortem were known and, risky though it was, he decided he wanted to detain Sam until then. He could detain him on suspicion without charge for forty-eight hours, and that might just take him up to the results of the post-mortem. After all, only Sam knew where the seal was, and there was no telling what he might get up to if he were released. It seemed to be so valuable that if it were lost, some influential people on the Council, as well as his superior officers, might make life very difficult for Stuart.

When Stuart returned, he stated, quickly and smoothly, that Mr Hosking was correct. He paused long enough for Jim to insist that his client was released. Then, having summoned a policeman from another room to act as a witness, he said he was re-arresting Sam on suspicion of the murder of Mary Dyer and gave him the customary warning about relevant evidence.

The effect on Sam and Jim Hosking was one of utter bewilderment and shock. Sam could hardly believe his ears. He had not had the faintest idea that that was what was in Stuart Cooke's mind. Jim Hosking was electrified into action. He jumped up from his chair.

'On what grounds are you arresting my client?' he demanded.

'I have enough circumstantial evidence as grounds for suspicion,' Stuart replied.

'The circumstantial evidence is as weak as it can be,' came the instant retort. 'It doesn't amount to a case and would not stand up in court.' Then another thought seemed to strike

174

Jim, and he leaned right across the table, and peered into Sam's face.

'Is there something else you haven't told me?' he asked in his strongest, full-throated courtroom manner. Stuart reflected that he might have been trying to cross-examine and intimidate a hostile witness. Sam realised his actions were caused by his sudden shock at this turn of events.

'No,' replied Sam, when he had found his voice. 'I can't believe this. She was my friend and I was doing all I could to help her. That's what this whole thing is about.' Jim Hosking sat down, realising that Sam's reaction was credible, and that he was as shocked as Jim himself.

'What on earth are you thinking about?' Sam thrust the question straight across the table at Stuart.

'All along, I have been suspicious of the fact that you found the body, that you had a key to the flat after knowing her for only five or six months, that you had been there for over two hours the day before, and I'm still not entirely happy about why you had the seal valued before you went to the museum.'

'All these circumstances have been explained,' said Jim Hosking, vigorously.

'I've told you why Mary gave me a key.' Sam stood up and rushed to his own defence. 'The whole point was that she wanted to have the thing valued to get the money she thought should be hers. And anyway, I would have thought it was pretty obvious that she died of a heart attack.' This poured out, loudly and passionately. Then Sam subsided and sat down.

'But there is always something unco-operative about you,' went on Stuart, quite undeterred by this emotional surge. 'We have only your word for it about what was said in the flat on Thursday, and how you got the key. I'm holding you on suspicion until we get the results of the post-mortem on Tuesday.'

Sam opened his mouth to say more, when Stuart stopped him by continuing to speak.

'Why won't you say where the seal is?' he asked with a sneering ferocity, even malice. 'And why did you run away from your family?' he added, to keep his side of the exchange going, before Sam could start again.

'Well, I'm telling you the truth about Mary and the key.' He forced the words through closed teeth and slapped the table with his open hand at the same time.

There followed some silence, while hard and bitter stares met each other across the room.

The silence was broken by Jim Hosking's even and measured tones. 'Well, you, as a police officer, have the right to hold a person on suspicion,' he said. 'It's now eleven-thirty on Sunday, so you can hold him only until eleven-thirty on Tuesday, and I must say that, after all you have been told, there are very thin grounds for suspicion. You put a foot wrong, young man, and I'll be after you for wrongful arrest.'

There was a grunt from Stuart, but nothing more needed to be said. Jim Hosking soon left, promising to let Hazel and Dave know what was happening. Sam was returned to his cell, having been told by Stuart that he would question him again. Stuart went home for his Sunday lunch.

Hazel had just finished the Sunday lunch she had prepared for herself and Andrew when the phone call came from Jim Hosking. Jim had not phoned the night before, knowing that Sam was not living at Brewster Lane and that there was nothing Hazel could do about the situation. Although he did not know her personally, he also hoped that she could have a good night's sleep. Therefore, his call now gave Hazel both pieces of news, the charge under the Treasure Act, and the holding of Sam on suspicion of murder. He pointed out that the Treasure charge could not possibly succeed if Sam handed in the seal by Wednesday afternoon, and he could not be held without charge for murder beyond eleven-thirty on Tuesday.

Hazel felt her knees go weak. She went and sat down and held her head in her hands. Oh, God, she thought. Whatever has he been up to?

Fortunately, Andrew had gone out immediately they had finished lunch to meet with one of his friends. Hazel made a mental note not to tell him. She did not know what lay ahead or how she was going to get through it, let alone loading it on to Andrew as well. He had seemed full of a speechless sorrow since Thursday night.

The weakness seemed to spread to Hazel's whole body. She felt drained of all energy and will power. She didn't want to make the effort to organise her thoughts or to decide what she should do. She just sat. There were no tears. This situation seemed beyond hope or help. Had their relationship come to this? That confident, intelligent, ambitious and well-organised man whom she had married: had he sunk to this? She hadn't even known about Mary dying until Mr Hosking told her, and that was a shock enough in itself. What on earth was there to be suspicious about as far as Sam was concerned? Was it all just an awful mistake, or had he secretly been doing things that he had told her nothing about?

The whole thing seemed too terrible to contemplate. Hazel just sat and allowed the knowledge of what Mr Hosking had told her to soak into her mind and settle there. She kept telling herself that she must make sure that she and Andrew carried on their lives as normally as possible. She repeated to herself that she must not tell Andrew: he could think that his dad was still at Dave's. She also thought this confirmed that she would be right not to have Sam back. He was intelligent and strong enough to look after himself, and there was something in his nature that was strange and unpredictable. But what if he was in really deep trouble? He would need her. He would have nobody else, and she couldn't just ignore him, pretend that she had no responsibility towards him. As she had said before he left on Thursday, they were now a part of each other. Yes. Her mind and body felt limp and weak, but for the moment she would have to admit to anyone outside the family that she was his wife and they were a couple.

Hazel dragged herself into the kitchen and spent the afternoon washing up and doing various other chores. She moved about slowly, as if she felt delicate. When Andrew returned, she just stayed quiet. She did the things he would normally expect her to do, and she kept her feelings inside.

The rest of the afternoon and evening passed in this listless and somewhat unreal way. She was glad Andrew was busy in his room. She hoped he was preparing for his Monday schoolwork. Everything to Hazel seemed languid and sluggish. When she finally dragged her weary mind and body to bed, she fell asleep much more quickly than she expected. The next morning, she thought she must have been past caring.

Sam, though, had no sleep at all. He had no comfort in the cell at the police station, – just a hard-sprung bed with a cushion at one end and a blanket if he wanted to use it. He sat and thought, he paced about, he lay down. Nothing brought any relief, and sleep for the second night running was out of the question. He was glad to see the dawn come, pale and grey.

He was irritated by the echoing sounds of activity along the corridor. He went over and over the events of the last two weeks in his mind until he thought he would be sick with the endless repetition. He tried looking at things from Stuart Cooke's point of view and at times convinced himself that he could see why Stuart should be so suspicious. But Stuart had not seen Mary's body. There was the initial shock of finding her, but then she looked so peaceful and serene that nobody could have had any doubt that she had just been taken by a heart attack while she was eating her breakfast.

Each time his mind went round and round in circles, Sam came back to his one point of comfort: the post-mortem would establish that Mary had died of natural causes, and then he would be released.

When Stuart came into work on Monday morning, he phoned the coroner's office to ask when the post-mortem would take place. He was told that it was scheduled for some time on Tuesday. He cursed under his breath. He pleaded with the coroner to persuade the pathologist to make sure it was in the morning, but was told that that was not possible. The pathologist, it was pointed out most emphatically, set his own schedules. He could never know exactly how long his work would take or what problems he might encounter. Therefore, it was not possible to predict the time of any result he announced.

Stuart, this time accompanied by Kevin, questioned Sam for two hours on Monday morning, and then again on Monday afternoon. Sam declined the invitation to have Mr Hosking present. On each occasion, Stuart went over the same ground again and again – looking for inconsistencies, Sam assumed. Sam, in a slow and tired but patient way, gave the same answers. Lack of sleep was affecting his responses and his thinking. Stuart was just waiting for the post-mortem. After each session, he and Kevin compared impressions, but did not notice anything new.

Then, at eleven o'clock on Tuesday morning, there was some relief for Stuart. There was a phone call from the coroner.

'I have some news for you, Inspector,' came the placid, solemn voice. 'The pathologist is early with his schedule and a short time ago carried out the post-mortem examination of Mrs Mary Dyer.' Stuart held his breath. 'Pulmonary thrombosis. Natural causes. If the next of kin is satisfied with that, I will not be holding an inquest.'

'Thank you, sir.' Stuart breathed a long sigh. So that was that. Sam Dent was right, after all. There was no evidence for suspicion.

Within fifteen minutes, just long enough to have his personal possessions returned to him, Sam was outside the police station, breathing freely. Stuart had warned him that he had one day to hand in the seal.

He had slept fitfully during the early hours of Tuesday, and now he felt fine. He could hardly believe it. After being cooped up, sleepless and airless, in that concrete box for two days and three nights, he was free.

He just walked up and down for the love of walking. He didn't want to think about anything. He just walked. He breathed deeply for the sheer joy of breathing. He just breathed. He never dreamed the Thorby air would seem so pure and fresh. He even found himself smiling for the first time in over two weeks.

He headed for People's Park, a peaceful and refreshing expanse of walkways, flowered gardens and meadows just north of the centre of town. A stream ran through the middle of it. He often went there during lunchtimes, especially if he was feeling at all under stress.

About a hundred years ago, the owner of a mansion with a vast garden had died and left it to the Council. The house had been turned into a museum of country life, and the garden had been transformed by the Parks and Public Gardens Department. There was a part of it that was still an urban garden, meticulously organised. It had a wide green sward, fringed by birch trees and pines, with an asphalt path around the edge, and outside that was a cycle track. An imaginative head gardener had also allowed part of it to grow naturally and mostly wild, with thickets and tangles, sycamores, hawthorns and brambles, and even an area of rough heathland.

There were still wide, grassed walkways, or 'rides', and it was here that Sam loved to walk, especially at this time of the year, early summer, when nature still retained some of the freshness of spring, and yet the sun had some power.

He loved the openness and spaciousness where he could breathe, relax and find peace. He loved escaping from the world of plastic and glass, tarmac and grid-locked queues of cars, to this living world, where the gentle exercise of walking, the light, the greenness and the space soothed his mind and raised his spirits. Here he felt so very small, a tiny speck in the endlessly revolving pageant of life. He loved to immerse himself in it. When he returned from a walk here, he felt that he had had an emotional bath.

These wilder parts were populated by silver birches, small coppices of hazels, hawthorns, and holly and elderberry bushes. Now, the blackthorn and hawthorn were in full leaf, working to produce the black sloes and red haws of the autumn. In the rough pastures that lay between the trees and bushes grew foxgloves, cowslips, teasels, meadowsweet, primroses, buttercups, clover and dog violets, all harbouring a rich harvest of insects for blackbirds and starlings, chaffinch and greenfinch. Even the thistles fed the goldfinches and linnets.

The air was thronged with the fizzing and buzzing and whizzing of insects, and life was shooting, twittering and burbling from every thicket.

Sam loved this area. As he walked, he yielded his senses to the sights and sounds of the birds. He filled his eyes with their colour and movement as they bustled about on the endless cycle of displaying, mating, preening and feeding. He filled his ears with the sound of birdsong. Wrens would skulk at the foot of thick and chunky bushes and sing their hearts out. Hidden woodlarks would add in their delicate, falling yodels, and willow warblers contributed the sweetness of their descending cadences. There was the staccato rhythm of the chiffchaff, and the liquid trills of the robin, shaken out at random on the breeze. The song thrush repeatedly shouted his bold and strident phrases from the top of bush or tree. And from the blackbird cascaded a fluent, melodic whistling: unhurried, full, rich and deeply musical.

Sam sat on a wooden seat and surrendered to the moment. The living beauty of the scene healed his wounded spirit. Then, later, he glanced at his watch: he had been there for two hours.

He thought about Hazel and Andrew. He suddenly realised that this was Tuesday, Hazel's day off. He got up and walked slowly down the green avenue towards the park exit. He thought about Mary, her life now spent, lying dead in the morgue, all that aspiration, all that emotion and affection gone forever.

What did it all matter? He felt the sunshine warm on his face. That was the source of all life and energy. It was indifferent to all human passion and feeling, will and ambition. It shone on everyone and everything, just and unjust, right and wrong. All that mattered was that great spectacle of life that he had soaked up in the park.

He remembered that his car was still parked at Dave's. He had been given back his mobile phone. He rang Jim Hosking to tell him he had been released because the post-mortem had said that Mary had died from a heart attack. There were now no charges, and he told Jim he would hand in the seal to Elaine Disbrey.

Then he rang Hazel and asked whether, if he walked to Andrew's school, as it was Tuesday, she would give him a lift to Dave's. She said that she was glad he was out and would meet him at the school. Sam thought that she sounded rather abrupt. Still, what could he expect? What did he deserve?

He had some time to kill, so he went to get something to eat in town and at four o'clock he walked to Andrew's school.

Hazel's car waited at the school, in a line of other parents' cars, for Andrew to come from cricket practice.

He walked apprehensively towards the car and peered nervously into the interior, and then Hazel saw him. She lowered the window. The stare was cold and hard.

'Get in the back,' she said roughly, and looked away, not inviting a reply.

Sam did so, meekly. He felt he wanted to say something to break the ice. 'Thanks for coming for me.' The tone was flat and expressionless. Hazel did not reply. She was not going to make it easy for him.

As they waited, neither of them spoke. The silence was deep and heavy. Healing would be slow this time.

Then they saw him, bantering with two or three other pupils as a little knot of boys spilled along the drive.

Andrew noticed Sam just as he opened the front passenger door. He threw his bag on to the front seat and climbed in the back. He buried his face into the side of Sam's chest. Tears scalded his eyes. Sam put his arm round him, unable to speak. His throat hurt.

Hazel watched for some moments in the rear view mirror. She was dry-eyed and she felt distant, a clinical observer.

'Can I move back in?' Sam asked. Hazel did not reply. She turned on the ignition, engaged the clutch and moved up through the gears.

Both Sam and Hazel knew that, with Andrew in the car, she was at her most vulnerable. 'I suppose so, but only for Andrew. I hope you've learnt your lesson. There's only us.'

Just you wait, though, she thought. There's something else I'm going to make you do before you move back in, and you'll suffer as you do it.

19

Hazel had intended to drive straight round to Dave's house, but Sam asked her to go via the Blacksmith's Arms so that he could buy Dave a crate of beer: that would be all the reward he would want for the accommodation he had provided. Then, at Dave's house, he left an explanatory note of thanks, with his key placed on top of it, gathered all his belongings and brought his car home. Andrew insisted on travelling home in Sam's car.

That evening, everything in the Dents' house seemed smothered in a quiet that had fallen like a cloak. Andrew stayed in the lounge to watch television with his parents. Apart from the occasional question and reply, there was silence. Hazel and Sam avoided each other's eyes.

Sam slept very soundly in the spare room, and the next morning he behaved submissively, as he had done the evening before. The family moved about their breakfast routines slowly and quietly.

Sam intended to go to work, and eventually looked for his car keys but they weren't on his desk in the dining-room, where he usually left them.

'Have you seen my car keys, Hazel?' he asked politely, almost deferentially.

Hazel did not answer him. 'Andrew, you'll have to catch the school bus today, and it's time you were going.'

Of course, he noticed the sharpness of the tone, but Andrew was not going to argue or question his mother. He didn't want anything to upset the atmosphere. Sam knew that Hazel was waiting without speaking until Andrew had gone.

Then Sam asked again, patiently: 'My car keys, Hazel, have you seen them?'

'I've got them. Here you are.' She took them from her pocket and tossed them to him. 'And before you find out for yourself, I'll tell you I've taken the door key off the ring.'

'But I thought I was moving in again.' Sam was bewildered.

'You can move in again,' Hazel said in the same strong tones, 'when you've done one thing for me, and I'm going to see that you do it.'

'What's that?'

'You know where that seal is, and now you're going to get in your car and go and get it. You'll bring it here, and then we'll go together to the Council offices in Thorby, where you'll hand it in to Elaine Disbrey.' Hazel paused slightly and then shouted: 'And we'll do that before either of us does anything else. I've got all the house keys in my pocket, and you don't get yours back until it's done.'

'Yes. I'm going to hand it in,' said Sam. For the first time, he increased his volume. 'The fourteen days is up this afternoon, and I've told Jim Hosking I'm handing it in.'

Hazel was not going to be shouted down. 'We'll do it together,' she repeated.

Sam did not want to stare her out, and so he turned and looked out of the window in some despair. He could see what Hazel was up to. She thought she was making him fetch the seal, and then he would have to be taken like a naughty schoolboy to hand it in officially.

He stood silently and thought for a minute. She'd got the key, because she had planned this, and he couldn't get back in the house without it. He couldn't keep running off to Dave's every time they had a row. There seemed no way out for the moment. Hazel was going to humiliate him and he

185

would just have to take it with as much dignity as he could manage. Should he take the key by force? That was out of the question. He would not stoop to that sort of thing. She had outwitted him this time because he had not expected it, and he'd have to go along with it. He had only a few hours left until the fourteen-day deadline.

'OK. I'll go and fetch it.'

As he drove to Loscar wood, Sam was running over this unexpected little scene in his mind. Was this how it was going to be from now on? Would she keep up with this sort of rather pointless and very trivial revenge? He decided he would have to go through with this one and just be humiliated, if it made her feel better. But then he wondered if it was her way of testing him. If he accepted this, and behaved quietly, she would think he was changing and they could think about a new start. Sam decided that that made the most sense. She could have her pound of flesh for now, and he would forget it. After all, she was letting him back into the house and into the family, and this was a small price to pay for that. She was an intelligent lady, and trivial revenge and tit-for-tat was not her style.

Having nothing suitable of his own to dig with, he had to go back to Dave's for the trowel. He soon got the job done without any problems, returned the trowel and went back to Hazel. Without a word, they both drove into Thorby, and Hazel watched from the car park as he took the seal and its pouch into the building. She guessed how he would be feeling and she was right. Degradation was a new experience for him, but he put up with it by thinking of things long-term.

Elaine Disbrey was polite. She smiled a lot and offered Sam tea or coffee, but he declined. He checked that she had Bridget's address and said that he thought the owner of the seal was now Mary's son, Howard, who lived in Australia. He wondered fleetingly how Sarah was going to manage now, but dismissed the thought, because he hadn't even met her.

186

He was soon back in the car park. As he approached Hazel, she got out of the car, threw his key to him, got back in and drove off to Pine Properties. When she was at work, she phoned the bank to enquire whether a large cheque had been drawn on the Dents' joint account that week. It had not.

Sam was able to resume his work easily and seamlessly at TCS after his four days' working 'at home'. It was a relief for him to settle into the regular daily routine again. He decided that was what he liked. His three nights in the police cell had been a traumatic shock. Hazel was right. That sort of thing might be all right for students, but not for a family man.

As the heat and excitement of the summer yielded to the gentleness and tranquillity of autumn, life was taken over by the daily and weekly routines again. Hazel worked on at Pine Properties as normal, and kept the family and house going by shopping, washing, cleaning, ironing and cooking, like millions of other wives and mothers. Wasn't it funny, she thought, how much could go on inside a house, while to the outside world all seemed calm and happy and normal?

Since Sam had left home for a short time in June, he and Hazel had something of a barrier between them. Hazel was still defensive. Something had changed in her state of mind towards him. She decided that if Sam did something so stupid that he got into trouble with the law, she would stand by him, and for Andrew's sake, she would have to let him back into the house. But she felt there was now a part of him that was no longer a part of her. There really was something irrational about a man who could leave his home and family and not tell them what he was doing. She decided that they would be partners now only in a legal sense, only on the surface, only for the world to see. There would not be a physical or spiritual partnership.

Sam wondered how he could repair permanently the

187

damage he had done to their relationship. It seemed to Sam that if he wanted to build bridges between himself and Hazel, the best way was to have more experiences in common, to do things together. He hoped that a better physical relationship might follow in the wake of a practical one.

Hazel had always been more active in the village community than Sam had. She loved meeting people and found it easy to get to know them and generate small talk. Sam told Hazel what he had been thinking one evening, and was surprised when she responded quite brightly.

'I'm glad you are beginning to think like that,' she said. 'You've been much happier and better to live with since the summer. It's because you haven't got some great issue to worry about, or some great cause to fight for.'

Sam smiled. 'Do you really think so?'

'Yes, of course I do.' Hazel encouraged him. 'Stop trying to take the world on. Just join it. Accept people for what they are.' Sam just sat quietly, and Hazel continued. 'I know it sounds simple, but it's the right way. Just give a bit, and people will meet you halfway.'

'Where shall I start, then?'

'Well, you do that newsletter every two months. You write about all the activities. Get involved in one of them.'

'But it's all over the phone and through the post. I don't distribute it, and so it never gets me out and into things,' he said. 'Isn't there one we could join together?'

Sam waited, hopeful, expectant.

'I'm not interested in sitting on committees and organising things. I'd rather get into doing things.'

Sam thought that was characteristic of Hazel, and he had a suggestion ready. 'In the last issue of the newsletter, a new group that is starting up gave me some material. It was the Thoreswood Environmental Group, TEG. They said they had elected a chair, vice chair and treasurer, and they wanted a secretary. They know I do the newsletter, and so they probably would be glad of me. I think there may be a bit of walking and improving local footpaths. Would you join in?'

Hazel's agreement, which she gave, was all Sam wanted. The group had had only one inaugural meeting, and they welcomed Sam with open arms. They quickly arranged another meeting in which they agreed a constitution, which would enable them to apply for sponsorship and grant funding. Contact had already been made with the Forestry Commission, which owned Loscar wood. The Thorby District Council and many local residents were full of ideas for improving aspects of the environment.

Once Sam had cleared some paperwork for them, he and Hazel joined in walking local footpaths and in helping with small improvements. Many signage repairs were necessary along public rights of way across local farmland. A footpath that led along the edge of a housing estate to the south of Rowle Road needed to be hard-surfaced by contractors, but volunteers were needed to cut back vegetation and prepare the area. An agreement had been reached for the diversion of a footpath around a farmyard where the stables were being extended. Then the volunteers moved in with forks, shovels, mattocks and wheelbarrows.

An incident occurred during the preparation of the footpath, which showed that Sam and Hazel were becoming a popular couple and were relaxing more. The farmer was glad that the TEG was not being awkward about the diversion of the footpath, but the volunteers were mucking in to create the new part of the path. So he lent them a rotavator, and Sam was standing nearby when he brought it for them to use.

'Are you going to take it, then?' he asked, beaming at Sam. 'I've filled the little tank in the middle with petrol. You start it by turning the flywheel with that cord. It's a bit like a motor mower.'

189

'OK. I'll try anything once,' Sam said, with good humour and a shrug.

'Where do you want it?'

'We're going in this direction. Just about here, I think.' Sam took over control of the handles from the farmer and moved the machine into position to start. The farmer went back to his stockyard. The idea was to go along and loosen the earth so that other people could move it away with shovels and wheelbarrows, and lower the surface so that they could put some hardcore along the top.

Sam could see where the flywheel was, wrapped round with a cord, the end of which dangled down. Sam gripped it and, with a glance at Hazel, who was watching nearby, pulled. The wheel spun and the engine stuttered and then died.

Sam pulled again, harder and faster, and it started with quite a roar. Not only did the engine start, but the whole thing lurched forward. Sam kept his grip on the handles. If it's going, he thought, I'd better steer it in the right direction.

So, he steered. The machine pitched and juddered forward at a quick walking pace. Sam hung on and followed. It suddenly occurred to him that he didn't know how to stop it.

It carried on, Sam stumbling after it. He was aware of some of the volunteers keeping pace beside him. He noticed Hazel. He got to the end of that stretch of path and there was a gate in front of him. What to do? He got nearer the gate. Then he was almost on it.

He could think of nothing better to do than turn left into a cultivated field. Then he let the rotavator pull him along for a short distance. But he couldn't cross the whole field. So he turned left again. By now, those people near him realised he couldn't stop, and laughter began.

'Keep going, Sam.'

'The farmer wants the whole field done.'

'Stopping's not allowed.'

'You'll run out of petrol eventually.'

'This'll give you some exercise.'

'Faster, faster.'

Sam didn't know whether to laugh with them or curse them. He just hung on, and turned left again.

Hazel thought that she'd better go and try to help him. She walked beside him and looked for any likely looking levers on top of the compact little engine. She saw one and reached down. Sam looked down, too, and didn't see the concrete post.

Wham!

The rotavator hit the post; the laughter from everyone increased. Sam bashed into the back of the rotavator, Hazel fell sideways, Sam bounced sideways from the machine and fell on top of her. Laughter was all around. Sam closed his eyes.

What a fool I've been – he nearly said it – but then he seemed to fall about even more, and he stopped trying to do anything. He relaxed and thought he might as well enjoy it. He felt parts of Hazel all around him – a leg, a hip, her stomach just beneath her breasts.

'Have a good time, Sam.'

'Don't worry about us, Sam. We won't look.'

'Grovelling on the ground at your age, Sam.'

'You could get arrested, you know.'

The laughter went on. Then he opened his eyes and Hazel's face was about three inches away.

'Good afternoon. Fancy meeting you like this.' They joined in the laughter and began to get up. Sam had got to his knees when he realised the rotavator engine had stopped. The farmer, attracted by the general hubbub, arrived.

'Well, anyway, the engine's stopped,' said Sam.

'Of course it has,' said the farmer, laughing with all the

others. 'If you want to stop the engine, you just let go of both handles.'

Afterwards, and later at home when they told Andrew, Sam and Hazel realised what a release of tension there had been. They, and everyone else, had laughed into each other's faces. Merriment and good spirits filled the air. Rancour couldn't exist. The silly little scene had done a power of good.

Another activity, which involved much walking round the village with clipboards, was the assessment of access for the disabled to the local shops, the doctor's surgery, the pub and public transport. At some points, kerbstones needed to be replaced by low-level, ribbed paving slabs.

Sam and Hazel found time to take part in most of these projects, and it was good, healthy, open-air work, with much good-natured banter to raise everyone's spirits.

There was a two-day village festival in mid-October, and Sam and Hazel not only helped to staff the Environmental Group's stall, but joined in the general activities with gusto. The entertainments included a ferris wheel, a kite-flying demonstration, a brass band and a jazz band, along with the usual craft and charity stalls in the marquee. There were children's sports, a fun run, a parade, a hog roast and a bouncy castle. A disco, augmented by an entertaining steel band, occupied the marquee on the Saturday evening, and Hazel bravely entered the limbo dancing competition.

Sam entered for the fun run on the Sunday morning. Forty-six villagers and two dogs ran the two-mile course round the village. The winner completed it in thirteen minutes, twenty-eight seconds, and Sam came second in fourteen minutes, forty-two seconds. All the entrants, including the dogs, received a medal, and there was even a toddle round the recreation ground for the under-fives.

Immersing himself in all this local social activity provided an emotional release for Sam, and his happiness increased.

Because he was happy and relaxed, Hazel's attitude to him relented, and she warmed a little. A fortnight after the festival, the Environmental Group held a quiz night with a pea-and-pie supper and a glass of wine in the church rooms. They both thoroughly enjoyed it, and as they walked home, Hazel clung to Sam's arm like she used to do in their younger days. It was just one of the little things that they did that gave them both pleasure: Hazel would hold on to Sam's arm almost as if it were a maypole, and continually feel it up and down. Sam felt accepted physically again.

Later in the year, Hazel suggested another physical activity, which she knew Sam would find difficult. In spite of many seaside holidays when he was a boy, and looking after Andrew on his own family's holidays, Sam had always been frightened of water, and could not swim. Sometimes, as he stood on the shore and looked at a calm and peaceful sea stretching away towards the horizon, he would feel a vague panic inside. It was illogical. He knew that, but he felt it in his stomach.

Hazel had suggested a few times that she should teach Sam to swim, but she could see him curl away from her mentally as the fear took root, and she did not press it. She thought he might be less afraid if he could do it off the crest of this new-found happiness.

She was right. He agreed to go to the public swimming pool in Thorby. As they approached the building, his stomach clenched into a tight knot of fear. He deliberately unclenched his fists. His mind was full of shouting, bullying, pushy PE teachers at school, who threw a float into the pool and then bawled at people to go after it. They would soon get the idea, they said; they would soon get their confidence in the water. It made Sam worse. He had once choked in a swimming lesson, and had to be pulled out of the water, convulsed with fright. He recovered in spite of the fussing around him, but he never forgot it.

When they had changed and had got into the swimming area itself, Sam was going to turn back. The smell of the chlorine brought fearful memories flooding into his mind. Stinging echoes of children shouting bounced off the tiled walls and the surface of the water.

Hazel got to him quickly, and put her hand on his arm, hoping it would soothe him. She noticed that it stopped him turning back.

'Just walk into the water,' she said, earnestly but calmly. 'That will be enough for today if it's all you can do.'

Sam did walk into the water and kept the surface at waist level, while Hazel went away and returned to him, smiling. He just looked about him, taking in the scene, and watched Hazel as she had a few short spells of swimming. She was as gentle with him as she knew how, and insisted that just to walk in was enough. 'It was helping to overcome the fear,' she said, as they drove home.

The result was that Sam agreed to go again. On the second occasion, Hazel got him to lie on his back in shallow water when no other swimmers were near. She completely supported his weight by putting her hands under his back and hips, or sometimes under his back and neck. Gently, gently, she kept telling him to relax, just to lie back as if he was in bed, but to keep his back hollow, and his head well back, resting in the water. She could hear the quick and jerky intakes of breath, and saw his restless eyes flitting in all directions, but she was patient. For an hour, that was all they did, and at the end of it, she knew the fear had shrunk just a little.

They did the same again for a third time. The firmness of Hazel's supporting hands, the calm softness of her voice, her reassuring presence, and Sam's increasing control, finally pushed out the fear. He moved his arms by his side, still on his back, flipped his wrists, rotated his hands. As Hazel slid her hands gently away, Sam stayed there, his head right back and looking at the ceiling.

They both knew he had done it, and he practised calmly and slowly for another twenty minutes. Sam was thrilled. The effect on him was startling. He felt sheer elation. He had achieved this difficult physical thing, and Hazel had helped. Physically, mentally, she had helped him to overcome his fear. Emotion between them was unblocked. It flowed both ways.

It was such a physical thing that it relaxed them both: the physical support in the water, the touching of the skin and the hands, the looking up into Hazel's face for reassurance and control. As they walked back to the car, hands were held tightly, and finally, they hugged for fully two minutes before they drove off. That night, Sam felt able to go back into Hazel's bed for the first time for several months.

20

Suddenly, one Wednesday morning, in late November, Sam felt as if the life had been sucked out of him with a violence that left him bewildered and breathless. He was empty and lifeless, without energy or willpower. He sat in his car in the TCS car park and looked at the building where he had worked for over ten years. It was eleven o'clock, and he tried to collect his thoughts together by going over the traumatic events of the last half-hour.

When Sam arrived for work at TCS at about nine o'clock each morning, his routine was always the same. After parking and using his swipe card to come in through the staff entrance door, he quickly took in his stride the two short flights of stairs to the first floor. He walked briskly to his desk in the open plan office, exchanging greetings with those colleagues who were already at their desks, and switched on his computer. While it went through its clunking noises and various screens as the machine started up, he went to the corner of the office, put his overcoat or jacket on one of the many hangers there, and by the time he had returned to his desk, his working screen was ready. The email icon was the first to be clicked, so that he could see how many emails needed to be answered. Some he would answer straight away, and others he would leave until he had a lull later in the day. Then the email provider could be minimised so that he was alerted through the day by new arrivals, but at the same time he could make progress with the current project.

On this morning, Sam ran through this routine. He had been working on one large project for the last eight months. Motor Mobile – known around the office, and even on their own website and publicity flyers, as 'Momo' – was a car hire company that was very aggressive in its hire fee policy. It had quickly expanded in recent years from the UK to the whole of Western Europe, Canada, and had even made some inroads into the northern United States of America.

Eight months ago, TCS had won a data collection contract for them, which had grown in size ever since. Originally, Sam and one other person had worked on it. Now it occupied five workers full-time. Three of the others had been employed on short-term contracts especially for it. They worked not in the main office, but downstairs in a large area filled with row upon row of computer desks, and which looked like a warehouse. 'Momo' was thought by everyone to be a successful contract.

Motor Mobile had undercut almost every other car hire company with its cheap hire fee policy. It fed, by the day and by the hour, enormous quantities of data about its cash flow, workforce, hire availability and model availability from its accounts department to TCS. According to the status of these various factors of its business, it varied and reduced its fees to keep profits small by frequently offering existing customers percentage discounts. Depending on the accounts data processed and categorised by TCS and fed back to its management, fees were discounted according to the day of the week, and even the hour of the day. It was a complex operation and depended on quick results achieved and returned by TCS. It kept 'Momo' ahead of its rivals and enabled it to expand.

At about half-past ten on this morning, Sam's email icon beeped, and when he looked to see what it was, he saw it was from his line manager, Stephen Kirkham, one of the directors. He needed to see Sam in his office without delay.

Sam saved his current work and went downstairs to Stephen's ground-floor office.

Sam found it difficult to guess Stephen's mood as he went in. 'Good morning, Sam,' was spoken with a brief courtesy, but Sam noticed there was no energy in the smile, and his hands lay palms down on the desk in front of him. He had obviously been waiting for Sam, and no particular piece of work was being interrupted. He motioned Sam into the chair in front of the desk.

'Good morning, Stephen.' Sam returned the formal pleasantry.

'No. It's not too good, I'm afraid.' Stephen, still speaking softly but very firmly, moved straight to the heart of the matter. 'We've got trouble with the "Momo" contract.'

'What sort of trouble?' asked Sam, genuinely puzzled.

'They like to keep their profits small but widespread,' said Stephen. 'That way, they keep expanding, which means they increase the volume of the small profits.' He paused and was looking at his hands on the desk, and not into Sam's face. 'For two months now, the small profits have turned into small deficits. Because your six-factor analysis is based on national data, it has happened everywhere, and they are blaming us.'

'But they make the decisions about levels of fees,' protested Sam. 'We only provide the data to inform the decisions.'

'For the last four months, you have included predicted performance as part of the data.' Stephen had put his hands on the wooden chair arms now. He leaned forward slightly across the desk, and his tone was more vigorous.

'Well, the decisions were still theirs to make.' Sam also increased his volume, and felt he was keeping up his end of the argument. 'We don't determine the performance because we don't set the fees. They asked us to make provisional predictions, and that's all they are: provisional predictions based on their hypothetical decisions. We all accepted that we were providing them as a help.'

Stephen did not answer or contradict this, because it was true. He moved straight to further explanation.

'It seems that what has happened is that they appointed a new chief executive three months ago. The last one left to get a better job on the wave of the success that we helped him get. Since then, the regional managers have been taking your predictions and acting on them without reference to the new chief executive. Because profits are falling, they are blaming your predictions.'

Sam could easily see what had been happening, without Stephen spelling it out for him.

'Well, if the regional managers are not deferring to the new CE, that's his problem.' Sam's delivery was fast, and his tone was incisive, with a cutting edge. 'He ought to get on their backs and co-ordinate them properly, and not blame us.'

Stephen was looking fully into Sam's face now, and his gaze was level and unwavering. 'But he *is* blaming us, and specifically, he is blaming *your* figures.'

Suddenly, Sam had a feeling that Stephen was not exercising his usual flexibility and understanding. He usually discussed all aspects of a problem with his project managers, while they worked out the best solution together. Now, he seemed to be driving straight at Sam, without concessions, without taking any other perspectives.

'Well then, the solution is obvious,' said Sam. 'We'll send all the figures straight to the CE, and only the CE, so that his subordinates can't act on their own.'

'I don't think he can take all that in on his own,' said Stephen, raising his eyebrows to show the understanding Sam would normally expect. 'I think he knows he can't take it all in and act on it quickly enough.' Stephen resumed the driving flatness of his tone. 'These are his first three months' figures, and profits are diving compared to those of the previous CE. Now the chairman is gunning for him, and to save his own skin, he is blaming us.' Stephen leaned further forward in Sam's direction. 'And as you deal directly with "Momo", he's blaming you.'

Sam had a sinking feeling, and realised for the first time that Stephen had conducted this whole conversation with an air of inevitability. Now Sam saw it coming. He put his fingertips to his forehead between his eyebrows and looked down into his lap for some seconds. Then he looked up at Stephen.

'What does TCS say to that?' he asked. There was a slight shake in his voice. Emotion was rising.

Stephen looked back at him in silence. He let the silence hang for a full six seconds. It seemed like an age to Sam. Then he said, softly, clearly and steadily: 'He has pulled the plug on the whole contract.'

Sam jumped back in quickly: 'He's already done it? Well, then, don't we have any compensation?'

'We'll get some, yes, but it won't make any difference to the position we're in,' said Stephen, unperturbed by Sam's quick response. 'I think this man's on his way out and will quickly be gone, but it still leaves us without a contract.'

'Will they get someone else to do their processing?' asked Sam.

'I doubt it. I don't think anyone else could do the job any better than we do, and I don't think they'll find another CE as good as the last one. They'll probably stop this fast adjustment policy and just consolidate their position.'

Again, there was silence. The seconds started to tick away again. Sam could not bear another long silence. He put his fingers to his forehead again.

'So where does that leave me?'
'Without a project to manage.'
'Any others?'

Now, for the first time, Stephen could not look directly at Sam.

'Things have been more difficult for us for some time than the management have dared to let on,' he said. 'We have no other projects, and no likelihood of any.'

Sam had had a feeling for some minutes that this was coming. 'So,' he said, more loudly, his emotion rising again, 'I've done nothing wrong. I've not even made an error of judgment. They run their company, not me. And yet you're going to get rid of me. Right?'

'We'll have to let you go, Sam. What we're suggesting you do is to agree to voluntary redundancy.' Stephen ignored the signs of distress Sam was now showing, and continued to control his own tone of voice. He still spoke softly. Sam realised that, like a fool, he had spoken the words for him.

Then Stephen continued, before there was any more reaction from Sam. 'We'll go through the normal procedures, in fairness to you,' he said. 'Please understand that it is your project that has disappeared. It is nothing to do with you personally. We're giving you your stipulated month's notice, starting from today. There'll also be a consultation period, in which we consider all other options that we could employ you on. Finally, though, in the absence of any projects for you, we would have to pay you off with redundancy money. As you've been here for ten years, the statutory minimum would be about four months salary, but we would increase that to at least six months. However, we haven't worked things out precisely yet. I'm just trying to give you an idea of what you'll get if you agree to the voluntary redundancy. At the end of it all, I'd give you a good reference.'

Sam knew that, in spite of the procedures Stephen had outlined – notice, consultation, ostensible help to find other employment within the company – this was the end. He could hardly believe he was hearing the words. Everything seemed unreal. It was as if he was looking at this from a distance, hearing these words that were going to end his career at TCS.

'So what do you say, then? Will you go along with voluntary redundancy?' Sam had rather got lost in his own thoughts, and Stephen's words seemed to register a few seconds after he had spoken them. He did not bother to reply straight away. He just continued with his own thoughts. There was not much he could do to fight this, even if he wanted to. He supposed they were trying to make it easy for him, and he might as well take some of their money with him.

'Could I just reserve my position until I've talked it over with my wife?'

Stephen smiled for the first time. 'OK,' he said, 'but you hardly need me to tell you the procedure now. Because we are a very vulnerable industry, when I say we are giving you notice, that means in the form of garden leave, and we'll be in touch about the consultation period and the redundancy terms, should you wish to consider them.'

Sam nodded. Stephen drew a deep breath.

'OK, Gary,' he called loudly, and at once his door was opened and Gary, the chief IT support engineer, stood in the doorway, looking not at Stephen, but at Sam. He had obviously been waiting outside for some minutes.

Sam climbed wearily out of his chair and made for the door without a word or even a nod to Stephen or Gary. He went through the doorway as Gary stood aside, and Sam realised that Gary was looking at him with some sympathy. Sam did not return the friendliness.

He had seen this happen to other people, never dreaming that one day it would happen to him. The feeling of unreality was still with Sam, as Gary walked with him up to his desk in the office on the first floor. As Sam reached his desk and turned to face the documents laid out on it, he raised his eyes and looked darkly, and with his face set hard, at Gary.

'Half an hour to clear the desk?' he asked, roughly. He was

dimly aware of one or two people looking at him from adjacent desks.

'Yeah,' replied Gary. 'The phone has been disconnected and all authorisations and passwords cancelled at the server.'

'All right. You don't have to tell me,' Sam snapped back. He knew it was unnecessary, and that Gary was only doing what he had been told to do, but a dark mood had already descended, and Sam just did not feel like being civil to anyone. He knew without Stephen Kirkham saying so, and before he left his office, that he would be gone in half an hour. He knew it was a necessary security precaution for TCS, but it felt humiliating all the same. He knew he would now be on 'garden leave'. The consultation would be just going through the motions. He knew there were people around him who were feeling for him, but his barriers had gone up, and he didn't care.

He made sure he had put all his personal possessions and CDs and disks in his case, and had put all his working documents reasonably neatly in his drawers. Then he went and collected his jacket and coat, and made his way to the door without looking to right or left. At the outer door, he gave his swipe card to Gary.

'Bye, Sam. All the best,' said Gary.

Sam did not reply, and was gone.

So now, at eleven o'clock, he sat in his car, looking back at the building.

He was bitter. He had seen it happen to others. It was just one of those things that happened to people. You do your job well. You do nothing wrong. Then suddenly, circumstances seem to gather up and kick you in the teeth. And nobody else seems to care. You are now yesterday's man, no use to anyone else because you have no more influence over anyone or anything. The network of contacts you have built up will sever their ties with you. You are out and on your own.

'Oh well, to hell with them all,' thought Sam, as he started the engine and reversed out of his parking lot. 'If you're on your own, it means you can start again.'

He turned the car in the direction of home. He was glad his personal life was in order, going better than it had done for some time. He was glad he had a family to go home to. That was his anchor.

He would tell Hazel all about it and discuss the inevitable decision with her. Now they had something they really had to co-operate over.

21

Sam felt a range of emotions as he drove home late on Wednesday morning. He felt strange. It was as if he had been cast adrift on an inland sea. There was no immediate danger, and yet he had lost his bearings. He had no idea what was going to happen next, or in which direction he was supposed to be going.

He also felt light-hearted and light-headed. He was not used to this kind of freedom. After over twenty years of routine, working within parameters and to specifications, it seemed odd to think he was suddenly free from it all. He no longer had to worry about the 'Momo' contract, or any other contract. He would not have to go back to TCS at nine o'clock tomorrow morning, switch on his computer, hang up his coat, greet his colleagues, answer his emails and plan his day. Tomorrow there would be an unfilled, day-long period of time stretching in front of him. He could fill it in whatever way he wanted.

He also felt slightly anxious, even guilty. Would he spend his time usefully if it were not structured for him? Somehow or other, he would have to find another routine, other restrictions and parameters. His days could not just be formless and open-ended. Where would he go? What would he do? Who else would give him a job? Could he employ himself for a while?

One thing he was sure of was that Hazel would have some sympathy. She would support him. There was a time when she would have blamed him and attacked him. She would have been sure he had done something wrong, made some mistake, and so it was his fault. But not any more. They had a new level of understanding recently. Now, he was sure she would listen and be on his side. He would just wait for her to come home, and then explain in every detail. Then he would explain to Andrew.

Then he could start again.

So, with this mixture of thoughts and feelings, he arrived home to an empty house, put the car in the barn, made himself a light lunch and went for a walk in Loscar wood. It was a quiet time in the wood. Everything was bedding down for the winter. The season's life force had been spent. Sam didn't even see any squirrels.

It was not too cold. It was a dull, windless day, and Sam enjoyed the fresh air and gentle exercise. He still had a sense of a strange freedom.

Neither Hazel nor Andrew thought anything was unusual when they arrived home. According to the ebb and flow of the work, Sam sometimes came home early, sometimes very late. It was as they all ate their evening meal that he told them of the morning's events. They both listened with silent attention, their eyes on Sam as they wondered what he was feeling at the time, and when he had finished, they made encouraging comments.

It was later, when Andrew was again upstairs at his work, that Sam started the conversation by asking Hazel what she thought about it all.

'You said when we were eating that you thought all that stuff about consultation procedures was going through the legal requirements and that Kirkham was telling you politely that you were finished at TCS.'

'Yes. I think so,' said Sam, quietly. 'Kirkham might have thought that the management have been hiding it from the staff, but we've all been saying amongst ourselves for some time that there isn't much work around, and I'm not surprised that they've got to start getting rid of people, even senior people, starting with me, because mine's the first project to pack up, and they have nothing else as far as they can see ahead. Anyway, after ten years there, I think a change would do me good.'

'What's the alternative to voluntary redundancy?'

'Compulsory redundancy,' said Sam, with a shrug. 'It always looks better on your CV if it's voluntary, and they might give you better terms.'

Some moments of silent reflection followed, when Sam and Hazel were of one mind. This seemed inevitable, and they would have to do the best they could together.

'Well, I think my job's pretty safe at the moment,' said Hazel, 'so whatever happens we'll be OK. What are you going to do?'

'All I can do,' said Sam. 'Tomorrow I'll go to the library and look through this month's edition of *The Keyboard*, and there are bound to be plenty of project manager jobs in IT,' he said. 'The only trouble will be finding one that is within travelling distance of here.'

That was all that was said. If there were any jobs going, the specialist magazine would be sure to carry the advertisements, and Sam could take his time.

The next day, though, Sam drew a blank at the library. There were no advertised jobs at his level within fifty miles. There were plenty such jobs in London and the south of England, especially along the M4 corridor, but Sam did not want to uproot Andrew from his school now that he had started his GCSE courses, and Pine Properties was a regional estate agent, and so Hazel would have to start job-hunting if they moved. Of course, salaries were high enough to enable him to stay in a modest hotel during the week and come home at weekends, but he thought it best to leave that option for the moment.

To entertain himself in the reading room, however, Sam cast a casual eye through some of the newspapers, and eventually came to the Situations Vacant section of the local paper, the *Thorby Recorder*. His attention was attracted by a medium-sized framed advertisement asking for applications for teaching posts at a secondary school called Jamia Atif Akram.

There were vacancies for teachers of English, Mathematics and ICT, to start as soon as possible in the New Year. Sam had never thought of teaching, and he would not normally have been interested. He was qualified only in his subject; there must be an extra professional qualification needed to teach it. Anyway, the stories in the press and on television about bad behaviour in secondary schools nowadays were enough to put anyone off. He had better things to do than try to teach yobs who did not want to learn.

But something made him pause and look back at the advertisement again. It was obviously an independent school, with a name that was Asian, and probably Muslim. What about the language? If they all spoke in Urdu, that was another barrier.

Sam thought that it was not worth considering, but then looked at the address at the bottom of the advertisement: Musk Hall, Thorby. Well, that was near, and in the absence of any other vacancies, Sam wondered if it was worth an enquiry.

He knew something about Musk Hall, from an article he had read in the *Recorder* some time ago. About eighty years ago, it had been a grand mansion owned by a socialite of the time who was well known for having lavish weekend parties for a high society set from London. Nearby, there was a field with a grass landing strip for the planes of the period. The Hall had a wooded park with a small lake, and was one of the first buildings in England to have an indoor swimming pool. It also had a large ballroom, and there was even a golf course not far away.

Then the owner had lost his wealth in the late 1930s, and during the Second World War the building had been converted to a hospital for wounded troops. After the war, the newly nationalised Coal Board had acquired it and used it as a sanatorium for miners with spinal injuries and those needing hydrotherapy. Later, they had converted the sanatorium to a conference centre, turning the wards into small halls and lecture theatres. With the demise of British Coal, it had been left empty and abandoned for a while, and had obviously been bought by these people, who had used it as a school.

Sam thought all this was interesting. The small halls and lecture theatres would make good classrooms, and there were lots of small rooms for domestic or office accommodation. He knew the Hall was situated just off the main road to the west of Thorby, about seven or eight miles away from the town, and in the absence of anything else to do, he drove out there during the afternoon, to see what the place looked like.

He was most impressed. He parked just off the road, and walked along a tree-lined drive to the Hall. The grand old house formed the nucleus of a complex central building, and the various wings, which radiated from the centre, would have housed the indoor pool and hospital wards at one time.

The buildings looked to be in good repair and gave quite a palatial aspect to visitors as Sam walked along the drive. At this time of the day, the students would be in session, but Sam saw nothing of them as he strolled around. He wandered slowly down the winding path to the lake, which was placid and had a moored rowing boat on the near edge. The boat looked as if it was used for maintenance, and there was no sign of any yachts or any kind of pleasure craft.

There was some wildlife on the lake – a few mallards and a pair of coots, with a lone great-crested grebe at the far end. Sam strolled round the path that bordered the lake until he was stopped by a fence that skirted some trees and went down to the water's edge. Then he retraced his steps, found his car and drove home, having had a satisfying afternoon's relaxation.

In the evening, he discussed the whole situation with Hazel. They both agreed that moving house was out of the question with Andrew having started his GCSE courses, and with Hazel's job to consider. There was something about the rural setting of this school that attracted Sam. He kept thinking what a refreshing change it would be to work in the countryside. His life at university, and his work in city centre office blocks had made him very much an urban animal, and yet he loved his walks in Loscar wood and People's Park in Thorby. This rural aspect of things, irrelevant though it would be to any job offered, kept presenting itself to Sam's mind.

To Sam's surprise, Hazel was enthusiastic, and her comments were light-hearted. 'Anything to keep you busy,' she said, smiling, 'and it will certainly broaden your mind.'

When Sam rang the school for further information, they sent a prospectus and asked him to apply by letter and CV if he was interested. Another two weeks went by, and there were no jobs in IT advertised at the level he wanted within a radius of fifty miles of Thorby, which was the limit he had set. In early December, he posted a letter of application along with his CV, and he received a phone call the day his letter arrived. The Principal invited him to attend for an interview as soon as was convenient. Sam had posted the letter in a spirit of having nothing to lose, and being curious rather than interested, but the school seemed very keen.

He drove over that afternoon, and had what amounted to an informal conversation with the Principal, Dr Fazeel Ahmed and his Deputy, Dr Imran Patel. They explained that Atif Akram was a highly respected Muslim scholar and had been a teacher of both Dr Ahmed and Dr Patel. They had founded the school in his honour two years ago, having bought the empty building and grounds at an auction at which there were no other bidders, and so they had it at a bargain price.

Sam was impressed by the quiet dignity with which they both spoke, and with the respect and consideration they showed towards him. Dr Ahmed was thin and gentle in manner, probably in his mid-fifties, his hair grey and his hands long and bony with prominent blue veins across the backs. Dr Patel was much younger, heavily built with very thick, black hair. He smiled a lot and was excessively courteous in everything he did and said.

They told Sam that, as they were independent, just the two of them appointed whatever staff they wanted, and they could employ him on the strength of his degree alone, although if he wanted to stay long-term, they hoped he would study for a Postgraduate Certificate in Education.

It was an all boys' school and was a hundred per cent boarding. Two things about the school were made clear to Sam. The first was that all official business was conducted in English, except for classes for the boys in Arabic. He would find, if he came, that the boys often spoke to each other in Urdu, but they were not to do so to a teacher, and everything they wrote was in English. The second was that, although the Muslim staff and the pupils observed all the normal Muslim practices such as five prayer times a day and the health and cleanliness codes, a teacher such as Sam would not have anything to do with the Islamic or boarding side of the school. He would be expected only to deliver his subject, and in years ten and eleven, that meant the OCR CLAIT course. The English National Curriculum was taught throughout the whole school.

When Sam had been shown the one IT room with thirty Dell computers of moderate capacity, which were networked and had a Windows operating system, there seemed to be nothing he could complain about. They admitted that they could not pay anything like the salary Sam had been earning, but they tried to match the salary structure used in state schools.

They offered the post to Sam without writing to the referees he offered. They asked for his National Insurance number and also told him they would have to get a CRB check.

He went away to think about it.

In discussion with Hazel, he repeated that he felt he had nothing to lose and that he would not stay long if he did not like it. He said that he felt, above all, that it would do him good to have a complete change and a new start, even if it did mean less money. It was, after all, better than no money at all, or unemployment pay.

He accepted the post, and started the new term in the New Year.

For the first month, he was rushed off his feet. He tried to establish how far the students had got with the previous teacher. This was not easy because he had left precious few records. He had left because he was seriously ill at the end of September, and since then, all IT lessons had been covered in a rather disjointed way.

He started again with the CLAIT classes in years ten and eleven, and began to organise the whole curriculum by writing out programmes of study and schemes of work for all years. He devised an assessment, recording and reporting policy, having made sure that it fitted the school's overall policy in those matters. He did the same with policies for homework, discipline, health & safety, and display. Finally, he made a lengthy inventory of his resources and wrote a development plan. He was sure that all these things would change continually, but he had to make a start somewhere.

One thing that did surprise him was that the students showed considerable respect and courtesy towards him from the beginning, even when he did not know any of their names. Many of them told him they were glad to have a 'proper' IT teacher again, because they liked the subject and wanted to do well. They all wore a uniform of black trousers and blue jumpers around the school, with, of course, the traditional white *taqiyah* – or skull cap.

Sam learned that the boys' fathers were ambitious for them, and thought it was an honour for them to be accepted by the school. Their fathers were not rich, being mostly taxi drivers and shopkeepers, but the school was partly financed by money raised at the network of mosques that covered the country. Part of a good Muslim's disposable income was given to charity, and that included schools.

Being, as it were, 'on show' in front of twenty-five teenagers for six teaching hours a day, however, was such a different working environment for Sam, that at first he used to feel really tired at the end of each day. He realised he needed to be alert to all that was going on around him in a way that he had not had to be when he just sat in front of his own computer most of the day. In his subject, he did not often need to write instructions for a whole class on the board, but when he did he wrote on a white board with a marker pen. He used to like to hang his jacket on the back of his teacher's chair. One day, as he wrote on this board, there was a low buzz of conversation, but he distinctly heard above it the voice of Iqbal, on his left: 'Your jacket, sir,' and as he spun quickly round, he saw that a boy who had thought of a reason to walk by his chair suddenly pulled his dangling hand away from his jacket. As the boy carried on, to go back to his seat, Sam noticed him point at Iqbal, and dart a poisonous look at him.

'You don't scare me,' he heard Iqbal say to the boy, and Sam reflected, as he put on his jacket and felt for his wallet in

213

the inside pocket, that some of the boys probably did not lead an easy life.

Sam learned how to be firm without being aggressive, to lay down his own rules, and to make it clear where the lines were that were not to be crossed. He learned how to deal with something sharply without making a fuss or interrupting the flow of a lesson. 'Four on the floor,' he would snap if a boy tipped his chair back as he sat on it. 'Have you got arms?' he would ask if a boy blurted out without raising his hand to be asked. He sometimes used a bit of sarcasm as well: 'Pretend you're normal,' he would sneer at a persistent troublemaker.

For serious misdemeanours, a boy would do one or more detentions, and because it was a boarding school, this would go on until nine or ten at night. There was also a system of being 'on report'. But if there was serious bullying or theft or insubordination, the culprit would be expelled by Dr Ahmed. Shahid, one of the boarding Muslim teachers, told Sam how this was usually done. When the pupil reported to Dr Ahmed, he simply told him that he would consider what punishment might be appropriate, without telling him that he had already made up his mind. Then, as the boy was finishing his Sunday morning breakfast, the duty teacher would approach him. 'Finish that quickly,' he would say, 'and then I will come with you to your room. Pack quickly while I watch. Your father is on his way, and you will be gone in half an hour.'

'Wow!' said Sam. 'No room for any nonsense, then.'

'No,' said Shahid, 'and he will have behaved well up to that point, in the hope that he might be allowed to stay.'

And so Sam began to assert himself, to play his role in the school, and gradually to earn the respect of pupils and staff.

They had a very long lunch hour. Because they all went into the mosque for prayers at one o'clock, lunchtime stretched from twelve-thirty until about a quarter to two, and lessons finished at half-past three. There was a staff meeting after lessons on Tuesdays, but on other days, Sam could do a full two hours' marking and preparation before he went home for tea. He made full use of it, and really enjoyed this flexibility in working hours at the end of the day.

Sam found that he was welcomed very warmly by the rest of the teachers. There were two in particular, Iqbal and Atif, that were very friendly, who always looked into his eyes and smiled whenever they met him in the corridor or the staff room. They stopped what they were doing to answer any questions on administration or organisation that Sam had, and were always willing to talk socially.

One day, Sam asked Atif about reports in the media about violence in Muslim countries in the Middle East and Asia. He asked him if the media were right in calling this 'Jihad' or 'holy war'.

Atif shook his head. 'The word,' he said, sounding authoritative, 'means "struggle", but not an armed struggle or a war, a struggle of the intellect and mind. There is a constant struggle to improve the intellect, to dispel ignorance and to make the world a better place for all mankind.'

Atif reached into his bag and pulled out a small booklet. He said, 'I will read you a short passage from this booklet, which was written by our Principal. He writes that Islam is "a faith whose foundations lie firmly within the concepts of peace and compassion. *Jihad* in Islam refers to individual or collective attempts made for the betterment, prosperity, protection and welfare of the individual or society. A person struggles to refrain from all manner of evil such as lying and theft, and strives to remain on the path of good. This struggle is called *al-Jihad al-akbar* (the greatest *Jihad*) and *al-Jihad al-afdal* (the best *Jihad*). There is sanction for the justified use of force in ensuring peace and security, which is called *al-Jihad al-asghar* (the lesser *Jihad*). By ignoring the ninety per cent peaceful struggle and promoting the ten per cent forceful struggle, some people are guilty of misusing this key term.'

'So you see,' concluded Atif, 'the Qur'an essentially teaches peace and love.'

This was one of the few occasions when Atif was able to correct misconceptions Sam had got from the western media about Islam. As time went on, all the Islamic staff, and the religion itself, grew massively in his esteem and respect.

As he grew more accustomed to the pattern and pace of life as a teacher, Sam grew more relaxed and happier. There were times when there was a rush of work, but mostly, Sam found that it was a routine that was not too taxing.

The feelings that Sam had had last December about a change of atmosphere, a change of scene, a chance to drive into the countryside every day to work, had turned out to be true. Sam certainly had to work hard at the job without let-up, and the hours were longer than he imagined they would be, but he began to find a kind of peace and happiness and fulfilment that was a bit warmer than he had found at TCS.

Hazel, of course, noticed every shade of change in Sam. She had been surprised how calmly and equably Sam had ridden the shock of his redundancy at TCS. He had, though, been in quite a tense and apprehensive mood over Christmas and the New Year, as he waited to start an entirely new type of job. The winter had not been easy, but things had slowly improved, and by the end of July, Hazel felt that the family was almost back to the spirit of last autumn.

They decided to take a hot, sunny holiday in early August. In their younger days, Sam and Hazel had scorned package holidays conducted by tour operators, but now they were happy just to sit and be organised. They had a very relaxing holiday based in a hotel in Sorrento and they were taken to Capri, Pompeii, Vesuvius and Naples. On the small beach at Amalfi, Sam just sat and baked in the sun all day while Hazel and Andrew browsed the shops for souvenirs, explored the narrow, white alleyways and harbour, and visited the ninth-century duomo standing in the central piazza of the town.

Sam's skin became a deep mahogany colour. He turned brown very quickly in the hot summer sun, ignoring any sunscreen offered to him, and was the envy of friends. Hazel was particularly fair-skinned. She always used sun cream and even then had to be careful not to develop a heat rash.

The holiday culminated in a two-day visit to Rome, a place Sam and Hazel had always wanted to visit. They had to stand in many queues, but thought that the spectacular views of the Trevi fountain, the Spanish steps and the Colosseum were worth it. So also was the wealth of art treasures in the Vatican museum and St Peter's basilica.

The school's GCSE results, published in the third week of August, were very good. Sam's ICT results were not as good as those of the other subjects, but were quite reasonable.

The Principal, Dr Ahmed, was quite complimentary, accepting that Sam had had only one term and a few weeks before the examinations to move the department forward again after the untidiness of the autumn term.

As the autumn term started, Sam was in a settled state of mind. The new timetable started smoothly. Football took over from cricket as the boys' main interest. The work progressed steadily, the evenings grew dark and the leaves fell. Sam felt that he was in touch with the eternal cycle of the seasons more than he had ever been in an office block in a town centre or in a unit of an industrial estate. He felt fulfilled. The pace of life was steady and strong.

22

As Sam knelt by the toilet bowl in his pyjamas, he wondered how many more times he would retch. He had not much sense of the time, but thought he must have been there at least half an hour, as he looked wearily towards the window yet again. His whole body ached, and he felt that all the strength had been drained out of it by the constant vomiting.

Then, at last, the powerful thumps from deep inside him subsided, and there was a period of calm. He gave one final flush, put on his pyjama jacket, shivered, gathered himself together and moved slowly out of the bathroom to the spare bedroom where he had been sleeping, fitfully, for the first part of the night. He was aware of Hazel watching from her bedroom door, a pained expression on her anxious face.

'All right?' It was just a whisper. Sam gave a slight nod.

But he was not all right. He shivered violently again as he got into bed. He pulled the bedclothes tightly around him. His teeth chattered. He tried to snuggle and relax, but sleep would not come, and soon he was so hot, he threw off the duvet. Eventually, he got up and sat in a chair by the window – until he shivered again and got back into bed.

The dark night crawled towards a cold, grey November dawn.

Hazel looked in on her way down to get breakfast for Andrew and herself.

'Going to work?'

Sam shook his head. He had no energy left. It was not like

him to give in. He had not taken more than about three or four days off because of illness in the whole of his working life: a flu epidemic about ten years ago. Now, though, the fight seemed to have gone out of him.

'The funny thing is,' Hazel was saying, 'that you had hardly anything to eat last night. I can't think what you can be bringing up.'

'Only froth.' Sam shook his head again.

Hazel went down to the kitchen. She had a constant, nagging anxiety about Sam. He hadn't eaten properly for weeks. She knew he had lost weight around his neck and stomach, and he had precious little surplus flesh anyway. Since the October half-term, he had not enthused about his work at the school, as he had done in the summer. Some days, she could tell that he had to drag himself off in the mornings, and he looked so pale and tired in the evenings.

After breakfast, Hazel came up again.

'Can you manage to get to the doctor's or shall I ask her to call?'

'It's probably just a bug.' Sam summoned up the energy to sound firm. 'If I stay in bed for the day, I'll be all right tomorrow. Will you ring the school?'

'It's not just a bug,' came the retort. 'You've had this night sickness before. You're right off your food, and the way you're going hot and cold, you seem feverish. I'll ask Dr McCurrach if she'll call.' She waited for the protest that did not come. 'But if she comes, I'll have to wait in,' she continued. 'I'll phone the school, and then I'll phone Pine Properties and tell them they'll have to manage until I can get there.'

Hazel shook her head as she went downstairs again. He doesn't fight any more, she thought, and that's something else that's worrying. She told Andrew that he would have to go to school on the bus that day because she had decided to get the doctor to Sam, and wouldn't be going into Thorby until she had called.

Dr McCurrach called just after eleven, took Sam's temperature, felt his pulse and listened while Hazel told her the story of sickness in spite of very little food, and Sam's lack of his usual drive and energy. She seemed concerned about the shivering and feverishness, but was non-committal about everything. Then she decided to make a fingertip examination of Sam's stomach, and, after that, asked him to lean forward.

As she touched his ribs, he winced.

'What's the matter?'

'It's just that I've been feeling uncomfortable on that side, and I've got a bit of a pain in my right shoulder,' said Sam, quickly.

Dr McCurrach seemed suddenly much more alert, felt along the top of his collar bone, and lightly grasped the top of the right lung.

'Ooh!' A quick intake of breath.

'How long have you had this pain?'

'About three weeks or so. I lifted some benches in the gym at school, and thought I'd twisted it, but it's not improving.'

'I don't think it's anything to do with benches,' said Dr McCurrach, suddenly much more decisive. 'I'm a bit concerned about this, and I think I'll send you to the hospital for some tests.'

'Outpatients?' asked Sam, as he replaced his pyjama jacket.

'No. I want you admitted today.' She turned to Hazel. 'I'm not sure about this, but I want to be safe. Can I sit at a table downstairs and write a letter?'

'Yes, certainly,' said Hazel, as she stood aside for the doctor to go through the door, shooting a rather hard glance at Sam. Sam knew it was a reproach for not mentioning the shoulder pain.

Dr McCurrach sealed the letter as soon as she had written it.

'You must see that Dr Evans gets this when you get to the hospital,' she said briskly. 'I'll phone to get Sam admitted for tests now. Can you take him in?' she asked, almost as an after-thought. 'I'll phone for transport if you like, but it will be much quicker if you take him.'

'Yes. I'll do that,' said Hazel, and there was a slight pause. 'Could you tell me why you think it is so urgent?'

'Well, in that letter, I've asked Dr Evans to do some tests,' she replied. 'I can't be certain without the results of the tests, but it is possible that his liver could be enlarged or diseased. We'll have to wait for the tests.'

Ever the diplomat, thought Hazel. She won't commit herself.

Dr McCurrach's phone call was brief, and then the next two hours were busy for Hazel. She packed all she could think Sam would need, patiently helped him dress and made sure he was warmly wrapped, and drove him to the hospital in Thorby. The admission procedures were slow and tedious, but she finally left Sam in Ward G1, and got to Pine Properties at about the middle of the afternoon.

At the end of the day, she called back at the hospital, but Sam was not on the ward. A nurse told her that they had taken some blood for a test, and that at the moment he was in radiology having an MRI scan. Hazel was welcome to wait for Sam's return.

She waited, and when he returned she made sure he was comfortable and had all he needed. She left as they were bringing round the meal trolleys. She did hope he would eat something. She hoped even more that he would not be sick again.

It was a very quiet meal shared by Hazel and Andrew in the early evening. Andrew then worked in his room for two or three hours. Hazel did some ironing, had a bath and went to bed early.

The next day, Hazel called at the hospital in a lengthened lunch hour, and, before she saw Sam, was given a message that asked her to call on Dr Evans in his office before she left.

Sam forced a rather feeble smile when he saw Hazel, but she was a bit shocked at how tired and listless he seemed. He told her, slowly and quietly, that he had been down to radiography again, but he didn't know much about the tests they had been doing. He seemed really quite exhausted. After a few minutes, Hazel kissed him lightly on the forehead, said she hoped he could get some rest in the afternoon, and went along to Dr Evans' office.

Dr Evans was courtesy itself. He shook hands and greeted Hazel warmly. He was tall and thin, a bit too thin in Hazel's opinion because his cheeks were hollow, and yet they seemed to fit in with the rest of his gaunt and rangy appearance. Beneath moderately bushy eyebrows were clear, light blue eyes, which Hazel decided were his most attractive feature.

'Good afternoon, Mrs Dent.' He spoke slowly, clearly and very deliberately. 'Your GP referred your husband to me yesterday because she suspected liver damage or liver disease, and now I have to tell you that Dr McCurrach was right. She was quick to spot the significance of the pain in the right shoulder, and the imaging scan does show that your husband has an enlarged liver. This causes pain when it presses on nerves in the diaphragm, which are connected to the shoulder. A poor quality of the liver is consistent with the other clinical symptoms.'

Here he rummaged on his desk to find yesterday's letter and held it fairly close to his face as he read it. 'Loss of appetite, weight loss, sickness and tiredness, and also' – he looked up at Hazel with those blue eyes beneath those bushy eyebrows – 'a high temperature and shivering symptomatic of a feverish condition.

'Now I must come straight to the point, Mrs Dent.' He put the letter down and looked across the desk with a sharp intensity at Hazel. 'We have not yet completed all the tests I want to do on your husband. For one thing, we don't yet have the results of the blood test, but the signs so far are very serious. I did a hepatic arteriography test this morning, and it shows what we call angiosarcomas on the liver. These could be malignant growths and they appear to be quite widespread. If they are too widespread, it may not be possible to remove them surgically, and chemotherapy and radiation therapy, which are alternative treatments, may not help much, either.'

Hazel's eyes were focussed hard on Dr Evans' face. Seconds passed in silence. The silence seemed like minutes.

'Are you telling me,' she asked in little more than a whisper, 'that it's terminal?'

He did not deny or confirm it.

'For the moment, I'm saying that it's very serious and I want to finish the tests before making a judgment,' he said. 'I just wanted to tell you directly about his condition, and tell you at the earliest possible moment.'

'Yes. Thank you.' Hazel put the heel of her right hand to her forehead and looked down at her lap. There was something about the intensity of Dr Evans' gaze that she could not keep returning without some respite.

'Of course, it won't have started in the liver,' the doctor was saying, and Hazel looked up again sharply. 'We found a large, dark melanoma on his forearm, and the suspicion is that it has released cancerous cells into the lymph. Hadn't you noticed the melanoma, Mrs Dent?'

Hazel suffered a deep, sinking feeling. 'No. I'm sorry.' Just after they were married, Hazel would have known about every mole and mark on Sam's body, but not in recent years. What a thing to happen, just for the sake of not noticing.

'He seems to have quite a good skin, though. Does he sunbathe excessively?'

'Normally, not much,' replied Hazel, shaking her head

and giving a little sigh, 'but he fried himself to a crisp one day this summer in Italy.'

Dr Evans made no reply.

'Well, there's nothing more to tell you at the moment,' the doctor continued, in his measured and precise and yet, Hazel sensed, sympathetic and compassionate tones. 'I'll let you know when we have the results of all the tests, and I'll also have to tell your husband at that time, too.'

'Yes. Thank you,' said Hazel, and rose quickly from her chair. She made for the door, stopped, turned and said 'Thank you' again, and then she was through the door and walking towards the exit. She would be very late back at Pine Properties, but what did it matter?

She walked down the corridor in a daze, looking ahead, not noticing anything to the left or right. She could barely take in what she had just been told. Why did it have to happen to Sam? Why did it have to happen to us, just because of sunbathing in Italy?

Oh, hell. I just wish, for God's sake, I could turn the clock back.

23

'Could I have a word, please, Mrs Dent?'

It was Christine Dugget, Hazel's deputy. Hazel had come from her office at the back of the premises, to look in a filing cabinet in the main office, and was just turning to go back, when Christine intercepted her.

'Yes, certainly, Christine.' Hazel tried to sound bright enough to be polite.

Christine stood silently for a moment.

'In private, please, Mrs Dent?'

'Oh, yes. OK.' Hazel turned and walked to her office. Christine followed. Once inside, Hazel motioned Christine to the 'customer' chair in front of her desk, while she manoeuvred round to sit behind it. Then she looked up, expectantly.

'I'd just like to say, Mrs Dent,' said Christine, deferentially, but in a clear and firm tone, 'that all the people in the office, and I, would not mind at all if you just stayed at home at the present time.'

She could see that she had taken Hazel by surprise, and rushed on before she could reply. 'I mean this in the nicest possible way, Mrs Dent, but you are looking very much under the weather. We know your husband is ill, and you visit him in hospital each day, because you've told us, and we'd like you to know that we don't mind covering for you. If you don't mind my saying so, you look as if you're not getting any sleep at all. You must be under a great deal of stress.'

Christine was relieved to have said it all in one go. She had been rehearsing the speech in her mind for two days now, ever since a few people in the office had discussed Hazel's situation one lunchtime, when she was out.

Hazel did not reply immediately. Now she realised that Christine had said all she wanted to say, she held her head in her hands for a moment and looked down at the blotter on her desk.

'That's very sweet of you, and I appreciate it,' she said, looking up at Christine, 'but the situation is not all that simple. I had better explain.'

She moved a small pile of letters away from the blotter, and rested her elbows in the space she had made, while she leaned forward to speak candidly to Christine.

'Yes. It's true that I am getting about one hour's sleep a night, and I had better tell you openly and plainly that my husband has gone through tests at the hospital and has been diagnosed as having terminal cancer of the liver.'

Christine gasped. 'Oh, I'm so sorry, Mrs Dent. We had no idea it was that serious. No wonder you're not sleeping. But you only had those three days off a few weeks ago, didn't you?'

'It's all right.' Hazel waved an arm rather impatiently at Christine. 'Let me tell you the rest of the story. The cancer is too widespread for an operation, but he is having some radiation therapy, which is the treatment we both opted for. The consultant has told me, though, that it only delays the inevitable. Neither of us wants to tell them to stop the treatment.'

Hazel was surprised that she was able to speak so fluently to Christine about it, but she realised that her mouth had gone very dry. She reached down for the bottle of mineral water she kept behind her desk, deftly unscrewed the cap, and took a mouthful.

'But I'm not visiting the hospital every day,' she continued.

'It's about a month since he was first admitted, and he was only in there for a week. Once everyone knew what the situation was, Sam asked if he could go home for a while, and just come back for his treatment, or when things…' Hazel could feel the tears pricking the backs of her eyes, and her throat was closing, and so she took two or three gulps from the water bottle – 'or when things get too bad.' Christine felt embarrassed, but had no idea what to do or say. There was another pause. The silence settled heavily. Hazel took another gulp of water.

'So that's where he is now,' she continued, 'because that's where he wants to be.' Her throat felt a little easier and she felt she could continue. Indeed, she was glad to be able to talk like this to her closest colleague. It was as if the slightly tense feeling that everyone had during the working day had relaxed, and there was suddenly a personal feeling inside her bare and austere office.

'Of course, when I knew he was coming home, I decided I would stay with him all the time, and not come to work. They could take it out of my holiday allowance if they wanted, but I thought that was what I would do, and I did, as you know, have three days off. Then Sam insisted that I came in as normal. He said he felt he had said all he wanted to say, and he wanted to see me off in the morning and have the house to himself during the day. It was the same with Andrew. He also said he wanted to stay at home with his dad in case he wanted anything, but Sam told him to get off in the mornings as well. We are all together in the evenings, of course, and Sam doesn't want the TV on. We just sit and talk. Andrew won't go up to his room. He sits and talks, too. But Sam has gone so thin, and he looks grey and tired all the time, with that slight yellowish tint in his eyes and face. He's very calm, though, and he's always very sweet. He has just accepted it. That makes it a little easier.' It was not so hard to talk now, and Hazel was happy to keep the flow going.

'The funny thing is,' she said, 'at the very beginning, one thing that kept me awake at night was wondering how I would tell Andrew the terrible truth, but, you know, Christine, the odd thing is that I never have. Dr Evans has told Sam, but I have not told Andrew, and yet we all know. None of the three of us has said it out loud, in so many words. It's as if an unspoken message has passed between us. We all just know.'

The emotion was swelling again. She drank more water.

Christine felt compelled to say something. 'It must be awful for you, though,' she said, putting all the sympathy she could muster into her face and voice. Christine felt inadequate. She had felt that before, how she could never find words good enough to match her feelings. She wondered if anyone else could.

'Each night when I get home, I can tell how he has spent his day. He comes downstairs probably about the middle of the day, and he's usually had some soup or even a bit of toast for his lunch, and then there are photograph albums lying all over the floor. He's gone so thin. I don't think he has the strength to gather them up again. There are CDs everywhere as well. He's obviously decided he wants to spend his days looking at the photos we've taken over the years, most of them on holidays, and about five albums' full when Andrew was a baby.' She paused and took a sip of water while Christine waited again.

'I got home a little early one day, though, and I think I took him by surprise. His eyes were very bloodshot. I didn't say anything, but I knew he'd been crying, and the albums were all over the place, as usual. He's always been a bit like that, though. He can get quite weepy when he gets emotional.'

Hazel stopped the flow of talk. That was as personal as she wanted to get with Christine. She could have opened a floodgate of feelings and memories with another person and in another place, but now she became aware that she was, after all, still at work. She stood and looked over the frosted glass and through the clear glass into the office beyond. Christine stood, too, and was the first to speak.

'Well, remember what I said, Mrs Dent. If there comes a day when you don't want to come in ...'

'Yes. Thank you, Christine,' Hazel replied, quickly. 'I'll remember.'

Just as Christine was reaching for the door handle, Hazel stopped her, urgently and quickly calling her name.

'Christine!' She stopped and turned. 'Christine,' she said, much more softly. 'There will come a terrible day ...'

She couldn't finish the sentence. The tears sprang suddenly, and stabbed the backs of her eyes. An unseen force seized her throat, making it hurt. Her face crumpled as she covered it with both hands.

Christine managed to say, 'Yes, Mrs Dent,' and turned away quickly from the stricken woman in front of her. She went rapidly through the door and closed it behind her quietly. She stood and took two very deep breaths before she was able to walk away down the office.

24

'Hello. It's me.'

The voice at the other end of the line was just a whisper, but Hazel recognised it instantly.

'Hello, Sam. What is it?'

There was a pause. Then the whisper again: 'You know what.'

'Oh, no.' Hazel didn't really want to say that, but she blurted it out, on reflex.

'It's time to go time,' breathed Sam again. Now it was just a murmur, no louder than the rustling of leaves.

'OK. I'll come.' Hazel looked across the office. It was a great relief that Christine was looking straight back at her, and Hazel beckoned.

'Sam's phoned,' she told Christine, and the look straight into her eyes told Christine everything.

'I'm going home now. Would you phone Clarke's taxis and send them to my house? I'm not sure I'll be able to drive when I take him to the hospital, and I'm certain I won't be able to drive back home on my own.'

Christine nodded. Hazel picked up her bag and briefcase, and was gone.

Sam greeted her with a pallid smile when she went into the house, and he had managed to get dressed. Hazel kissed him very tenderly – just a light brushing of the lips. Then she helped him on with his shoes and coat, and quickly filled a bag with the things he would need.

She had not really expected this today. Sam had seemed the same as usual when she had left, giving Andrew a lift, as she did most days. Many times they had talked about when this moment would come. Sam said he would just know, and Hazel accepted that.

Sam seemed very calm. Hazel glanced at him a few times as she scurried about, and especially as she phoned the hospital. He kept his eyes looking down most of the time, and when he moved it was so painfully slowly. He seemed surprised when the taxi drew up outside, and glanced at Hazel.

'I thought it was best,' she said, and that's all she could say.

She grabbed Sam's bag and helped him move carefully through the door. It was a slow process getting him settled into the back seat of the taxi. He waited patiently while Hazel dealt with the bag, and had to tug twice at the door on his side to open it. The driver closed it. It occurred to him that this was the last time he would leave the house and travel the few yards down Brewster Lane to Rowle Road. He looked across at the part of the barn he could just see past the Davies' house. Then they moved off.

They held hands as they sat together in the back seat. Sam's hands felt cold to Hazel, but she clasped them as firmly as she could, and hoped that he got some warmth from her.

They took things very slowly when they reached the hospital. Hazel found a wheelchair and used the lift. Sam sat passively. She remembered how he had spurned the lift and galloped up the stairs two at a time when they had visited Andrew, not so long ago.

Admission did not take long this time, and they had set aside one of the rooms off the main ward, G1, for Sam. He was exhausted by the time he was installed in bed, and rested, his head lying well back into the pillow. As she had done so many times, Hazel thought how tired he looked. His closed eyelids were the colour of lead.

Hazel managed to have a brief talk with the staff nurse as he rested, but when he stirred, she was quickly back at the side of the bed. Sam asked her to plump the pillows so that he could sit forward a little.

'The nurse says the doctor hasn't been round yet today, and he'll be here maybe in about an hour.' Sam did not respond, but just closed his eyes again.

Hazel moved very close. 'Now what would you like me to do,' she asked gently, 'stay here for the afternoon, or go away for a while?'

'Stay here,' he replied, eyes still closed. 'I just want you to be here.' He fumbled with the bedclothes and moved his arm out and laid it softly on the duvet. Hazel held his hand in both hers.

'Thanks,' he said, and drew a deeper breath. 'Could you just stay here?'

'Of course I will.'

Sam dozed for a little while, but roused himself when the doctor came. He was quite lucid as they spoke briefly. Sam told him he felt 'pretty bad' when he asked, but shook his head when the doctor asked if he wanted extra morphine.

When they were on their own, Sam leaned forward again and looked at Hazel. She thought he seemed to be a bit more lively now.

'Just one thing I want to let you know,' he said. 'While I was at home, I wrote two letters, one for you and one for Andrew. You'll find them in the top drawer of my desk in the dining-room.' Then he paused while he took several more breaths. Then he lay back again, and added, quietly, but with deliberate clarity: 'Don't open them just now, though.'

That hurt Hazel a little. She knew what he meant by that. She wondered how he could be so calm about it, but he had been calm all day. It was as if he had found a peace that was beyond her experience. She grasped his one protruding hand in both hers again, and held it firmly and warmly.

'OK,' she said. 'We'll open them later.'

'Thanks,' he replied. 'You'll find I've tried to work on the next newsletter as well, but I couldn't finish it. Tell people I'm sorry.'

'They don't need to be told that,' she said. 'People know how hard it's been for you.'

Sam rolled his head wearily on the pillow. 'What did the school say last time you phoned them?'

'They said not to worry about them, and how good you were,' said Hazel.

'Yeah, but they were good to me, too.' He rolled his head back to face her and opened his eyes again. 'Everybody's been good to me,' he murmured, 'especially you.' He gave Hazel a weak smile. He closed his eyes again, and she felt a slight pressure from his hand. 'Thanks, Haze.' He hadn't called her that since before they were married, when he used to do it playfully, as if to tease. Now it fell, like a drop of soothing oil, straight upon her heart.

Those were the last words he spoke to her. He dropped into a doze, and then into a deeper sleep.

Hazel sat for another two hours, holding his hand and watching his face. She thought how serene and placid he looked as he slept, just as his life had been serene and placid for these past few weeks. Her mind ranged over a myriad of memories, while her gaze stayed fixed on the face she had loved for over twenty years.

There was no drama, no final speech. She decided that 'Thanks, Haze' was all she wanted to hear echoing down the corridors of her memory, as the future stretched away from this moment.

Finally, she gathered her things, and told the nurse she would leave now, as Sam was sleeping. She made her way out of the hospital in a cocoon of her own making. She knew the way, and kept her eyes on the floor. She didn't want to see anyone else, and she hoped no one else would notice her.

233

She watched the familiar route home through the taxi window in a daze. It suddenly occurred to her that she should try to pray, but she found she couldn't. The man who had been half her life for twenty years was slipping away from her, and the thought filled her. She dwelt on it. Nothing else mattered. Tears washed her cheeks, and every so often she licked the salt water from her lips.

Andrew was waiting at the door as she paid the taxi. Her red eyes and crumpling face told him all he needed to know. They clasped each other for support and strength, and sobbed quietly into each other's shoulders for some minutes, until they gently pulled apart.

Andrew did nothing during the evening. He didn't really want to go and hide in his room and leave his mum on her own. But he didn't want to do anything else, either. Just as with Hazel, the one thought filled his mind, and there was no room for anything else. His spirit was crushed, and he felt hollow inside. Every so often, his brown eyes brimmed over, and he wept a little, silently.

Hazel was the same. She felt bruised and exhausted. Quite early, they both had a warm drink and went to bed, knowing they would not sleep. Hazel looked at the clock every ten minutes until about four o'clock.

The ringing of the telephone startled Hazel from a shallow sleep just after five. The hospital told her that Sam had passed into a coma, and they thought she had better come.

She decided that at that hour of the morning there would be little traffic, and so she could manage to drive herself. She told Andrew that she would go alone, and that there was no need for him to go to school. He simply shook his head. He said nothing, but went with her.

Sam seemed to be as she had left him. One arm was outside the bedclothes, and so she held it while she looked once more into his pale and placid face. The greyness that she had got used to seemed to be of a slightly lighter shade now.

And so they sat for hour after hour, Hazel on one side and Andrew on the other side of the bed. Occasionally, one of them stirred and took a few steps round the room, or visited the toilet. The nurses brought drinks.

The end came early the following morning. Hazel sensed when he stopped breathing. She glanced across at Andrew, and the shattered brown eyes told her he had noticed, too. She let go of Sam's hand and held that of her son, as he reached towards her. She let the tears flow for some minutes. Then she dabbed her eyes with yet another tissue, regained some composure and went for the nurse.

Hazel felt a sense of unreality for the next few days. She and Andrew shared the telephoning of friends and relatives until all had been told, and arrangements were soon made. But she lost track of the time and had to keep checking on the day of the week. She tried to get some sleep, but knew that it wouldn't come. Andrew was the same. They tried to eat, but just sat and picked at the food. Occasionally, they went for a short walk together.

For Hazel, the final three days with Sam were like a scene that kept replaying before her eyes. She recalled every word that had passed between them. She took an unexpected pleasure in the fact that he had called her 'Haze' at the end. It reminded her of the uninhibited joy that had been theirs at around the time they got married.

Hazel also recalled many times the fact that she had promised Sam that she and Andrew would open his two letters 'later'. Eventually, when there were no more pressing phone calls to make, she decided it was the right time.

She quickly found them in the top drawer of his desk. They were both sealed, and so she explained to Andrew, who took his upstairs to read it privately. Hazel opened hers. He had typed it, and it was dated two weeks before that final afternoon.

Darling Hazel,

I have been feeling at peace these last few days. It seems ironical that this illness should have happened just when I had found a new level of happiness.

Anyway, I thought I would write some final words to you while I can still think clearly. I don't know how bad it will be at the end, but it may be that I can't say much, or at least not much that is clear or logical. So it's better if I tell you my thoughts this way.

I am sorry that we had some ups and downs in recent years, especially the last two years. Everything I did and said, I thought it was for the best. Everything was done out of love for you and Andrew.

I don't want you to be sad when I have gone. You still have half your life in front of you, and I would like to think that there will be many years of happiness for you.

Now, I am going into my last battle. I am bound to lose, but I know that you will be with me, giving me your strength. That is where you have always been.

Whatever I was doing, wherever I was going, I knew I could always come back to you. You were the warm centre of my life. You were the beat of my heart for twenty years.

I love you forever.

Sam.

Hazel read it over and over. It was not long, and it was simple. She sat until she felt she had really taken it in, until it had become part of her.

A long time later, Andrew came downstairs. He, too, was red-eyed. Wordless, he gave Hazel his letter.

'This one's about me, but you can read it,' she said, giving him hers. Then she read Andrew's, typed and with the same date.

Dear Andrew,

As you know, I will be leaving you soon. Please don't be unhappy or sad. As I write this, I am thinking of a handsome, strong young man, making his way in the world.

There is enough money in my life assurance policy to see you through your A-level studies and university. You make sure you succeed, but enjoy it along the way.

I am sorry you had no brothers or sisters, but that's just the way it worked out, and so there were just the three of us. Only the three of us.

Soon, there will be only the two of you. Please look after your mother. She is the best mother in the world.

The best thing a parent can give is independence. When you are a parent, and you give love unconditionally, you will know this. And so, shortly, you will have your independence, completely.

Please listen to your mother, and listen to others that you trust, as well. But above all, be true to yourself.

Then you will truly be my son.

I love you forever.

Dad.

There was a long silence in the house, while mother and son read and re-read their own and each other's letters.

Eventually there was, as always, coffee.

Epilogue

Hazel went back to look for the unfinished newsletter. It, too, had been put in the drawer of Sam's desk. By a quick glance at the front page, she noticed that Sam was trying to write an account of his recent experience at Jamia Atif Akram, the Muslim school.

He wrote that it was only eight miles away, and therefore the pupils and staff were neighbours. He quoted from a booklet written by the Principal:

Neighbours mean not only those who live next door, but any with whom we interact socially. People of one street are neighbours of the people in the next street; people from one town are the neighbours of the people in the adjacent town.

The article went on to plead for mutual tolerance by all people:

When there is mutual understanding, mutual confidence and respect will automatically prosper.

This mutual understanding, Sam argued, spread outwards from the family:

Occasionally, there are heated arguments between husband and wife; however, it is tolerated by both of them because each is aware that they have to live together. We should all tolerate behaviour reciprocally. In this way, an atmosphere of peace and tranquillity will flourish that will benefit society generally.

That was all there was. Hazel was not sure whether it was the beginning or the end of an article.

But in the end, she thought, that was what he believed. I think I'll have it read out at his funeral.

Author's Note

Quotations in the epilogue and on pages 238 and 239 are reproduced from Pirzada, M.I.H. (2005) *Muslims in a Multicultural Society*. Al-Karam Publications, British Muslim Forum. ISBN: 0 9547694 49.